DARK DISCOVERIES

Spring 2014, Issue Number 27, www.DarkDiscoveries.

Publisher
JournalStone Publishing, LLC

Editor-in-Chief
Aaron J. French

Consulting Editor
James R. Beach (Consulting Editor)

Assistant Editors
Kenneth Heard (Reviews Editor)
Lacey Friedly (Senior Submissions Editor)

**Art Director,
Layout, and Design**
Cyrus Wraith Walker

Contributors
Brian Evenson   Geoffrey H. Goodwin
Bentley Little   Robert Morrish
Maurice Broaddus   Joel B. Kirkpatrick
Tom Piccirilli   Yvonne Navarro
John R. Little   James R. Beach
Douglas Clegg   Michael R. Collings
                         Aaron J. French
        Richard Dansky
        Amy Shane
Joe McKinney and Patrick Freivald
Frank M. Robinson & Lawrence Davidson

Special Thanks
Brian Evenson
Jeffrey Sackett
Tom Piccirilli
Geoffrey H. Goodwin

**Contributing
Artists/Photographers**

Cyrus Wraith Walker (Cover and Story Art
pgs.10, 27, 40, 59, 77, 83)
_____

DARK DISCOVERIES
(ISSN 1548-6842) is published (Qtrly) by
JournalStone Publications, 1261 Peachwood
Court, San Bruno, CA 94066

Christopher C. Payne
JournalStone Publications
1261 Peachwood Court, San Bruno, CA 94066
U.S.A.
christophercpayne@journalstone.com.

Please make check or money order payable to:
JournalStone Publishing and send to the address above.
Credit/Debit cards via Paypal at:
christophercpayne@journalstone.com. Advertising
rates available. Discounts for bulk and standing retail
orders.

Fiction

Interviews

Features

Hellnotes Reviews

SAMHAIN KNOWS WHAT SCARES YOU!

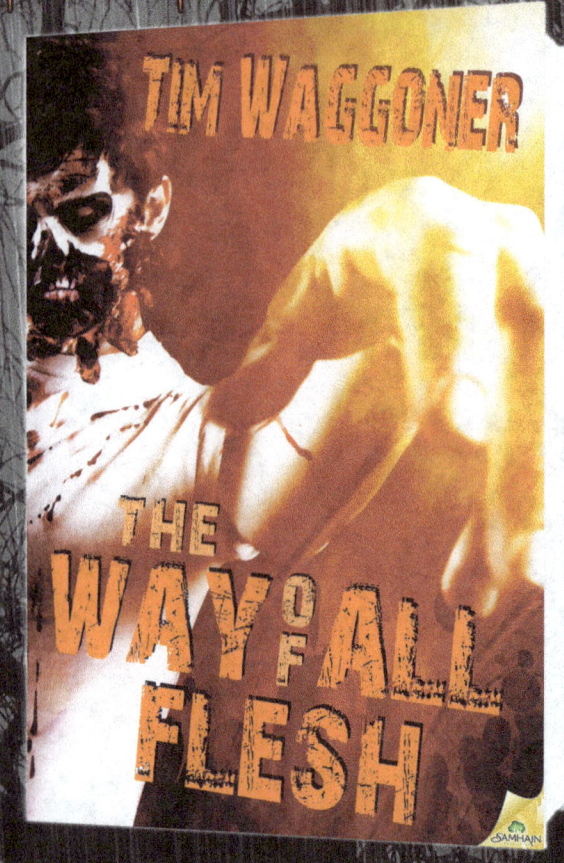

TIM WAGGONER

THE WAY OF ALL FLESH

A PLACE FOR SINNERS

AARON DRIES

HUNTER SHEA

THE WAITING

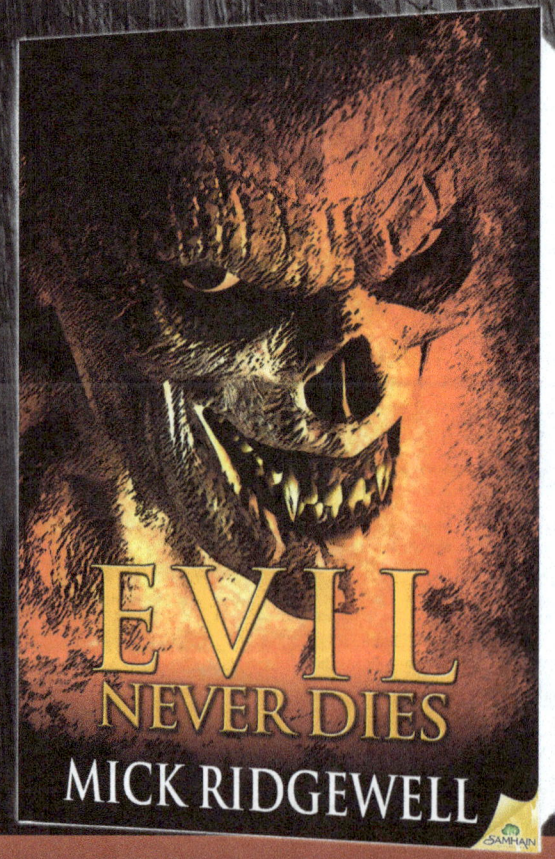

EVIL NEVER DIES

MICK RIDGEWELL

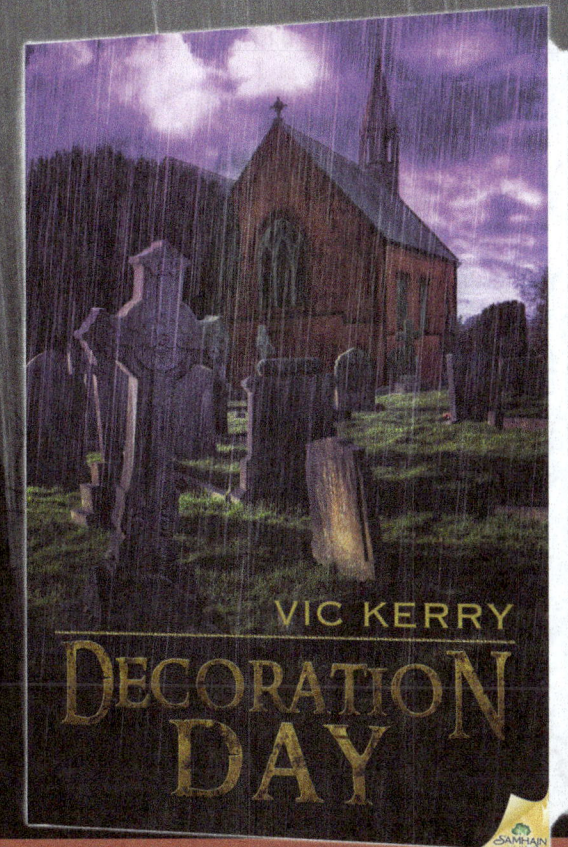
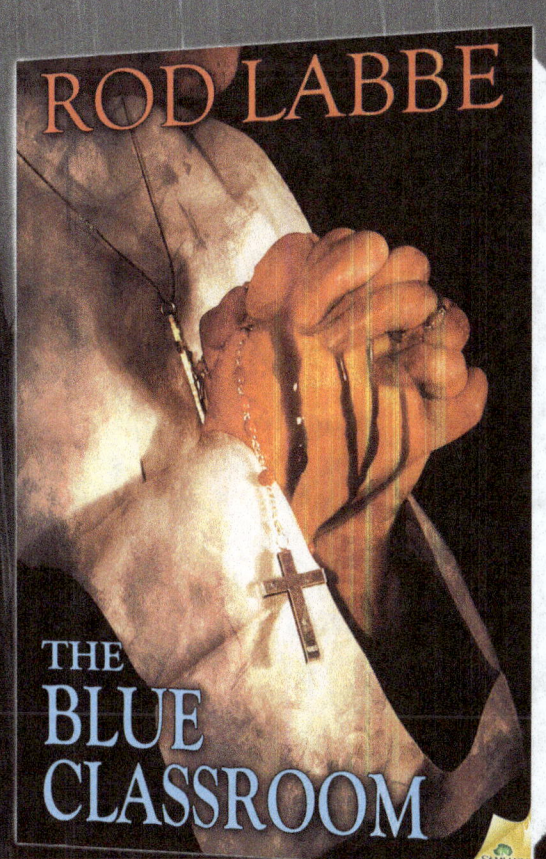

Updates
from the Fantastique...

Greetings... Welcome to issue #27 of *Dark Discoveries*, where our focus is Dark Mystery and the interplay between horror and suspense thrillers. Before we dig into the theme, I would like to address my new role as the Editor-in-Chief of the magazine. As James mentioned in the last issue, although I am taking over for him, he will remain on the team as a "creative consultant," contributing regular articles, offering his input on themes and content, and assisting with distribution and advertising. So there's no need to fear; the man who singlehandedly started DD, kept it going, and—with considerable help from former Managing Editor Jason V Brock—raised it to the level of professionalism in which we find it today, is not going anywhere. DD readers can still expect his presence to be felt in the issues. I'm extremely grateful to James Beach and Chris Payne of JournalStone Publishing for trusting me with this position, and I look forward to putting some of my creative ideas into action. *Dark Discoveries* is going to pay witness to some of the most wild, unusual, and interesting content ever to grace its pages in future years. We are starting a journey. I hope you will come along for the ride.

Now, the issue you hold in your hands (or electronic device) is the first one where I have managed the content as Editor-in-Chief, with the help of James and the rest of our wonderful staff. We have crafted something amazing, and I'm sure you will enjoy it. This time around we are exploring the theme of Dark Mystery, with a mixture of suspense, horror, and intrigue. It is possible that something of a dichotomy exists between thriller and horror readers; but nonetheless we have attempted to cross-combine the two. The fiction in this issue is not primarily centered on the *whodunit* quality of mystery literature, even though that is one aspect present in the stories; rather, they explore the "mystery" component in a more literal sense, while remaining true to their horror roots. "What is the mystery?" or "How might we figure out this mystery?" are the questions these authors address in their tales—not content with simply solving a murder, but trying to understand the "mystery" of the circumstances—which are possibly supernatural. *Dark Discoveries* is a horror magazine. The stories contained herein will always be some variant of horror. Simple as that.

The fiction in this issue is all original and can be found nowhere else. We have a new story from the weird and versatile pen of Brian Evenson about a mysterious teddy bear, as well as a new interview with him; a horrific tale from Bentley Little involving murder in the Israeli desert; Maurice Broaddus, co-editor of the Bram Stoker nominated *Dark Faith* anthologies, grants us an unsettling look into the agoraphobic life of online marriage and divorce; the great Tom Piccirilli shows us spousal abuse and something much worse; John R. Little offers his fast-paced suspense thriller with hints of science fiction and futurism; and finally, we have a brand-new novella from the one and only Douglas Clegg, which is probably one of the most enthralling and unconventional pieces I've read in some time.

Dr. Hannibal Lecter is explored in my article as an example of a literary character that straddles the line between mystery and horror, and James Beach contributes to the international influence of the two genres with his article on the Italian film connection. You'll find an interview with Tom Piccirilli, plus a fabulous new comic series by Joe McKinney and Patrick Freivald, and an interesting look at the shudder pulps by legendary genre writer and critic Frank M. Robinson. Additionally we have recurring columns, each of which offer thoughtful insights into this issue's theme.

As you can see there's plenty to chew on here, so you might as well turn the pages and get started. I want to reiterate how excited and honored I feel to be stepping up as Editor-in-Chief of *Dark Discoveries*, and I would like to thank the longstanding subscribers and readers for their time and support; DD is going strong and planning some great things for the future, so we're glad to have you with us. I would also like to thank our newer readers for checking out DD and giving us a chance. You won't be disappointed.

So without further ado, on with the issue. Catch me back here next time.

—Aaron J. French
Editor-in-Chief

A Career in Misperception:
An Interview with Brian Evenson

by Geoffrey H. Goodwin

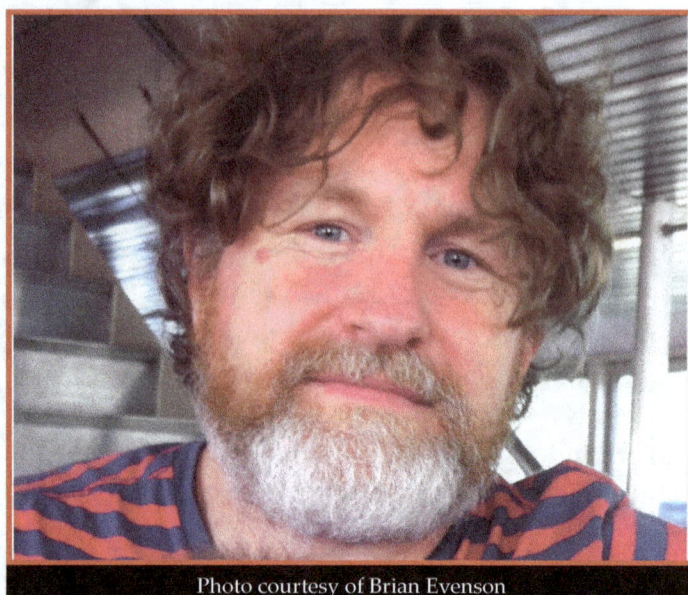

Photo courtesy of Brian Evenson

Geoffrey H. Goodwin: With over a dozen books of fiction under your belt, you have now successfully established yourself as a professional author. I wonder… what are you interested in as a writer? What do you want to do when you sit down at the blank page?

Brian Evenson: When I sit down at the blank page, I want to write a story that I would like to read. That's a big part of it. Since I read pretty eccentrically, I think possibilities for doing that are quite open. I'm very interested in stories that are related to understanding the way in which we perceive the world, as well as stories that call into question the way in which we perceive the world. I'm very interested in stories that put characters in moral and ethical dilemmas which the story just doesn't resolve. I think, in some cases, this can put the readers in a position where they have to deal with trying to continue to think through the problem. There is a philosophical element to my fiction, but I'm interested in perception and the relationship of the body to perception. I'm interested in misperception, too. I'm interested in the way in which reality is suspect or questionable. That's something I go back to again and again. There's the experience that probably a lot of people have had, some version of where you're out and it's an autumn day and you see a bird and it seems to be moving strangely. It's kind of shuffling and you don't really have a sense of what's wrong with it, but you're sure something's wrong with it—and then you come closer and you realize that, no, it's not a bird at all, it's a leaf and the wind has been blowing it around

in a particularly strange way. That moment where you, literally, are seeing something that's not there and then it becomes something else is really interesting to me. My fiction is fiction that's going to try to make you see the bird, again, in what you now think is the leaf.

GHG: When people could read about happy bunnies and cheerful stories, why on earth do people read things like horror? It's so dark and creepy.

BE: It *is* dark and creepy. I really like stories that stick with me. As a reader, I'm looking for stories that have an effect on me, that continue to work within my head after I put them down and continue to percolate within me. A lot of the stories that are not creepy but happy reinforce the status quo. I'm more interested in shaking things up and making people think about who they are and what life is to them and whether the reality we think we live in is real. Things like that. Ultimately, what that does is strengthen your sense of the world and your sense of who you are—but it does so by destabilizing it first, and it makes you a more complex and interesting person. That's the reason to read it.

GHG: You've stayed true to dark fiction even though you went through an experience in academia where some writers might've sacrificed their vision or compromised their aesthetics…

BE: I'm stubborn. I think that's part of it. I felt strongly about what I was doing and felt good about doing it, so I wasn't willing to back down. What it ended up doing, ultimately, was make me realize that I could be attacked for what I did, that what I did mattered in some ways as a writer. If I was going to write the way I do, I needed to be committed to it fully. It did clarify a lot of things for me. It wasn't a pleasant experience. I didn't enjoy it. I was really unhappy the last little bit I was there at the school, because it was an uncomfortable environment. But I think it served me well as a writer. We have these moments in our lives as writers, and in our lives in general, where we have to decide whether we're going to capitulate to pressures or if we're going to resist them and there are moments in which either of those approaches are viable. There are some things that you should capitulate to and other things you shouldn't. I didn't feel like I should have in that case. I've been lucky enough to go on and move from there to a much better university, a much better job, and a much better career than I would've had if I had given in and pulled my writing back in various ways.

GHG: That commitment certainly comes through in your writing. Given the aforementioned love for the dark and creepy, who are some of your favorite contemporary horror writers?

BE: In terms of what's going on in contemporary horror stuff, I'm very interested in Laird Barron and what he's doing. I think *The Croning* is really an interesting book. He's one of the most exciting of the new voices. I also think Peter Straub's recent book, *The Ballad of Ballard and Sandrine*, is terrific. It's a very thin novella and very weird, but also combines different sorts of genres and overlaps them in a way that I find smart and appealing. I like Caitlin R. Kiernan's work, as well. She's someone I really admire. I think Jesse Bullington is doing some interesting work, and I always like Jeff VanderMeer. He and Ann VanderMeer are both great editors, obviously, but he's a very interesting prose writer. I love Robert Aickman's work, and I find myself often going back to it.

GHG: We've talked about Thomas Ligotti in the past and *Dark Discoveries* quoted both of us in an appreciation they did for Ligotti. Is there anything else you can say about him?

BE: Thomas Ligotti is definitely someone who is underappreciated. I understand why he has a cult following and I think his writing's uncompromising in a way that I really admire. He has a distinctive voice. As a story writer, he's as good as anybody working in the field that can be loosely described as *horror*. I love *My Work Is Not Yet Done*, partly because I like novels about workplaces gone wrong, but I think it's masterful in the way it approaches things. My only complaint about Ligotti is that I wish there was more of his work out there, but I understand there's only so many hours in a day. The stories remain consistently strong over the course of his career, so in that sense, as someone who is working in a fairly obsessive way and in a fairly uncompromising way, I find him to be a tremen-

dous inspiration, and I would think that most writers who are serious writers would. I dedicated *Immobility* to him and one of the characters is playing around with certain ideas from Ligotti's *The Conspiracy Against the Human Race*, even though it's not in any way meant to be a depiction of him or a depiction even of his ideas. But I do see him as a misanthropic kindred spirit.

GHG: *Immobility*, your newest novel, has an interesting origin myth.

BE: Charles Orr was running a website called *The Hypothetical Library* and asked me to write a description for a fake book that I hadn't written and that I wouldn't write but that sounded like something I *could* write. I had this idea I'd been thinking about for a while which ended up being very much like *Immobility*. It was about an apocalyptic detective who was trying to sort some things out about his reality, who didn't know what was going on, and who was paralyzed and confused. It kind of started from a story of mine called "The Adjudicator," which I see as the most direct antecedent of *Immobility*. I'd set down and written the description of this book, chosen a name at random, Horkai, and put this fake description together. It's just a paragraph or two, and Charles did a fake cover for it. We asked Jeff VanderMeer to do a fake blurb for it, and we put it up on the website. And then I found I was thinking about what would happen if I really did write this book and different ideas about it would come to me. As that was going on, I heard from Eric Raab at Tor. He had read the posting and said, "Hey, you know this is a really good idea. You should write it as a book." That was enough to make me think, "Why not?" So I started working on it, and once I started going with it, it actually came really quickly and came really well, and, in some ways, wrote itself. So *Immobility* started as an imaginary book and developed into a real book, and changed over time. The description of it is a little different than the end product, even though it's not radically different.

GHG: And, in what some might describe as another extratextual component of your recent writing, your newest short story collection, *Windeye*, is dedicated to your lost sister.

BE: I did that for two reasons. The title story, "Windeye," has a sister who is lost and then "The Dismal Mirror" has this sister who disappears, and the relationship of the main character to the sister was clearly very strange, so I liked the idea of dedicating the book to a sister who was missing and may in fact be imaginary as well. I don't have a sister who's dead. I have several sisters, but they're all in perfectly good health. That dedication was part of the game of extending the fiction outside the bounds of the stories.

GHG: In terms of extending the fiction outside the bounds of the stories, would you say that it's a collision between genre and literature?

BE: Well, I do think there is a *connection* between genre and literature. In the past, I've tended to use the world "collision," but in this case I think it's more of an intermixing or melding of the two. Genre and literature are very friendly in *Windeye*. It's a way of trying to get all the satisfactions of genre and all the satisfactions of literature together, so that the stories can be read on both levels and still appeal. I've been moving in that direction for a while. It's only recently that I've figured out the balance in a way that I'm happy with. I think a lot of writers use "genre" as raw material so that you go in and mine genre and smelt that into something which is very different from a generic object. I would argue that someone like my colleague Robert Coover uses genre in this way. For me, in this book, it's really trying to have one foot in literature and one foot in genre at the same time, and realize it's the same terrain ultimately. That's the tricky thing: trying to find a way in which those two meld, where the seam is not visible.

GHG: It demonstrates that you're informed by reading many different literary traditions.

BE: My reading is really eccentric. I tend to read in all sorts of directions and I tend to read a lot. That's the thing I love most about the audience who read horror fiction or science fiction: they *love* to read. That audience has a lot of people who read intensely, and they read not only in their genre but literature as well, and they are very informed. I grew up reading horror, mystery,

and literature and had all of those things in my head at the same time, so it makes sense that my own work would cross those things. I was influenced by people like Lovecraft early on. Peter Straub in terms of more recent fiction. This was when I was first starting out as a writer. People like Gene Wolfe. Michael Moorcock—his novel *Behold the Man* was very important to me. Ultimately, I think those things percolated in me over time and made me realize there could be this synthesis of what people saw as literature and what people saw as genre in a way that took the best of both worlds and combined them into a powerful piece that could be read in several ways.

GHG: Samuel R. "Chip" Delany once said that we bombard ourselves with particles until we emit one of our own.

BE: I think that's a good way to say it. Chip, of course, was another writer who was important in my development. I think, for me, reading is a huge part of writing. What I pursue in terms of reading is very critical.

GHG: Who's B. K. Evenson?

BE: A name I use when I'm writing videogame novels and movie tie-ins. B. K. Evenson has written two *Deadspace* novels, one *Halo* novella, and an *Aliens* tie-in. What I would say about him is that he's very much like me, but those books are much more interested in reveling in the space that they occupy. B. K. Evenson is setting out to write an unashamedly unapologetic videogame novel but to do it in the best possible way he can. I like those projects quite a bit. They're fun to write, and they write quickly. Before, I'd never written a project and had the editor say to me, "Well, this could be more violent." The worlds of the videogames are actually well-created and well-imagined, so they are fun to work in. The other thing I've done under that name is co-write a novel with Rob Zombie. That one just came out recently, and it's based on Zombie's movie. Maybe B. K. Evenson has the ability to have more fun than Brian Evenson. The main reason I used B. K. instead of Brian is because I thought it would sort things out a little more.

GHG: Did Rob Zombie just call you on the phone?

BE: No, it was all done through agents. I think the novel we co-wrote is pretty strong and pretty interesting. It's called *Lords of Salem* and it's based on the movie of the same name. I got to watch a rough cut of the film. Interesting to see the way Zombie's developing as a director. I think there are things about that film that surprised the people who knew his work.

GHG: What's next for you?

BE: The thing I'd really like to do—I did a reading a few weeks ago and figured out how I could do it—is write a sequel to *Immobility*. I have an idea for how that's going to work. I'm hoping I can get a substantial start on it. I think the perspective will shift and it will be from the character Rikte's perspective instead of from Horkai's perspective. In terms of what's going on with contemporary stuff besides that, I'm spending a lot of time with graphic novels. I'm writing a book about Chester Brown's *Ed the Happy Clown* and am extremely intrigued by that world, which manages to do amazing things with surreal images and still has a nice verbal component to it. It's like the best of both worlds.

❦ ❦ ❦

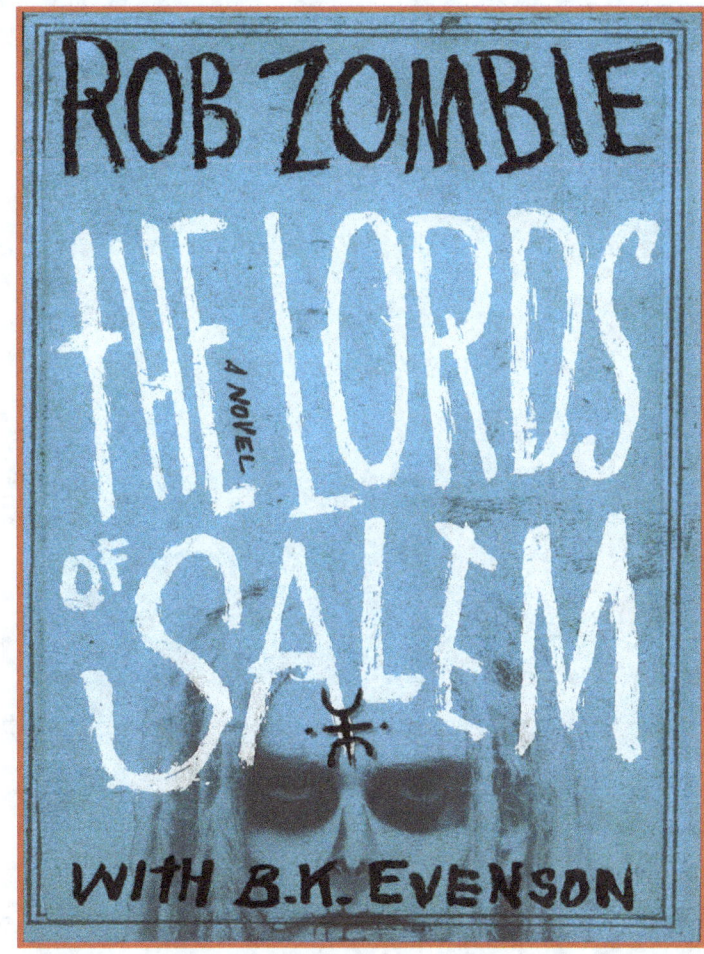

Photo courtesy of Brian Evenson

9

BearHeart™

by Brian Evenson

I.

The Donners, Michael and Lisa, first heard about BearHeart™ when they were at the obstetrician's office, about four months into the pregnancy. They were waiting at the counter, behind an almost-due Portuguese woman, and while the receptionist tried to locate some staff member named Marlie who apparently could speak broken Portuguese, Michael started looking at the brochures and flyers spread to one side of the reception window. There was an invitation to be part of a study on weight gain and pregnancy, and a flyer for an exercise class. There were glossy tri-fold pamphlets for IUDs and other contraceptives, as well as special hi-resolution color ultrasound packages that produced the image of your baby in the womb matted with a pink or blue border, or, if you wanted to keep relatives guessing as to the gender, yellow.

And then there was BearHeart™. There was a single flyer for it, battered and a little wrinkled, with phone numbers at the bottom that you could tear off. BearHeart™ offered an ultrasound that would, they claimed, be covered by most insurance. They would provide the client the usual ultrasound image but in addition, for a small fee of $50, they would make a high-resolution recording of the heart of the baby in question. This would be placed in a device that would be sewn into a silken fabric heart. This in turn would be placed inside of a teddy bear, in its chest. Squeezing the chest just right would start the recording of the heart beating, which would run for thirty minutes.

"A perfect gift for your newborn!" it exclaimed near the bottom of the flyer. "Babies find great comfort sleeping next to a bear that beats with the rhythm of their own heart! Give your child the gift of post-womb womb-like comfort! Only 50 American dollars!"

Grinning, he showed the flyer to the other half of the Donners, to Lisa, and watched as she read it.

"Weird, right?" he said.

"That can't be good for the baby," said Lisa. "Having its heart both inside and out of it at the same time. It'd be confusing."

"Sweetheart," said Michael. "The heart's not actually outside of it. It's just a recording."

"Still," said Lisa. "Would you want to curl up with a recording of your own heart?"

"I don't know," said Michael. "How do I know? I've never tried it."

They kept talking about it in the waiting room once they were checked in. It was just something weird to talk about. They talked about it too once they were in the examination room and waiting for her doctor to come, and then the doctor came. Among other things, she squirted gel on Lisa's belly and pushed a pocket ultrasound against it. It was connected to a little speaker in her jacket pocket. She turned the sound up and they heard the rapid, rhythmic sound of the baby's heart.

"Some people think it sounds like a stampede of horses," said the doctor.

There were other things, measurements, questions about diet, a little discussion, and then the visit was done. The doctor was gone and Michael was helping Lisa into her clothes again.

"Maybe we should just record a stampede of horses and put that in a bear," said Michael.

"Very funny," said Lisa.

But on the way out, after giving the receptionist his credit card for the co-pay, Michael reached over and tore off one of the tabs from the BearHeart™ flyer. "Just as a joke," he explained to his wife as she rolled her eyes. "Just so we have a story we can tell at parties. Just so we can say we did."

***

Which was why, when the baby was born premature and stillborn at six and a half months, they still had a bear containing a recording of the baby's heartbeat. They had called the number on the paper tab and made an appointment. They had gone to a body imaging facility at around 8 one night where a nervous technician wearing ash-colored scrubs had met them at the front door, unlocking it for them and locking it again after them. He hustled them into a basement ultrasound room and did a quick sonic scan. He put a binder with laminated pictures of bears in front of them and told them to choose one. They were obviously not supposed to be there.

"But that wasn't thirty minutes of heartbeat," said Michael.

"What?" said the technician. "Oh, no, we only need about 15 seconds. We just take that and loop it."

Michael wondered if he should complain. It felt like a mistake now to have come; what had started as a joke now just seemed odd. But they were far enough into it, far enough along with it, that it seemed like they should finish. Lisa was just barely tolerating it—this was not her thing, but Michael's, she had made that very clear on the drive over. And now, when he tried to get her involved in choosing a bear, she just waved the book away.

He looked quickly through them, but what did he know about choosing a bear? He hadn't even had one when he was a child. They looked all more or less the same as far as he was concerned. In the end he chose one with small black eyes and dark brown fur that was described "tight nap." He chose it partly because of the thought that he'd be able to make a joke about it when the baby was napping with the tight nap bear.

Before they left, the technician took Michael's fifty dollars, then took his insurance card and wrote down the numbers.

"It'll show up as tomorrow," he said.

"Why?" asked Michael. "Why not today?"

The technician looked furtive. "That's just the way we do it. Anything freelance shows up as tomorrow."

And then they were standing out in the improperly paved parking lot watching the technician lock the door.

***

The bear, when it arrived in the mail, wasn't dark brown at all but more a kind of streaked pale brown. The nap too couldn't be properly described as tight since it was basically not a nap at all but just fabric. It was, no question, a cheap bear. It looked worn, too, like maybe the technician had just gone and bought the first used bear he'd seen out of a thrift store.

"That's it?" said Lisa, rubbing her stomach. She was maybe six months pregnant at the time. "Hideous."

But she had stayed and listened as Michael had pushed on the bear's chest repeatedly, trying to switch on the heartbeat. It took a while to make it go, but when it finally started, even she had to admit it sounded remarkably clear.

"But even so, why would a baby want to listen to it?" asked Lisa.

Michael shrugged. He had no answer. He toyed with it a while, turning the heart on and off, and then he'd tossed it in one corner of the crib, to wait for the baby.

***

For all intents and purposes, the Donners forgot about the bear. Instead, they prepared for the baby. They read online about what they needed and what they should expect. They filled the house with baby things, slowly settled into the idea of a baby coming. They did another ultrasound, this one at the obstetrician's office, and found out they were having a girl. Michael was surprised—he'd expected a boy, had directed his thinking toward that the whole way along. But then he began to get his mind around the idea of having a girl and grew to like it.

Indeed, it was all going smoothly—a *textbook pregnancy* the obstetrician liked to say—and then, suddenly, it was not. Michael Donner came home from work and called out to Lisa Donner and there was no answer. He thought she'd gone out. He went into the kitchen and poured himself a drink. He took off his tie and placed it over the back of a chair. He wandered into the bedroom, and then he saw her, collapsed on the floor, unconscious, her thighs stained with blood.

He called 911. Then he checked to see if she was still breathing. She was. He slapped her and talked to her and chafed her hands until she started to come around but even then she was confused and didn't seem to know where she was. And then she saw the blood and became hysterical and it was all that he could do to control her

until the paramedics arrived and sedated her and bundled her off to the hospital.

***

"Sometimes," the pediatrician told them a few hours later, "the pregnancy just doesn't take." It wasn't their fault, there was nothing they could have done differently, sometimes the body just decided to let the developing fetus go.

"But we heard the heart," protested Lisa. "We saw her on the monitor. She was alive."

The pediatrician shook her head. Who knew what had gone wrong with the fetus? Something had, and that had stopped the baby from going to term. They shouldn't blame themselves, they should just understand that this was something that happened.

***

But Lisa had a hard time not blaming herself. It was her body after all that had been holding the baby and thus, she reasoned, her body that had killed it. Michael tried to comfort her, to hold her, but quickly came to realize that she did not want to be comforted or held. She wanted to be alone with her grief.

There followed days when she almost didn't leave the bed, days when Michael had to force her to eat. They were told, after the loss of the baby, that she was old enough that they could get a birth certificate, and so they filled out a birth certificate and a death certificate at the same time, marking a one minute difference between when she had been born and when she had died, even though to Michael it seemed like the baby had been born dead. But this, they were told in the hospital, was the custom. They were asked if they wanted to have a funeral, were told that that too was something that could be allowed, but Lisa couldn't face it. Instead they had the body cremated and took the ashes home. He didn't know what to do with them and couldn't get Lisa to say what she wanted done, so he placed the urn temporarily upstairs, on the changing table in the nursery.

When the baby had been born stillborn she had held it—one of the nurses said that this was sometimes done, was one way of saying goodbye—but it hadn't seemed to do Lisa any good. And it had ended up giving Michael nightmares. It was hard not to think about: the child, obviously dead and not fully formed, pressed against his wife's skin as she wept.

They left the baby things just as they were. At first Michael had suggested taking them away, storing them in the basement, but when he began to gather them his wife had given a strange keening cry that had frightened him as much as anything ever had, and he had put everything back.

So there they were: Lisa barely functional, Michael trying to live on tiptoe so as not to make it worse for her, the baby things for a missing baby all neatly arrayed in the nursery, both of the Donners waiting and hoping for a time when they would feel better.

II.

About three months after losing the baby, Michael woke up to hear a noise. He could barely hear it, wasn't even sure for a while that he wasn't imagining it. He lay in bed, his wife crumpled beside him, either asleep or pretending to be, and listened. For a while he thought he might drift off, but there was something about the sound that he couldn't quite put his finger on that continued to keep him awake.

Yawning, he finally got up and went in pursuit of it. He opened the bedroom door and went into the living room, but he wasn't hearing it nearly as well there. He went into the kitchen and stood holding his breath. Still nothing. Same in his office.

In the end, he went back into the bedroom and lay down. Immediately he started to hear it again.

He was wide awake now. He tried to find the sound and this time walked from place to place in the room, listened. Until, finally, he realized he was hearing it through the heating register in the ceiling, that it was coming from upstairs, from the nursery.

He went upstairs and opened the nursery door and waited. There it was, a sound like white noise, but softer, a strange thrumming to it. He walked around the darkened room, slowly homing in on it, only realizing at the last moment that it was coming from the crib.

For a moment he experienced sheer panic. It flashed through his mind that they had had the baby after all, but that both he and his wife were in denial that the baby existed. They had left it up here, alone, to die. And then he reached out and felt around and found the body of the bear.

Its heart was beating, slowly and regularly. Its borrowed heart, rather, since it was the sound of his dead child's heart. He'd completely forgotten about it. There must be something wrong with the mechanism that had caused it to go off at random, he thought.

He held the bear for a few minutes until, as suddenly as it had begun, the beating of the heart stopped. Had it really been thirty minutes? Perhaps there was a glitch somewhere. He placed the bear gently back in the crib and went back to bed.

***

The next day he didn't think about it. He left as usual to go to work, spent the day at the office. But when he came home for lunch he found that his wife wasn't asleep. She

was up and functioning, had showered, had even tidied the house. Something had begun to change. For the better.

He took a deep breath. In the months after the baby's death, watching his wife struggle, struggling himself, he had told himself that they, the Donners, would make it through, but he hadn't exactly believed it. But now he thought it might be possible.

He kissed her, they ate the lunch he'd picked up at the Vietnamese place, then he went back to work, whistling. The rest of the day was a good day, one of the best he'd had in a while. He felt good all the way up to the moment when, at the end of the workday, he walked through the door and found his wife sitting in the living room, rocking the bear, listening to the beating of its heart.

"Ssshh," she said. "She's almost asleep." And smiled.

He had stopped dead in the doorway. He just watched her from there, wondering what he should say, what, if anything, he could say.

"Do you want to hold her?" she asked.

"Lisa," he said. "You know that's just a toy, right?"

She looked down at the bear in her lap. "Yes," she said. "You're mostly right."

"Mostly?"

She nodded. "Only it has her heart," she said.

"Just the sound of her heartbeat," he said. "It's a recording."

"Sure," she said, after a long pause. "I know that."

He waited for her to go on, but she didn't say anything more, just kept rocking softly, looking down at the bear.

"Lisa," he said.

"She was calling to me," she said finally.

"Oh, honey," he said, and moved to take the bear, but she was clutching it now, not letting it go.

***

In the end, after a lot of talking, he got her to relinquish it of her own accord. Yes, she said, she understood. She hadn't meant to scare him. Of course she understood—it wasn't their daughter, it was just a teddy bear. She hadn't meant to suggest anything beyond that, she claimed.

"What did you mean when you said it was calling to you?" asked Michael.

"She, you mean," said Lisa, her eyes not meeting his.

"What?"

"I didn't say *it*," she said. "I said *she*."

He gestured with his hand. "Does it matter?" he said.

For a moment she looked at him with a shocked expression, but then slowly it vanished and she looked away. "No," she said. "Not really."

And then she became listless again, like she had been before. He led her back to bed and she let him. Maybe it would have been better to let her keep the bear, he couldn't help but think. But another part of him was worried about what would happen if he did.

"What did you mean when you said she was calling to you?" he asked again, tucking her in.

"Just that," she said. "I heard it. I heard something and went up to see what it was. It was the beating of her heart."

"It just started on its own?"

She nodded. "I didn't do anything. It just started on its own."

Having experienced something similar himself, he felt he had no choice but to believe her. There was something wrong with the player inside the bear, some sort of glitch. They would have to fix it. Either that or get rid of the bear. Probably better to do that, he thought, to just get rid of it.

***

But a few days later, he still hadn't gotten rid of the bear. Once it was back in the nursery, he again simply forgot about it. Lisa was spending most of her time back in bed again, but she was getting up a little more, and Michael told himself she was slowly getting better.

He would have completely forgotten about the bear if, three days later, he hadn't awoken in bed again knowing he had heard something. It was louder this time. Half in a daze, head throbbing, he made his way out of the bedroom and up the stairs to the nursery, but when he got there, the bear was nowhere to be seen. The sound, too, had diminished. He looked for the bear for a few minutes before returning to the bedroom. Only then did he realize that the bear was in the bed.

Furious, he woke Lisa up. She looked sleepy and confused. He brandished the bear at her.

"What do you have to say about this?" he said.

"About what?" she said.

Couldn't she just admit that she'd gone and got the bear and brought it into the bed? What was wrong with her?

"But I—" she said.

"No buts," he said, and continued to excoriate her until, furious herself she yelled:

"But I didn't go get it!"

Then how did it get here? he wanted to know. Stuffed animals don't just walk around the house. One of the two of them got it and God knew it wasn't him. Which left her.

"No," she shouted. "I swear. I didn't get it!"

He took a deep breath. All right, he said finally calming down a little, maybe she didn't go get it. Or didn't know she had. He was willing to accept that as a possibility. Maybe she had done it in her sleep, without thinking.

"No," she said, calming down a little herself. She had been in the bed the whole time. She was sure of it.

He shook his head. There just wasn't, he told her, any other explanation.

"What about you?" she said. "Why couldn't you have been the one to do it in your sleep?"

Without thinking, he said, "I'm not the one who's sick." He immediately regretted it, but it was too late. It was the beginning of an argument that ended up with the bear in the outside trash, his wife livid, and him having to sleep upstairs on a pile of blankets in the nursery.

***

The first thing he saw when he woke up was the bear, in the crib, pressed against the bars, like it was watching him. He realized, with a dull fury, that his wife must have gotten up once he was asleep and got the bear out of the trash and put it back in the crib. It had been a bad idea ever to get the bear, he told himself. At the time it had just seemed like a joke, and it would have been a joke if their child had survived. But considering all that had happened, it was a very bad idea.

He thought about going down and yelling at her about it, but wasn't that exactly what she wanted? No, he told himself, he would handle it like a grown-up: he would pretend not even to have seen the bear. He would simply put it back in the trash where it belonged, and then, since today was trash pickup, stay home long enough to make sure it was taken away. Then that would be the end of the bear. They wouldn't have to think about it anymore. They could go on with getting back to the way their lives had been.

***

And indeed, he managed to do all that. He showered, had some breakfast. He took a bowl of cereal in to his wife but she was still asleep—or perhaps pretending to be asleep so she wouldn't have to speak to him. He kissed her on the cheek and then went upstairs and got the bear and put it, heart now beating, in the trashcan. Then he got into his car and waited there behind the wheel in the driveway until he saw in the rearview mirror the trash truck arrive, the mechanical arm pick up and dump the can. *There,* he thought, starting up the car, *over and done*.

***

And that might have been the end of it. In normal circumstances it would have been. When he came home that night, he apologized to his wife and she apologized to him. She cried, and he had the decency, if that was what it was, not to accuse her of bringing the bear back into the house. And she, in turn, had the decency not to acknowledge that he had put the bear back in the trash again. She promised to make more of an effort, and he promised to be more patient. In short, they did all the things that each half of a couple does, out of fear or out of love, after being afraid of having gone too far.

***

But that was not the end. Three nights later, or four, when Michael had let his guard down, when he was beginning to feel that they were returning to their normal life, he again awoke in the middle of the night knowing he had heard something.

No, he thought, still mostly asleep. *Just imagining it. Dream.*

He tried to go back to sleep, he really did, but the sound wouldn't let him. Not a sound, really. More the ghost of a sound. But it would not leave him alone. Slowly, it began to fill him with dread.

He got out of bed. He listened in the bedroom, but the sound wasn't coming from there. He listened in the living room, even though he knew the sound wasn't there either. He listened everywhere in the house except for where he expected the sound to be coming from and then, in the end, he went to listen there too.

***

He opened the door to the nursery. Yes, there it was, the sound was here, the faint beating of a heart. There was the bear, in the crib, just as it had been for months now. But how had his wife gotten the bear back? Had it somehow gotten caught in the can and hadn't been thrown away? Had it ended up not making it into the garbage truck and she'd found it in the street? There must, he hoped, be some logical explanation.

***

He turned on the light and stared at the bear through the bars. The heart now had stopped, just as suddenly as it had begun. The bear, he saw, was filthy, covered with a layer of gray dust as fine as ash. He would have to destroy it, but before he did, he felt his wife owed him an explanation. He would wipe the bear off and then show it to her, get her to explain, and then, in front of her, he would destroy it.

But when he picked it up to clean it, he realized something had changed. The bear felt different now, heavier and when he moved it something seemed to sift through its body, like it was filled with sand. He moved it closer to his face and sniffed it and realized that no, it wasn't an ashy layer of dust, it was simply ash, and when, with a face, he laid the bear on the changing table to wipe it clean, he realized where the ash had come from.

The lid was loose on the urn there, a scattering of ash spilled around the urn's base, and when he looked in, he realized it was mostly empty.

His limbs felt very heavy. He could see, now that he was looking for it, where the seam in the fabric had been torn open and clumsily unstitched to fill the bear with his daughter's ashes. Things were, he suddenly knew, much worse than he'd realized.

Trying to think, he opened the urn and held it just under the edge of the changing table, slowly sweeping the loose ash into it. Then he put it back on the table and began to unpluck the new seam on the bear.

As soon as he did, the heart began beating again. And then, in a way that he didn't understand and that he found he never properly could describe later to the police when they were questioning him as to the death of his wife, the bear smiled at him.

He pulled his hand back, as if bitten. He stared at the bear. *This is the moment*, he thought hopefully, *when I wake up.*

But he did not wake up. He was already awake. And as he reached out again, this time to tear the head off the bear that had stuffed itself with his child's ashes and that contained a sonic replica of his child's heart, he had no way of knowing that this would be the last moment where he still felt like he had control of his life, that from here on out, things would only get worse.

☙☙☙

DOUBLE X CHROMOSOME:

By Yvonne Navarro

I'm told that the theme for this issue is dark/mystery. Dark...mystery. Dark mystery.

Dark.

Mystery.

How fitting. I think I'll write about writers and taxes.

Yeah, you're running. You're hiding. Why? Because to writers, taxes *are* the mystery. Taxes *are* the dark. Taxes are the *monster* in the dark.

All I can say is start young.

Paying? Maybe. Saving receipts? Definitely. Organizing? *Absolutely.*

When it comes to a writer doing taxes, you—not the IRS—are your own worst enemy. You can be the gal who on April 1st (yeah, you're a fool) takes an antacid when she looks at a manila envelope bulging with random, crumpled, and coffee-stained receipts coupled with cryptic, half-ripped Post-It Notes. Or you can be the Queen (Hail You!) who hits **Submit Tax Return Now** on your electronic form on March 15th, then goes out to have pizza and wings instead of yanking out precious clumps of quickly graying hair. And all because you labeled some folders, did your filing, made a few math (::gasp!::) calculations, and bought a copy of TurboTax Home and Small Business. In fact, you might even be paying for those wings with a refund. Imagine *that!*

I am not a tax woman, and I don't play one on TV. But

THE MAMMOTH BOOK OF

GHOST STORIES BY WOMEN

25 CHILLING TALES OF THE SUPERNATURAL

KELLEY ARMSTRONG, MURIEL GRAY, SARAH PINBOROUGH, LILITH SAINTCROW, LISA TUTTLE AND MANY MORE

EDITED BY MARIE O'REGAN

I *am* a writer and I've filed as such since the mid-eighties. (I'm only twenty-six, but you'll have to send me lots of money to see how I managed that. I accept PayPal.) You don't have to show a profit as a writer to take reasonable deductions; the intent to make a profit is what counts. So if you deduct a bedroom in your house as an office, it has to be an office. It can't be half office, half nursery, or half office, half exercise room. If you have a two foot by three foot pressboard desk with a computer on it in a corner of the family room, you cannot deduct your family room as your office. The *room* is it, not a corner of it, or the portion of it that you stick your laptop in when you're not using it. Putting a baby gate up between the chair and the couch does not an office make.

What else. Postage used to be a big deal. Now, not so much. Sure, a very few people still want submissions via mail, and some publishers still want signed original contracts. For the most part, though, this is the age of electronic transmissions, so even paper and printer ink are passé. What does that mean? It means you can deduct the cost of your internet service, and provided you actually *talk* to people instead of cower in the closet, perhaps a portion of your telephone bill. And your electric bill. And your heating and air-conditioning bill. I am not kidding. It all gets figured out on a percentage basis (yep, this is where that part comes in about how your office is *only* an office and not a shared space where you also stash all the 1950s stuff you inherited from dear, departed Aunt Edwina).

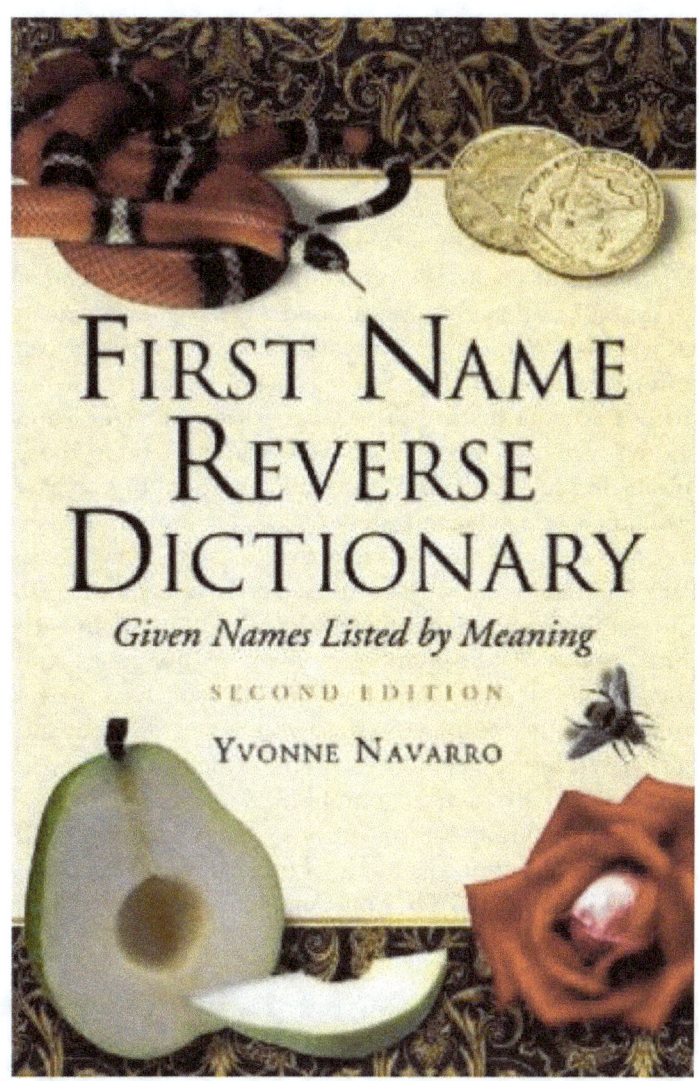

FIRST NAME
REVERSE
DICTIONARY
Given Names Listed by Meaning
SECOND EDITION
YVONNE NAVARRO

Do you go to conventions? A weekly writers' group? Book signings? Lots of deductions there: registration fees, travel (airfare or rental car, mileage if you drive yourself), and a portion of meals and those endless coconut-flavored, umbrella-wielding drinks you buy in the hotel bar. Don't get caught in the trap that you can deduct all this foodage and use it as an excuse to gorge on lobster and champagne. Again, only a *portion* is deductible. My trick? I find a liquor store close by and stock up on Barefoot White Zinfandel, then I ask the lobby bar for a wine glass. Maybe I should've titled this column "Cons on the Cheap."

There are a bazillion things that go into a writer's tax return but a finite amount of space here. So let's talk about a dirty word. *A-U-D-I-T*. Oh yeah, excluding the actual acronym IRS, that's probably the only word that can elicit as much fear as the word *lawyer*. But here's the thing: you know that scrunchy feeling in your gut? That little flipping butterfly that beats against your stomach wall when you type in the deduction for the $3,000 gaming computer? Yeah, that one. If you pay attention to it, it'll make you backspace out that deduction so that if you *do* get audited, you won't get dropped into a pot of merrily boiling water. Keep it honest, keep it reasonable, and you'll be fine. My friend Kevin J. Anderson survived an audit many years ago, and the only point he lost to the tax man was the deduction for a super spiffy sound system for his office. He had everything in order, he had all his receipts, he had intent to make a profit. At this point, he's done a helluva lot better than that, but that is his story, not this column.

Intent to make a profit. Hmmmmm.

What intent to make a profit is NOT:

Sitting at your desk for a couple of hours after dinner every night and screwing around on Facebook instead of writing. Writing long emails to friends in fourteen different states and Uganda instead of writing. Starting to research the history of Sasquatch for your story and ending up sixty-five clicks later reading about those interesting red-spotted mushrooms you thought you saw growing between the monster's toes in a photograph thirty websites earlier. You now know they're poisonous only to Peruvian women who've borne two boys, one middle girl, and eat them on the night of the fourth full moon in each third month of odd-numbered years in Mongolia. And guess what? It's a quarter to midnight, you have to get up at six in the morning because you have a day job, and you've written two sentences. If you're lucky.

What intent to make a profit IS:

It's writing: essays, articles, blogs, stories, and novels. It's *submitting* as many of those things as you can to **PAYING MARKETS**. You can't make a profit if you don't get paid, and if you give away your work, you're not going to get paid. It doesn't get any clearer than that. You can't trade a contributor's copy for a loaf of bread, and the IRS isn't going to think much of your home office and incidental deductions if all you ever received in return were/are contributor's copies. And remember that age of technology thing? Nowadays you might not even get those.

Intent to make a profit means intent to get paid in *real money*.

Make enough of it, and real money is taxable, even after deductions. And taxes make the IRS happy.

Not such a mystery after all.

~~~~~~~~~~~~~~~~~~~~~~~~~~~~~~~~~~

Check out Yvonne's story, "Return" in *The Mammoth Book of Ghost Stories by Women*, edited by Marie O'Regan. Her *First Name Reverse Dictionary* has been a favorite tool for writers for decades.

Comments? Questions? Suggestions? Yvonne Navarro can be reached via her website, Facebook page, or at her Dark Discoveries email: yvonne@journalstone.com.

Picture of Yvonne not writing taken by Ann Ochse.

~~~~~~~~~~~~~~~~~~~~~~~~~~~~~~~~~~

THE ITALIAN CONNECTION: CRIME FILMS OF THE 1970s

By James R. Beach

As part of a series of articles on European cinema in Dark Discoveries (the first being a two-part piece on giallo films by Scott Stine in issues #19 and #20, the second an article on giallo actresses in issue #25, Derek Botelho, and lastly my own piece on spaghetti westerns in issue #26), here is the latest on Italian crime films for our Dark Mystery special.

Drawing a bit of a parallel to America, Italy in the late 1960s was in a state of upheaval. Riots, protests and bombings shook the Italian citizens and, also much like the US, students were starting to question authority, distrust the government and especially the police force. Cinema was primed for a change as well. Films that blurred the boundaries between law enforcement and criminals became increasing popular in the late 1960s and early 1970s in Italy and the rest of the world. These became known as "polizieschi" or "crime" movies. This article is an attempt to take a look at how the horror genre is broader than people usually think and to show our readers that horror is ever-present in various forms of films, fiction and entertainment. Crime and fear of violence to ourselves, loved ones, our property, and our psyche is something that affects all of our lives.

A big influence for this new Italian genre comes from both the American and French cinema. One of the first movies to make an impact was *Bullet* (Peter Yates, 1968), featuring Steve McQueen, which showed a reckless cop driven to catch a criminal at any cost. *French Connection* (William Friedkin, 1971), *Dirty Harry* (Don Siegel, 1971) and *Magnum Force* (Ted Post, 1973) were extensions of this premise and were all very popular worldwide. (They especially made a big impact in Italy on both audiences and filmmakers.) The former starred Gene Hackman as a detective pursuing a drug ring and the latter films starred Clint Eastwood from Sergio Leone's popular spaghetti western trilogy (and whose presence certainly helped the Harry series' popularity in Italy). *Serpico* (1973) starring Al Pacino also made a big splash worldwide and was an American/Italian co-production (something which continually blurred the lines in that regard, as well as the proliferation of American actors in Italian films and vice versa). The French films *Dirty Money* (Jean-Pierre Melville, 1970) and *Borsalino* (Jacques Deray, 1970) were a big influence (the latter also co-produced by an Italian production company). And of course the adaptation of Mario Puzo's *Godfather* by director Francis Ford Coppola (1972) and Marlon Brando's Oscar-refused performance (as well as Pacino's career-defining turn) cannot be understated for their impact on the world and introduction for many to the Italian and American Mafia.

Not all of the influence was from outside of the big boot, either. *The Violent Four* (Carlo Lizzani, 1968) featuring Thomas Milan and Margret Lee (a Jess Franco regular) and *Mafia* (aka: *Day of the Owl*, Damiano Damiani, 1968), starring Franco Nero (*Django*) were the first to set the tone, with the former a tale of four bank

and Mussolini's defeat, Italy would face another sinister force—the Sicilian Mafia. Within a few years, writers would take on these villains in their fiction and eventually be part of the foundation of the crime genre.

The Day of the Owl (1961), by Leonardo Sciacia, more than any other novel helped set the blueprint for the crime films to come close to a decade later. The premise involves the police investigating the murder of a local businessman and how they run into the mafia at every turn. It showed implicitly how deeply imbedded into the Italian society the crime force was at that time—as well as their influence on the community in the form of culture, the arts, etc. It reflected the burgeoning paranoia and how it was becoming tough to trust anybody. In other words, it reflected the real world in many ways: crimes go unsolved, criminals go unpunished and so on. By the late 1960s Sciacia also started injecting politics into his books. Equal Danger (1971) blamed the murders of high-level judges on left-wing extremists (a reflection of the growing unease around the bombings and riots).

Of course the Italian crime films don't really fit in any outright "horror" category, or have any nod toward the supernatural part of our genre, but in terms of realistic fears, paranoia and horrors of violence were a big influence. And the level of violence grew in both the crime and giallo films, and both were influential on the horror and terror/suspense films to come later. Much of the slasher films and police procedural films of the next couple of decades in the US felt this shadow. There was one main difference between the two genres (although they often overlapped and blurred the lines of those boundaries). Whereas gialli took a bit more of the traditional mystery blueprint (influenced strongly by German writer Edgar Wallace and the Krimi films of the late 50s/early 60s) and mostly focused on a psycho killer (often times fetishist and sexually disturbed) and kept you guessing about their identity—with the police force often being ineffectual or nonexistent or at least somewhat in the background. In gialli it was not uncommon for a suspect to take up the mantle and become a detective themselves. The crime films put the police right in front and focused mainly on the crime world and mafia influence, and/or police and political corruption. The violence and sex was pushed to the forefront of both types of films and also helped to break down barriers in the rest of the world. Although the giallo and crime films were often cut by the time they reached our shores (sometimes quite heavily), they continually wore the censors down and eventually more and more violence and sex became acceptable in the US and other countries.

robbers and the latter an early police vs. mobsters story by a director who continued to do fine work in the genre throughout the seventies. Romolo Guerrieri, director of the pioneering giallo, The Sweet Body of Deborah (1968), helmed Detective Belli (Un Detective, 1969) again starring popular actor Nero. It was very well received and three months later, the influential Violent City (Sergio Sollima, 1970) hit the streets. Starring Telly Savalas and Charles Bronson, it made a big impact and inspired other spaghetti western directors to switch gears (much like giallo films also did around that time).

Other films that were made in Italy in the late 1960s that were influential include: Liliana Cavani's I Cannibali (1970)—an art school, modern take on a Sophocles tragedy set during the protest years of 1967-1969; and Elio Petri's Investigation of A Citizen Under Suspicion (1970)—which focuses on a fascist police inspector who murders his mistress and questions the authority of our leaders in general and the power they often wield.

A lot of the socio-political aspects of the genre actually date back as far as 1927 and the novel That Awful Mess on the Via Merluna by Italian author Carlo Emilio Gadda. Gadda employed a crime story framework to explore the fascism of Mussolini's regime. The story showed how hard it was to investigate a murder when society was so corrupt around the protagonists. After World War II

Let's take a look at some of the standout directors, actors, writers and musical composers in the field:

Probably the best director of crime films is **Fernando di Leo**. Starting out writing spaghetti western screenplays for Sergio Leone (*A Fistful of Dollars* and *For A Few Dollars More*), Sergio Corbucci (*Navajo Joe* and *Johnny Yuma*) and even Lucio Fulci (*Massacre Time*), di Leo eventually moved on to directing his own films. He initially did some sex comedies and dramas and later ventured into giallo and terror territory with films like: *Slaughter Hotel* (1971), *To Be Twenty* (1978) and *Madness* (1979), but his oeuvre of polizieschi ranks high. He was also one of the few to embrace the noir genre of the 30s and 40s and his films are often dark and downbeat.

Di Leo's noir trilogy is especially good and took the American and French genre into the modern Italian world. The first film, *Caliber 9* (1972), is the standout of the bunch (though the other two are also very good) and stars comedian Gastone Moschin in a landmark performance as small time crook Ugo Piazza, recently out of a prison stint for a robbery gone bad. He wants to go straight, but the mob thinks he stole the $300,000 and they want it back. Everybody including the cops believe Ugo has the money and the noose tightens around his neck as the film progresses and he professes his innocence. Adapted from a story by Giorgio Scerbanenco, the fast-paced, stylized action sequences and plot twists (a big influence on Quentin Tarantino especially, and John Woo) make it not only one of the best *Italian* crime films, but also one of the best *crime* films ever. The supporting cast is excellent with Bond girl Barbara Bouchet (*Don't Torture A Duckling, Amuck!, The Black Belly of the Tarantula*) as his go-go dancer girlfriend (with a very memorable dance sequence), Mario Adorf as one of the vicious gangsters, character-actor Lionel Standell as the cruel mafia boss (*The Americano*), French star Phillippe Leroy as an ex-partner and one of Ugo's only friends, and Luigi Pistilli (*A Bay of Blood, Case of the Scorpion's Tail*) as a radical cop with ideas of societal reform in mind. Di Leo quickly followed up with *The Italian Connection* (1972) starring Mario Adorf (from *Caliber 9*) and Henry Silva and Woody Strode as a pair of merciless hitmen (Tarantino modeled John Travolta and Samuel Jackson's characters in *Pulp Fiction* after them). Like *Caliber 9*, it tells the story of a small-time crook who is framed—only this time for the theft of a shipment of heroin. He is pursued through Milan by the aforementioned gunmen, but eventually fights back. The final film in the trilogy is *The Boss* (1973) and stars Henry Silva, Richard Conte and Gianni Garko. A bomb attack kills all the members of a mafia family except

Cocchi. He soon figures out it was an attack from a rival family and seeks revenge by hiring a hitman who starts a mob war. Based on a true story, or at least real people and events supposedly, it was a bold statement on corruption and the mafia at the time.

Di Leo also directed a number of other excellent crime films like: *Shoot First, Die Later* (1974) featuring an all-corrupt police force; *Loaded Guns* (1975); *Kidnap Syndicate* (1975); *Rulers of the City* (1976) starring Jack Palace and Fulci regular Al Cliver; and *Blood and Diamonds* (1977)—amongst others.

Starting out in westerns, **Enzo G. Castellari's** debut in the crime genre was with *Cold Eyes of Fear* (1971), starring Giovanna Ralli, Frank Wolff and Fernando Rey. Although interesting, it is a weaker effort by the director starting out somewhat like a giallo and then shifting to a crime/hostage film. His next film, *High Crime* (1972), starring Franco Nero is a much stronger effort. Nero plays a police inspector matching wits with an international drug ring. (Castellari also used his "Enzo Girolami" pseudonym on this which he used off and on during his career). He repeated that success with *Street Law* (1974), again starring Nero as a citizen beaten up by criminals and with the lack of police turns to vigilantism. Co-starring with Franco was the always beautiful and alluring Barbara Bach (a Bond girl, giallo regular and later wife of Beatle Ringo Starr). Castellari followed up with two efforts starring Fabio Testi, *The Big Racket* (1976) and *The Heroin Busters* (1977), before directing the hit war movie *Inglorious Bastards* in 1978 starring Bo Svenson and Fred Williamson (which Quentin Tarantino remade in 2009).

As mentioned previously, **Damiano Damiani** was an early pioneer in the Italian crime genre with his 1968 film *Mafia*. This started his relationship with Franco Nero that lasted a few years and also starred Claudia Cardinale (Fellini's *8 ½*) and crime movie regular Lee J. Cobb. Franco went on to star in: *Confessions of a Police Captain* (1970) co-starring Martin Balsam and Marilu Tolo; *The Case is Closed, Forget it* (1971) co-starring John Steiner; and *How to Kill A Judge* (1974). His *Confessions of a Police Captain* itself is a brilliant film and was extremely successful (with over 2 million people going to see it in 1970). It tells of a frustrated police captain who uses illegal means to put a criminal behind bars and along with *Dirty Harry* and *Dirty Money*, made the biggest impression on Italian audiences and filmmakers. The ambiguousness and questionable morals of the police in the film set the standard for later movies in the crime genre. Damiano went on to direct a number of films in other genres and eventually even took the reins for the underrated sequel *Amityville 2: The Possession* in 1982.

Stelvio Massi directed eleven films in the crime genre as well as worked as a cinematographer on others (which is also how he started out in the sixties on westerns, etc.). Although some consider Massi not as strong as di Leo, Lenzi, Castellari and other masters of the craft, he still delivered a number of entertaining crime films. His "Mark" trilogy is generally considered his best and certainly his most popular. Kicking off with *Mark* (aka: *Mark Il Poliziatto*, 1975) starring Franco Gasparri, Lee J. Cobb and Sara Sperati, it tells of a maverick cop who has a penchant for sunglasses and high caliber weaponry which he uses to blow the criminal element away. This was followed by two sequels, *Blood, Sweat and Fear* (1975) and *Mark Strikes Again* (1976) (all three written by Dardano Sacchetti—more on him later) and again starring Franco Gaspari and Lee J. Cobb (in the second one only and then John Saxon and John Steiner joined for the third). Massi handled the chair for an earlier giallo (*Five Women For the Killer*, 1974) and a number of other crime films such as: *The Last Round* (1976) starring Luc Miranda (*Puzzle, Torso*); *Cross Shot* (aka: *La Legge Violente Della Squadra Anticrime*, 1976) starring John Saxon and Lee J. Cobb again; *Destruction Force* (1977) again with Luc Miranda; *Convoy Busters* (1977) starring Maurizio Merli and Lilli Carati (*To Be Twenty*) and *Magnum Cop* (1978) starring Maurizio Merli and Joan Collins—amongst others. Massi later went on to direct a number of action films including the popular *Black Cobra* (1985) starring Fred Williamson (which led to three sequels).

Sergio Sollima was a regular practitioner in the crime genre, starting out writing westerns and eventually moved to the director's chair. Having early success with his *Violent City* (aka: *The Family*) featuring the acting forces of Savalas, Bronson and Jill Ireland in 1970, he then went on to helm *Devil in the Brain* (aka: *Il Diavolo Nel Cervello*, 1972)—an eerie psychological thriller (somewhat in the vein of Tessari's *Puzzle*) where a young boy witnesses a murder but due to traumatic events can't remember it—and *Revolver* (aka: *Blood in the Streets*, 1973) starring Oliver Reed as a prison warden forced to let inmate Fabio Testi out as his wife is held for ransom, and then both become trapped in a deadly conspiracy from the government to the streets (the latter films also featured excellent soundtracks by Ennio Morricone).

Another connection emerges between the number of Italian horror and giallo directors who also did crime films. **Umberto Lenzi**, who directed a number of pioneering gialli (*Paranoia, A Quiet Place To Kill, Knife of Ice, Spasmo*), cannibal (*Man From Deep River, Cannibal Ferox* (aka: *Make Them Die Slowly*) and horror films (*Nightmare City, Ghosthouse*), did a large number of crime films throughout the seventies—some of which are amongst not only the best of his own canon, but also of the field in general. Lenzi made ten

crime films in all (only Stelvio Massi made more with ten films in his canon). His first effort, *Gang War in Milan* (1973), was sandwiched in-between his giallo efforts and his highly influential cannibal film in 1972, and did firmly establish Lenzi as a credible crime director. It featured Antonio Sabato, crime film regular Philippe Leroy and the lovely Marisa Mell (*Seven Bloodstained Orchids*) and told of a small pimp's fight against the mob forces. Lenzi's next film, *Almost Human* (aka: *The Executioner*, 1974), established his violent, action-paced style and featured Thomas Milan (who became a regular and appeared in seven of Lenzi's crime flicks), Henry Silva and Laura Belli. It featured a great script by giallo and Gothic horror master Ernesto Gastaldi. Lenzi continued to do more crime films over the next few years with: *Syndicate Sadists* (1975); *Assault With A Deadly Weapon* (aka: *Rome Armed to the Teeth, Brutal Justice*, 1976); *Violent Naples* (1976); *Free Hand For a Tough Cop* (1976); *Brothers 'Till We Die* (1977); *The Cynic, The Rat and the Fist* (1977—also from a Gastaldi script) and *From Corleone To Brooklyn* (1978) rounding out his oeuvre. Often unfairly considered a hack and below the level of auteurs like Dario Argento and Mario Bava, Lenzi is not only a solid director, but quite excellent at, not only the crime film, but also pioneering in the giallo (after Bava who was the first, but predating Argento, Fulci and Martino) and cannibal genres (firing the first shot on the latter). Much like his gialli, Lenzi's crime films were often very violent and *Almost Human* was the first to get a V18 rating (adults only) in 1974. A fact which did nothing to deter over a million people from going to see it.

Sergio Martino, who helmed a number of excellent gialli (*The Strange Vice of Mrs. Wardh, Case of the Scorpion's*

Tail, All the Colors in the Dark, Torso) also directed *The Violent Professionals* (1973) starring Luc Miranda and Richard Conte, *Gambling City* (1975) also starring Miranda, and *The Suspicious Death of A Minor* (1975)—which fused the giallo, crime films and even comedy together (which Martino directed a number of—many starring Edwige Fenech). Martino was always a jack of all trades and eventually went on to do monster/adventure, cannibal and science fiction films in the late 1970s and early 1980s, but his giallo and crime films rank amongst some of his best, and also the best in the genres.

Ruggero Deodato, notorious for *Cannibal Holocaust* (1979) and *House at the Edge of the Park* (1981 starring *Last House on the Left's* David Hess), helmed one of the better, and also more violent crime films *Live Like A Cop, Die Like a Man* (1976). The two main police in Deodato's film are more like vigilantes who work for an agency, but would rather eliminate criminals than take them to jail (which they usually do in an extremely violent manner). The men look at women as sexual playthings and their attitude toward the females in the film predates the misogynistic efforts in his later films (like *Cannibal, House* and *Body Count*). Although an enjoyable and humorous action film in many ways, well-shot and nicely paced, the dark edge and attitude may turn some viewers off.

The grand old man of gore, **Lucio Fulci**, fired off a grisly crime film toward the end of the genre's run in 1980 (in-between his landmark *Zombie* and *City of the Living Dead*, and *The Beyond* and *House By the Cemetery*), *Contraband*, which reveled in violence, including a woman getting a blowtorch to the face. But Fulci dabbled in the crime film much earlier with his *Perversion Story* (aka: *One On Top of the Other*, 1969), *Lizard In a Woman's Skin* (1971) and *Don't Torture A Duckling* (1972)—blending elements of

both giallo and crime films together. Fulci, like Lenzi and Martino, was a jack of all trades and dabbled in various genres over the years and not surprisingly he tried crime films along with his horror films, gialli, comedies, sword & sorcery, dramas, etc.

Lastly, giallo director **Massimo Dallamano** (*What Have They Done To Solange, What Have They Done To Your Daughters, The Night Child*) also directed some great crime flicks such as: *Mafia Junction* (1973) starring giallo regular Ivan Rassimov (*Strange Vice of Mrs. Wardh, All The Colors in the Dark, Spasmo*) and British/Hammer films Stephanie Beacham (*Dracula A.D. 1972, And Now the Screaming Starts, Schizo, Inseminoid*) and *Colt .38 Special Squad* (1976) starring Ivan Rassimov again and also Carole Andre. His early effort *A Black Veil for Lisa* (1968) was very influential on the later crime and giallo genres and had a noir feel to it (something often lacking in some of the crime films of the seventies). Also of note is horror and exploitation director **Alberto De Martino** (*The Killer Is On the Phone, The Antichrist, Holocaust 2000*), who helmed a couple good crime films. *Crime Boss* (1972) starring Telly Savalas, Antonio Sabato and Paola Tedesco was his foray into the genre followed by *Counselor at Crime* (1973) starring Martin Balsam, Thomas Milan and Dagmar Lassander.

And the screenwriters for many of these efforts are not to be underestimated. Many of the directors wrote or co-wrote a number of their films (as well as adapted them from novels and stories), but a couple standout writers should be mentioned. One of the greatest Italian cinema writers was **Ernesto Gastaldi**—who not only wrote for Mario Bava (*Whip & The Body*), Riccardo Freda (*The Horrible Dr. Hitchcock*), Antonio Margheriti (*The Long Hair of Death*) and Paolo Heusch (*Werewolf In A Girl's Dormitory*) in the early days of Italian Gothic horror cinema—but also was a primary writer and influence in the gialli films. His contributions helped shape and define the genre—with directors like the aforementioned Martino, Luciano Ercoli (*Forbidden Photos of a Lady Under Suspicion, Death Walks on High Heels*), Lenzi, Giuliano Carnimeo (*Case of the Bloody Iris*) and others—by pioneering efforts like *Libido* (1965), *The Murder Clinic* (1966) and *The Sweet Body of Deborah* (1968). He also made a number of solid contributions on the crime side with *The Violent Professionals, Almost Human, Puzzle* (Duccio Tessari, 1974); *Gambling City, Kidnap Syndicate* and various others. His impact in the Italian cinema overall cannot be understated.

Prolific screenwriter **Dardano Sacchetti**, mainly known for his horror and giallo screenplays and story work with Mario Bava (*A Bay of Blood, Shock*), Dario Argento (*Cat O' Nine Tails, Demons*) and especially Lucio Fulci (*The Psychic, Zombie, City of the Living Dead, The Beyond, House By the Cemetery, The New York Ripper, Manhattan Baby*)—also wrote a number of crime films. His first was *Emergency Squad* (1974) for director Stelvio Massi and featured genre regular Thomas Milan, Gastone

Moschin and Ray Lovelock. A low-budget affair not well received, it still featured an interesting premise, but was weakened by a surprisingly dull performance by Milan. Next up was Lenzi's *The Manhunt* (1975) starring Henry Silva and Luciana Paluzzi, a much improved follow-up for Sacchetti. His remaining output in the crime genre includes: Massi's *Mark* trilogy and *Destruction Force* (1977), *Stunt Squad* (Domenico Paolella, 1977), and a few more for Lenzi (*Assault With A Deadly Weapon; Cross Shot; Free Hand For A tough Cop; The Cynic, The Rat and The Fist*).

Musically, **Ennio Morricone** lent his legendary talents to a number of crime films such as *Investigation of a Citizen under Suspicion, Cold Eyes of Fear, Revolver, Almost Human*, and others. Always recognizable for his style on his Leone westerns especially, Morricone went back and forth between gialli, crime, horror and art films in the seventies and also contributed to a number of Hollywood films including ones by John Carpenter (*The Thing*) and Brian De Palma (*The Untouchables*).

Also a jack of all trades, **Stelvio Cipriani** studied with Jazz legend Dave Brubeck in the US before embarking on work on movies. He's probably a bit more known for his soundtrack work with Mario Bava on classic horror films like *A Bay of Blood, Baron Blood* and *Rabid Dogs* (aka: *Kidnapped*), but he also worked on a number of gialli for directors such as Riccardo Freda (*Iguana With Tongue of Fire*), Luciano Ercoli (*Death Walks on High Heels*), Andrea Bianchi (*What the Peeper Saw*), Massimo Dallamano (*What Have They Done To Your Daughters, The Night Child*) and others. Cipriani's discordant and free-flowing jazzy scores influenced a number of filmmakers and he also did a number of excellent crime film soundtracks, including *Human Cobras, Execution Squad, Emergency Squad; Blood, Sweat and Fear;* and *Magnum Cop* amongst others.

Riz Ortolani was a frequent contributor to the Italian crime films. He lent his considerable talents to a number of westerns before turning to making scores for giallo films like *Perversion Story; So Sweet, So Perverse; The Dead Are Alive* (Armando Crispino, 1972); *Seven Bloodstained Orchids; Seven Deaths in A Cat's Eye* (Antonio Margheriti, 1973) and others. His soundtracks were featured on the crime films: *Confessions of a Police Captain, The Assassin of Rome, Mafia Junction, Counselor At Crime, How To Kill A Judge* and others.

Fernando Di Leo frequently used **Luis Enriquez Bacalov** in his films. Bacalov was born in Argentina and worked on a number of European productions during the seventies and eighties. Recently he scored Quentin Tarantino's *Django Unchained* along with Morricone, Ortolani and others.

Lastly, the **De Angelis** brothers, **Guido and Maurizio**, were in a number of crime films with their excellent soundtracks. Starting out scoring for Enzo Barboni's *Trinity* comedies (starring Terrence Hill and Bud Spencer), they went on to do the music for Martino's crime film *Violent Professionals* (along with his giallo *Torso*); Castellari's *High Crime* and *Street Law*; Mario Girolami's *Violent City; The Cop in Blue Jeans; The Big Racket* and others. They continued to work with Martino on a number of his films throughout the seventies like *Giovanna Long-Thigh, Sex with a Smile, Mannaja: Man with a Blade* and *Mountain of the Cannibal God*. They also continued to score films for Barboni, who continued his trend of fusing comedy into the western and crime genres with his popular Hill and Spencer characters.

***

So there you have it! A genre that explored the darker side of society, the human condition and psyche, and one that continually pushed the cinematic boundaries in Italy and the rest of the world.

Recommended Film List:

The Violent Four (1968) (Carlo Lizzani)

Mafia (1968) (Damiano Damiani)

Detective Belli (1969) (Romolo Guereri)

Violent City (1970) (Sergio Solima)

Investigation of a Citizen under Suspicion (1970) (Elio Petri)

Confessions of a Police Captain (1970) (Damiano Damiani)

The Burglars (aka: *Le Casse*) (1971) (Henry Verneuil) (Italian/French)

The Case is Closed, Forget it (1971) (Damiano Damiani)

Policemen (1971) (Stefano Rossi)

Human Cobras (1971) (Bitto Albertini)

Caliber 9 (1972) (Fernando Di Leo)

The Italian Connection (1972) (Fernando Di Leo)

Execution Squad (1972) (Stefano Vanzina)

Crime Boss (1972) (Alberto De Martino)

The Assassin of Rome (1972) (Damiano Damiani)

Sicilian Connection (1972) (Fernando Baldi)

High Crime (1973) (Enzo Girolami—aka: Enzo G. Castellari)

The Boss (1973) (Fernando Di Leo)

Revolver (aka: *Blood in the Streets*) (1973) (Sergio Solima)

Gang War in Milan (1973) (Umberto Lenzi)

Mafia Junction (1973) (Massimo Dallamano)

The Violent Professionals (1973) (Sergio Martino)

Bloody Hands of the Law (1973) (Mario Gariazzo)

The Ones Who Count (1973) (Andrea Bianchi)

Battle of the Godfathers (1973) (Jurgen Roland) (Italian/German)

Emergency Squad (1974) (Stelvio Massi)

Almost Human (aka: *Executioner*) (1974) (Umberto Lenzi)

Shoot First, Die Later (1974) (Fernando Di Leo)

Borsalino & Co. (1974) (Jacques Deray) (Italian/French)

Anonymous Avenger (1974) (Enzo Girolami—aka: Enzo G. Castellari)

How to Kill A Judge (1974) (Damiano Damiani)

Street Law (1974) (Enzo G. Castellari)

Gambling City (1974) (Sergio Martino)

The Manhunt (1975) (Umberto Lenzi)

Kidnap Syndicate (1975) (Fernando Di Leo)

Violent Rome (1975) (Marino Giralomi)

The Suspected Death of a Minor (1975) (Sergio Martino)

Mark (aka: *Mark IL Polizotto*) (1975) (Stelvio Massi)

Blood, Sweat and Fear (1975) (Stelvio Massi)

Flic Story (1975) (Jacques Deray) (Italian/French)

Syndicate Sadists (1975) (Umberto Lenzi)

Loaded Guns (1976) (Fernando Di Leo)

Rulers of the City (1976) (Fernando Di Leo)

Nick the Sting (1976) (Fernando Di Leo)

Colt .38 Special Squad (1976) (Massimo Dallamano)

Live Like A Cop, Die Like A Man (1976) (Ruggero Deodato)

The Big Racket (1976) (Enzo Girolami—aka: Enzo G. Castellari)

Cross Shot (1976) (Stelvio Massi)

The Last Round (1976) (Stelvio Massi)

Squadra Antifuro (1976) (Bruno Corbucci)

Cop in Blue Jeans (1976) (Bruno Corbucci)

Special Cop (1976) (Marino Girolami)

Rome Armed To The Teeth (aka: Brutal Justice) (1976) (Umberto Lenzi)

Violent Naples (1976) (Umberto Lenzi)

Free Hand for a Tough Cop (1976) (Umberto Lenzi)

Blood and Diamonds (1977) (Fernando Di Leo)

Convoy Busters (1977) (Stelvio Massi)

Dirty Gang (1977) (Stelvio Massi)

Weapons of Death (1977) (Mario Caiano)

Swindle (1977) (Bruno Corbucci)

The Heroin Busters (1977) (Enzo G. Castellari)

The Cynic, the Rat and the Fist (1977) (Umberto Lenzi)

Destruction Force (1977) (Stelvio Massi)

Stunt Squad (1977) (Domenico Paolella)

A Man Called Magnum (1977) (Michele Massimo Tarantini)

Magnum Cop (1978) (Stelvio Massi)

An Uncomfortable Cop (1978) (Stelvio Massi)

The Iron Commissioner (1978) (Stelvio Massi)

Brothers 'Till We Die (1978) (Umberto Lenzi)

From Corleone to Brooklyn (1978) (Umberto Lenzi)

Hunted City (1979) (Stelvio Massi)

Contraband (1980) (Lucio Fulci)

Day of the Cobra (1980) (Enzo Girolami—aka: Enzo G. Castellari)

✻ ✻ ✻

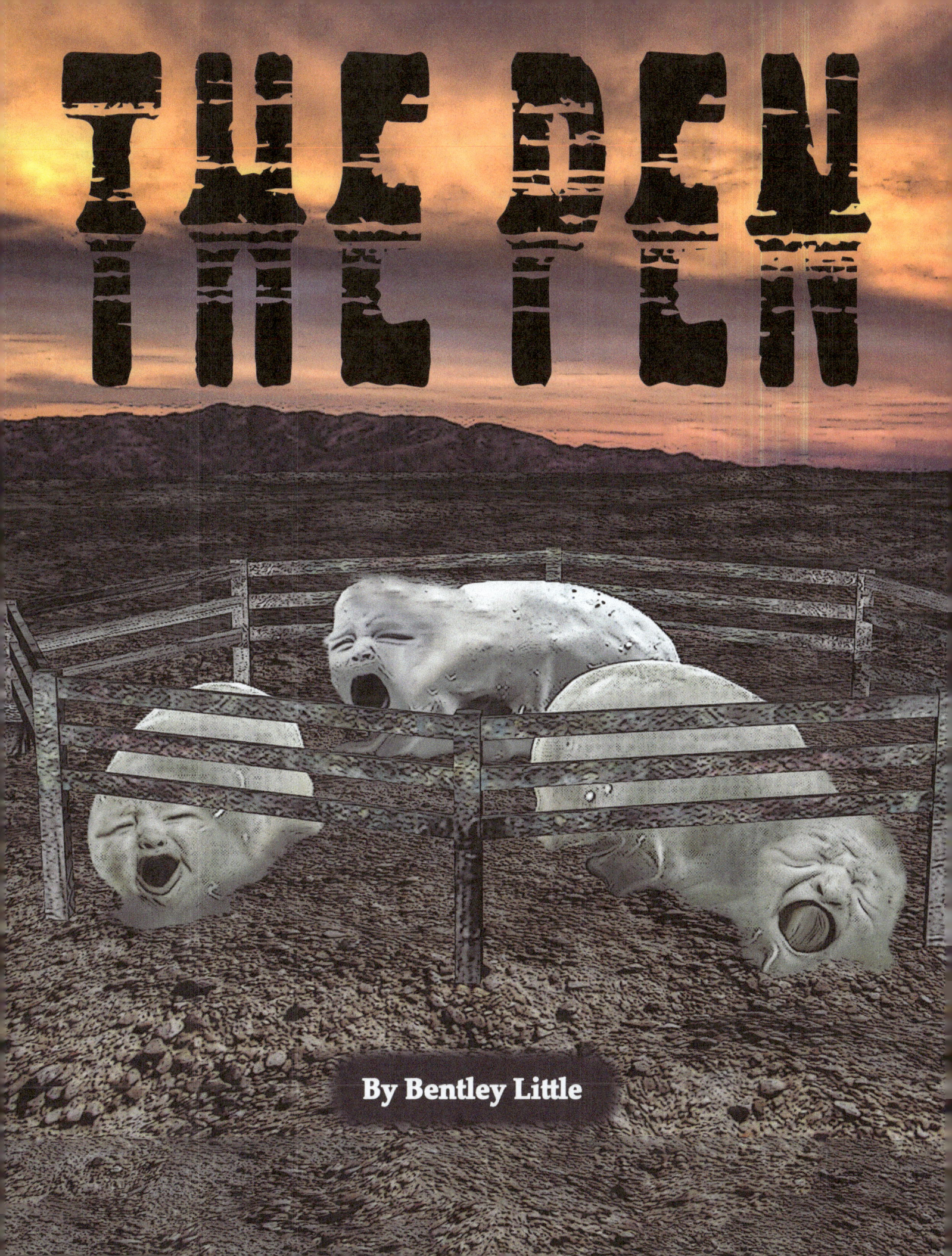

Jess wanted to backpack across Europe during his first year after high school. He wasn't sure if people still did that—it might have simply been one of those fleeting fads from the 1960s—but he'd read about it in books and seen it in movies, and making a trek across the continent had been a secret dream of his since sophomore year.

His parents had put the kibosh on those plans, however. *He* didn't have any money, they informed him, and *they* certainly weren't going to finance such a narcissistic indulgence, so he needed to just forget all about that foolishness. He refused to give up, however, and by the time he was in his second year at Grand Canyon College, he had actually convinced them to buy him a plane ticket to Israel. It wasn't Europe, true, and it wasn't for a year, but that was never going to happen, and since his parents were hardcore Christians, the Holy Land they were okay with, despite the perpetually unsettled politics of the region. Between the money he saved from his part-time job and the amount his parents were chipping in, he had enough for a summer's worth of footloose cross-country traveling, and that was good enough for him.

He'd been hoping to get a friend to go along on the journey—preferably a girl—but no one he knew was even remotely interested in such a trip, and, not wanting to go to a foreign country alone, he hooked up with a small group of guys he met on a "Backpacking American Friends" website sponsored by the Israeli tourist board. Unlike himself, they were all apparently religious (something of which his parents wholeheartedly approved), and they were each going as a sort of pilgrimage. He didn't inquire too deeply about the whys and wherefores, was content just having someone to travel with and help him deal with logistical headaches, and he corresponded online and spoke on the phone with all five of them in the weeks leading up to the trip. Finally, on June 21, he and his parents met up with the other young men and their assorted friends and family at LAX, getting to know each other in person for an hour or so before boarding the plane that was to take them to Tel Aviv.

The six of them had worked out a rough itinerary ahead of time. Or, rather, the three most devout had worked out an itinerary, since they had specific places they wanted to see, while the rest of them, Jess in particular, were content with a more free-form experience.

The first night in Israel was spent in a youth hostel, but after that, they were out of the city, taking a bus to a small settlement in the hinterlands, spending that night in a kibbutz, and then setting out on foot, hiking along various roads, visiting historical spots, camping out wherever they found themselves at the end of the day.

One of Jess' compatriots, it turned out, wasn't actually religious, but, even worse, was a hipster. Any hot indie band that anyone brought up, he claimed to have seen in some small club, before they made it, before they sold out, when they were still good. Jess was familiar with the type, and just to amuse himself, he brought up a few retro names in their music discussions, the ones no true hipster could resist. Van Morrison? Check. Velvet Underground? Check. Miles Davis, Thelonius Monk, Duke Ellington? Check, check, check. All of a sudden, the guy was his bosom buddy, convinced that he'd found a fellow traveler, and Jess strung him along for a while before letting his real tastes creep into their conversations: Metallica (still borderline acceptable; after all, they'd recorded an album with Lou Reed), Lady Gaga (puzzling…but… maybe…there was…a reason?), and then, the death knell for their fledgling friendship, the dreaded Rush.

It was a cruel joke to play on such a person, but Geddrick was a pretentious asshole and, as far as Jess was concerned, deserved it.

The truth was, Jess did not get along with any of the guys who'd come here with him, although, after the first four days, none of them seemed to get along with each other, either. The more time they spent together, the farther apart they drifted, and by the time their little band made its way to the country's arid interior, they weren't really speaking to one another. They were separate individuals within an ostensible group, together only because they were in a foreign land and were all from the United States. Jess was not sure why they didn't just go their separate ways and meet up again at the airport in August for the trip home, but they didn't, and he was actually glad about that. It turned out that he wasn't as independent as he originally thought himself to be, and even if he didn't like the other five, he still felt more secure being in their company.

It was Matthew, the most religious among them, who, after a sojourn to a remote and recently unearthed archeological site, suggested they cut across the desert, following in the footsteps of Jesus. Matthew claimed to know the path Christ had taken through the wilderness, and while that seemed highly unlikely to the rest of them, they were all up for the adventure and, using Matthew's map and Aaron's compass, they made their way between brown boulder-strewn hills and away from the road.

After stopping for a cold trail mix lunch at what passed for an oasis here—a spindly tree and some leafless bushes—Jess found himself in an awkward situation. He desperately had to go to the bathroom, but for the first time on the trip there was no restroom available, not even an outhouse. He'd been holding it in for some time, and finally he just blurted out, "Guys. I gotta take a dump."

"Do what you need to do," Geddrick said, uninterested.

Jess looked around. "Yeah, but where?"

"Dig a hole," Aaron suggested.

Matthew seemed shocked. "Not *here*!"

Geddrick snorted. "People have done it before. How do you think they took care of business before there were toilets? What do you think Jesus and his disciples did?"

"We're camping. That's how it's done," Aaron agreed. "Besides, I kind of have to go, too."

They took turns behind a rock, digging their own

holes and using their own toilet paper. Even though Jess was nonreligious, this still felt wrong. He was befouling the Holy Land, and for the first time, he wished he hadn't come here. He should have saved his money, waited a few years and gone on the European trip he'd always wanted. Or he should have banked what he'd accumulated and gotten a better car. *This,* all of a sudden, seemed like a huge mistake.

Matthew was reading his Bible aloud as he, Aaron, David and Paul attempted to determine where exactly they were in relation to Christ's wanderings. It was Geddrick who said, "Let's get a move on. I have no idea where we're supposed to be going, but let's get there."

They walked.

The desert didn't look the way Jess had thought it would. He'd been expecting a sand dune-y *Lawrence of Arabia* kind of place, but the land here was more varied and diverse, though still incredibly harsh and forbidding. It occurred to him as the sun was setting and they could see no evidence of human habitation in any direction, that hiking here had been an incredibly stupid and dangerous thing to do. There was no cell phone reception; no one knew where they were. If they ran out of food or water, died of dehydration or heat stroke, no one would come to rescue them. Their bodies might never be found.

Why had none of them objected when Matthew suggested they strike out on their own across this wilderness? He had no idea. It had seemed reasonable at the time, though now it seemed anything but.

They set up their tents in a warm steady wind as the sun went down. The silence was oppressive, stifling all conversation as they ate their MREs. Above, the stars were in different constellations than those with which he was familiar. It was, no doubt, because he was now on the other side of the earth, but there seemed something even more foreign to it than that. There was a sense that he was in a different world entirely, and that was not a feeling he liked.

In the morning, they awoke under a white sky, the clouds so high they had lost all definition and served merely as ceiling to the earth. Water rations were getting low, and once again Jess thought how idiotic it had been for them to hike out here.

"I think we should turn back," Jess said.

Matthew shook his head, consulting his map. "We need to go forward."

"To what?" Jess leaned over and looked at the map. "I don't see anything there. We are running out of food and water, and if we don't get some supplies *immediately*, we are going to die out here where no one even knows that we are. At least if we turn back, we know there's a road."

"This is the route Jesus took…"

"You made that up! No one knows that. You can't tell a specific path someone walked thousands of years ago from a few lines of poetry in a book!"

"He's right," Geddrick said. "I say we turn around."

"And I say we go forward," Paul chimed in.

"Then we split up." Geddrick raised a hand. "Everyone who wants to head back to civilization over here, everyone who wants to trek into oblivion over there." He pointed at Matthew.

It was settled. The two groups were uneven—Jess and Geddrick on one side, everyone else on the other—but that didn't matter. Jess did not like this desert, and the prospect of returning to civilization even made the thought of traveling with Geddrick seem bearable.

Aaron held out his compass. "Here," he said. "You guys take it."

Jess shook his head. "You need it more than we do. We're just backtracking the way we came."

"The desert can fool you. We're heading due west, so all we have to do is follow the path of the sun. You take it."

"Then we will," Geddrick said, grabbing the object from Aaron's hand. "Now let's get going." He slipped on his backpack and looked over his shoulder. "We'll tell the rescuers where you are."

"Peace be with you," Matthew said, although whether that was a serious wish or a snide comment, Jess could not tell.

They started off.

Aaron's compass died sometime around noon, its needle circling slowly around without ever finding a place to stop. Both of their watches died as well, and Geddrick wondered aloud whether they'd passed over some sort of magnetic rock. Overhead, the light seemed old, pale, spent, as though emanating from some dimmer, weaker sun. Beneath his feet, the earth felt strange and sticky, more like sugar than sand.

The two of them passed between a series of elephant-sized boulders. Jess was about to say that this area didn't look familiar, that he did not remember passing through here before, when he saw, ahead, a series of low buildings.

"Thank God," he said.

Moving quickly, grateful to have found people, they crossed the open space, entering a village that seemed to have no roads leading either in or out of it. Little more than a collection of huts, it was bisected by a flattened path of hardpacked earth that diffused into desert on either end of the settlement. Blank-faced women and half-naked children stood in the dark doorways, staring out at them.

"Hello!" Geddrick called.

No one returned the greeting.

"We're Americans! We're lost! Can any of you tell us where we are?"

Expressionless faces were the only response. One woman, holding her small son's shoulders, backed into her house, both of them disappearing into the gloom.

"Water," Jess said, looking at a woman with wild gray hair. "Food." He mimed eating and drinking in case they didn't understand English. "Do you have any water or food?"

No one moved, no one responded.

He was starting to get creeped out, and if they hadn't needed supplies, he would have left then and there, gotten as far away from this weird village as possible. But they *did* need supplies, and so the two of them walked slowly forward through the small collection of huts, looking for a store of some kind. There was no store, but at the opposite end of the path was a well, a well filled with water, and, looking at each other, they filled their canteens and extra bottles, first drinking gratefully until they were full.

They had no idea how to find food, but they still had two MREs apiece, as well as some trail mix and granola bars, so they could survive off that for a while now that they had water.

Geddrick tried to communicate one more time. "Road," he said, speaking slowly. "How do we get to a road?"

Only two women remained in their doorways, the rest having gone inside.

"Highway," Jess said. "City."

The two women stared impassively, not responding.

"Let's go," Geddrick said, and Jess could tell from his tone that his companion was just as unnerved as he himself was.

"Which way?" Jess asked, looking down at the slowly spinning compass needle.

"If they're following the sun, we'll go the opposite way. That must be where we came from, right?"

It made sense, and the two of them set off toward a low hill on the far side of the flat plain.

The hill was further away than it looked. Distance was impossible to judge here, with visibility great though unreliable, and the village had long disappeared into the distance, the sun nearly setting behind them by the time they reached their destination.

It was not a natural hill that stood before them but a purposefully sculpted mound, its sides bare and evenly sloped. On top of the mound was a pen, of the kind used to confine livestock. Made from unpainted weatherbeaten boards, it looked like a corral out of some old western movie, and while at first it appeared empty, as they made their way up the mound and drew closer, Jess saw that there were *creatures* within the enclosure. Three of them. They had to have been animals of some sort, but they looked like nothing so much as oversized human babies, babies without arms or legs. They snorted and snuffled in the dirt, whiter than they should be in this sun, their open mouths filled with small black teeth, their squinting eyes nearly invisible slits.

He shivered though the air was warm. There was something so fundamentally wrong about the scene before him that it was all he could do not to run away screaming.

"What the…?" Geddrick said.

The creatures began to speak in human voices, *familiar* voices, and Jess was chilled to the bone. Frozen in place, it took him a moment to realize that the voices were coming not from the writhing animals in the pen but from people on the far side of the hillock, behind the pen. He walked around the weathered fence, looked down the slope, and saw Matthew, Aaron, David and Paul setting up camp.

For the first time in his life, he understood what the expression "mixed emotions" meant. He was surprised to see the others, happy they were here, angry that they had split from Geddrick and himself, confused as to why they weren't ten miles away. Geddrick seemed to have no such internal conflicts. "Thank God!" he cried, hurrying down the slope.

Jess followed.

"How did you get here?" Geddrick asked, sliding down the hardpacked dirt.

"How did *you* get here?" Aaron responded.

Jess answered, meeting the group at the bottom of the mound. "We walked east."

"We headed west," Aaron said, frowning. "That doesn't make sense."

"Nothing makes sense around here," David muttered, and Jess wondered what the others had run into on their sojourn. He thought of that weird settlement with those silent people in their dark doorways and realized for the first time that there had been no men in the village. *Why?* he wondered, and was not sure he wanted an answer.

Only Matthew seemed unperturbed. "It is to be expected," he said smugly, as if he had indeed been expecting this all along.

Everyone ignored him.

"Good thing you guys are back," Geddrick said, gesturing toward Jess. "It's no party traveling with that nervous nellie, let me tell you."

They all laughed, and Jess wondered where that had come from. He and Geddrick had hardly spoken all day, and when they had, their interactions had been polite.

The two of them took off their packs and started to set up camp next to the others. Jess was definitely the odd man out, even more so than he had been before, and he did not understand why. The rest of them were acting as though this was some sort of reunion party. They all seemed to be ignoring where they were and what was happening. The six of them were lost in the middle of the Israeli desert, with dwindling food and water supplies, camping out next to a mound on top of which was a pen filled with freakish creatures none of them had ever seen before. The situation required a little more serious consideration than it was being given.

Although…

He himself was not filled with the sense of urgency that the circumstances demanded. He realized that intellectually, but it did not translate emotionally, and he was silent as he put out his bedroll.

Night fell quickly, the sun replaced by an odd sliver of moon and those wrongly positioned constellations, and Jess went to sleep soon after. Matthew was praying aloud, and Jess wanted to tell him to shut up, but he remained silent as he crawled into his sleeping bag. From the top of the mound to his right, he could hear sounds of movement: creaking boards, shuffling sand, animalistic grunting. Matthew's praying grew louder, as if to cover up those *other* sounds, and Paul's voice soon joined in.

"Shut up!" he finally said, after thinking the words for ten minutes.

Matthew's voice grew louder.

He could make out individual words here and there, and it was not until he heard his own name mentioned that he realized how angry all of this praying was making him feel.

He wanted to kill Matthew.

It was not merely a figure of speech, not an exaggeration of his feelings of annoyance. It was a genuine desire to end Matthew's life, and even as Jess acknowledged its strangeness, he realized that the impulse was not coming from him. Oh, Matthew was an annoying asshole, but, then, so were a lot of people. Being irritating didn't warrant the death penalty. And yet, he wanted Matthew dead, and he understood that he only wanted him dead because something *else* wanted him dead. The ground, the air, the rocks, the plants, the desert. The land was demanding a sacrifice, and in the middle of the night, while everyone was sleeping, Jess slipped out of his sleeping bag and tent.

Matthew was not in a tent, had his sleeping bag flat on the sand, probably so he could be closer to God, and Jess stood over him for a moment, looking down. The pious asshole's face was quiet in repose, and though his original idea had been to somehow cover Matthew's mouth and nose, smothering him, Jess decided that a bloodier end was far more appropriate.

Cautiously, and as silently as possible, he looked around the edges of their camp for a weapon, finally settling on a rock the size of a basketball. Still moving quietly, he brought the rock over to where Matthew was sleeping, knelt down, and smashed it into the young man's head. There was a sickening crunch, louder than it had any right to be, but Matthew let out no cry, and the noise was not enough to awaken any of the others. Carefully, Jess removed the rock, revealing, in the dark light of the tiny moon, a blackened mess. Picking up Matthew's feet and the opposite end of the sleeping bag, he dragged the body away from the camp and over to the edge of the mound before getting back into his own tent and sleeping bag and instantly falling asleep.

He was the first one awake in the morning, and he saw immediately that the body was gone. As was the rock. There was not even any blood on the ground. The only thing visible was a grooved furrow in the dirt, a shallow rut leading up the slope, as though the sleeping bag had been dragged to the top of the mound.

The others were wakening, but Jess ignored them and followed the trail up, the channel in the sand continuing to the very edge of the pen, where it suddenly disappeared. He walked forward slowly, seeing no sign of Matthew or the rock or the sleeping bag. The *things* within the pen, however,

had grown, changed, and with a sick feeling in his stomach, Jess thought they had eaten the body.

Why was that such a surprise? Matthew had been a sacrifice. He had understood that last night. What had he thought was going to happen? He wasn't sure, but in the harsh light of day, the gauzy vagueness of his feelings and actions the night before seemed to belong to a dream.

Gazing between the weathered wood slats, he saw the three baby-like creatures massed against the far side of the fence, staring at him with squinting piggy eyes. Shivering, he turned away and headed back down the slope.

"Where's Matthew?" Paul asked.

"I don't know," Jess said. "I was just looking for him."

"Up there?" Geddrick asked suspiciously.

"Yeah." He pointed to the track in the sand. "It looked like he went up."

They spent the next half-hour searching for Matthew and eating cold rations for breakfast as they looked. Each of them, at some point, went up to the top of the mound, and each of them eventually came down, but the strange thing was that none of them mentioned the pen or what was in it. It was as if the subject held no interest for anyone, as though that corral with those three horrible creatures was nothing more unusual than a bush or a boulder.

There was a serious debate, as the sun rose into the sky, whether they should wait here for Matthew to return or set off looking for him. Jess was the only one who knew that Matthew would *not* return, and he argued that they needed to get back to civilization. Once they found other people, they could send rescuers back to look for Matthew. Geddrick, not surprisingly, agreed. "He's probably wandering the desert hoping to be tempted by Satan. Let that fanatic do what he wants. We need to get out of here."

In the end, they left Matthew's pack, as well as his supply of food and water, and set off east, in the direction of the rising sun. After their lack of progress the day before, they moved quickly, not stopping to eat but snacking along the way, taking only occasional short piss stops, keeping always to the east, though they navigated by sun as the compass still would not work.

They had halfway decided to continue walking into the night, so long as their legs would carry them, but as the sun was setting behind them, its increasingly orange rays illuminated a low hillock in front of them, on top of which was…

The pen.

The four of them stopped as one, recognizing immediately what it was. They'd been walking in a circle, and a feeling of…what? Helplessness? Hopelessness? Fatigue? Despair? engulfed them. They would have to make camp again here tonight, Jess understood, and with the knowledge came the realization that he would have to kill—

sacrifice

—someone else, just as he had Matthew.

What had Matthew been praying for before he went to

sleep? Jess wondered. Had he prayed for his safety and the safety of their group? If so, God had not protected him.

None of them would be protected.

The demands of the land here were far older than any god.

Under the light of the too-small moon and the strangely aligned stars, Jess smothered Paul using one of Matthew's shirts, an execution that took longer and was less easy than using the rock, but through which the other three still slept. Once more, he dragged the body to the edge of the mound, and in the morning it was gone.

He climbed the slope in the light of the rising sun while the others remained asleep. The things in the pen looked different. He saw small arms and the beginnings of legs. The babyfat was morphing into muscle. Were they becoming people? Or were they becoming people *again*? The impression he had was that they were reverting to their original form, that, in the same way freeze-dried camping food was reconstituted with water, the blood and bodies of those they had eaten were reviving the creatures, thawing them out, letting them become what they once were, what they were supposed to be.

He looked to the left and the right, saw only desert in every direction. Was he to spend his days wandering the wilderness, his nights sacrificing his companions one by one? It suddenly seemed pointless to wait for that to play out, and he decided to move the clock forward and quickly dispatch those remaining in his party, but just before he was about to head back down, Geddrick came over the rise. In his hand was a trowel. "I know what you did," he said.

Jess looked at him. "What's that?"

"Did you kill Matthew, too?"

He did not have a chance to respond, because Geddrick lunged at him. Jess leaped to the left but was still clipped by the trowel and felt a sharp stab in his arm near the elbow. It hurt but was not deep or sharp enough to draw blood, and he immediately picked up a rock from the ground and threw it at Geddrick's head. He missed, but, as luck would have it, the rock hit Geddrick's hand, causing him to drop the trowel. Jess leaped, shoving him away from the weapon, and the two of them fought it out, rolling in the dirt. He was acutely aware of the things in the pen watching them, and he sensed from the creatures an anticipation, a *hunger*, that compelled him to fight harder, that gave him an incentive to triumph despite his hurt muscles and flagging energy. For he knew that if he did not kill Geddrick, Geddrick would kill him, and the loser would be fed to those things in the pen.

"Stop!"

"What are you guys doing?"

It was Aaron and David, who had climbed to the top of the mound to see what was going on. The two ran over, attempting to pull Jess and Geddrick apart, but somehow they got involved in the scuffle as well, and soon all four of them were fighting.

Geddrick succumbed first, although whether the fatal blow was delivered by David's punch or from the fact that Geddrick's head had slammed into the ground, Jess was not sure. All he knew was that while he himself was nearly tired out, Aaron and David were still strong, and he grabbed an apple-sized rock from the ground, held it in his hand as though it were a set of brass knuckles, and began whaling on the faces of the remaining combatants with a fierceness and fury he had never felt before. The rock connected more than it missed, and before Aaron or David could grab their own weapons, they fell to the side, one after the other, David first, their heads bashed in, blood gushing from the crushed pulp that had been their faces.

Exhausted, Jess collapsed, every cell in his body raging in agony. He lay on his back on the ground, breathing heavily, closing his eyes for a moment to rest.

When he opened them again, it was night, and yesterday evening's sliver of moon was now a full bright circle, blocking out all stars from the black surrounding sky. He sat up. The bodies around him were gone. He did not see any indication that they had been dragged along the ground, and it took him a moment to realize that he was now in the pen.

Had he been taken here or had the pen itself moved around him? The latter, it seemed, although he did not understand how that was possible.

The babylike creatures that had been in the pen had disappeared. There was no indication that they had ever existed, just as there was no evidence that Matthew, Paul, Geddrick, Aaron or David had ever been here.

Had they?

He wasn't sure. His brain seemed foggy, and it wasn't until he went to rub his eyes that he discovered he had no fingers. Or hands. Or arms. Panicked, he looked down, and in place of his legs saw only stubs. He was naked, and his clothes were nowhere in sight.

What had happened? What did this mean? He was afraid he knew, though he did not want to face it, and he cried out for help, but no sound came out. He had no voice, and his mouth opened and closed silently as tears rolled down his face. He thought of his parents, whom he knew he would never see again, thought of the world beyond this desert that was no longer his. The land here, this ancient land, was still demanding sacrifice. He knew it, *felt* it, but had no idea what that sacrifice was or why it should be required. He took comfort from the fact that the three previous tenants of the pen were now gone, even as he fell to the ground, losing what little control he had of his armless, legless body.

His last conscious thought was a practical one: if food *was* delivered to the mound, how would he be able to drag it into the pen?

And then he thought that maybe that was not his responsibility.

⚜ ⚜ ⚜

To Name the Genre

By Michael R. Collings

Recently I've heard, read, and participated in discussions of what to call this peculiar genre of ours, the one that readers of *Dark Discoveries* find so intriguing and exciting. Some aficionados refer to it simply by what many consider its primary component—*horror*, with (as noted on several panels I have served on) careful emphasis on the final syllable.

The name falls handily on the lips and offers an immediate guideline as to what readers might legitimately expect: blood and gore, the grisly and the gruesome, mayhem and monsters of all ilk. The name—along with the almost mandatory black cover—provides book sellers and book buyers a recognizable *kind*, directing both to the appropriate shelf, usually in the nether reaches of the store. On the whole, it serves as a handy moniker.

In some ways, though, *horror* seems a misnomer, a simplistic way to describe a complex kind of writing. If one were to state that Stephen King's *The Stand* or Robert McCammon's *Stinger* is horror, such a contention would be only partially true of those novels and would leave out hundreds of novels that do not resemble those two at all yet are demonstrably horrific.

Certainly alternative terms exist: *dark fantasy*, which I used frequently when addressing academic audiences that might have automatically bristled at the mention of *horror*; *speculative fiction*, which would undeniably include horror but which would also include much more; *dark speculative fiction*, which seems more to point out the difficulties in naming than resolve any of them; *dark fiction*, which would again include more than is conventionally intended by *horror*. Additional possibilities might include *supernatural fiction, weird fiction, monster fiction, slasher fiction*, and the cumbersome all-in-one of *dark psychological suspense thriller*. None of them define precisely the same approach to writing, and none of them quite work as a comprehensive identifier for this particular brand of writing. But then, apparently, neither does *horror*.

Using that single term as an umbrella label for such widely divergent novels as Stoker's *Dracula* and Jeff Strand's *A Bad Day for Voodoo* would be roughly equivalent to re-thinking *The Lord of the Rings* and simply calling it *Frodo*. Frodo is central to the key action, the destruction of the ring of power; and he does appear in a number of episodes, perhaps more than any other character. But as important as he is, his personal story cannot encompass the complexity of the whole. He does not destroy the ring, although he makes its destruction possible; he does not restore kingship to Middle Earth, although he does facilitate that restoration; he cannot fully redeem the Shire for himself after Sharkey's depredations, although he makes possible Sam's fulfillment as husband and father.

Similarly, to call a novel *horror* and expect it to provide horrors on every page would be like calling a play a tragedy and expecting the emotional intensity implicit in the term to show up in every line, every scene. Such a compression of powerful feelings would simply be too much; no audience would be able to endure it. Shakespeare was well aware of the unviability of constant, uninterrupted tragic power and consistently provided comic undercurrents to alleviate the strain...and paradoxically make the catastrophe that much more compelling, that much more cathartic. *Hamlet* without the grave-digger scene (as it is so frequently produced nowadays) becomes merely a litany of death without providing Hamlet the opportunity to first reconcile himself to its inevitability. *Macbeth* without the porter and his incessant "Knock! Knock! Knock!" devolves into a chaos of murder.

For all of these reasons—and no doubt more—a number of "horror" writers have chosen to set aside *horror* in favor of yet another alternative, referring to their works as *cross-generic fiction*.

The first time I heard the term was during a conversation with Dean Koontz some twenty years ago. He had graciously agreed to speak to one of my classes at Pepperdine, and afterward we talked at length about him, his writing career, and his books. I had brought along several for him to autograph and, when I opened *Phantoms* (1983) to the title page, he tapped it and told me that that one had been his "break-away book." When I asked what he meant by that, he began discussing it, not as a horror novel but as his first conscious effort to mix and merge genres.

In a new afterword to *Phantoms,* he writes at length about precisely what he meant by that and how the novel affected his career: "Writing *Phantoms* was one of the ten biggest mistakes of my life, ranking directly above the incident with the angry porcupine and the clown, about which I intend to say nothing more." The mistake, he continues, lies in the fact that that novel, more than any previous one, earned for him the label of "'horror writer,' which I never wanted, never embraced, and have ever since sought to shed."

More to the point, he says:

I believe, however, that 95 percent of my work is anything *but* horror. I am a suspense writer. I am a novelist. I write love stories now and then, sometimes humorous fiction, sometimes tales of adventure, sometimes all those things between the covers of a single volume. But *Phantoms* fixed me with a spooky-guy label as surely as if it had been stitched to my forehead by a highly skilled and diligent member of the United Garment Workers union—making a far better wage than that poor bastard crocheting license-plate cozies.

Because his previous novel, *Whispers* (1981), had been marketed as horror and had been a marked success, his publishers pressured him to produce another in the same mold:

I thought I would cleverly evade their horror-or-starve ultimatum by making *Phantoms* something of a tour de force, rolling virtually all the monsters of the genre into one beast, and also by providing a credible, scientific explanation for the creature's existence.... *Phantoms* would be a horror story, yes, but it would also be science fiction, an adventure tale, a wild mystery story, and an exploration of the nature and source of myth.

Phantoms does in fact provide a paradigm for cross-generic fiction:

- It has a monster; therefore it is horror;

- It has a developing relationship between two characters; therefore it is a romance;

- It looks directly to the past for information and themes; therefore it is historical;

- It has a lawman pursuing an evil-doer; therefore it is a police procedural;

- It has several chases, an apparent burglar, and missing jewels; therefore it is a thriller;

- It has a moment of hesitation before the monster is defeated—will it win or will it die?—and therefore the novel is suspense;

- It has a murderer and a victim; therefore it is a murder mystery;

- It has a scientist equipped with the latest cutting-edge apparatuses nudged slightly into the future; therefore it is science fiction;

- It has characters following clues to discover the underlying causes of an event; therefore it is detective fiction;

- It has a distinctive landscape, one recognizable to anyone familiar with the general area; therefore it is regional fiction;

- It deals with the disintegrating mental state of several characters; therefore it is psychological fiction;

- It persistently ties the story to contemporary life; therefore it is realistic fiction;

- It speaks of and through a sentience beyond human understanding; therefore it is a story about aliens, i.e., again science fiction;

• It points out occasions when the creature has interacted with humanity throughout history, imprinting itself on human memory as eternal and immortal and simultaneously sifting through human memory to find appropriate guises in which to appear; therefore it is mythic;

• It deals with characters that become larger than life and an enemy that potentially threatens the existence of all humanity; therefore it partakes of the epic;

• It has a dog in it (what self-respecting Dean Koontz novel doesn't?); therefore it is dog fiction;

• It deals in philosophical abstracts; therefore it is philosophical fiction;

• It covertly affirms the existence of the Devil, and thereby of God; therefore it is theological fiction.

And on. And on.

Of course, much of what I just listed is intended to be taken at least partially as tongue-in-cheek. Each item is a single *element* in a long, coherent, unified novel; and none—including *horror*—deserves to be elevated into the *sine qua non* of the story. To do so would result in a much narrower book, in several cases something along the lines of a novella or a short story. No single item could control the story without much of importance being lost.

Yet to remove *anything* from the list would also lessen the novel. *Phantoms* is an enduring story—as well as a bestseller—precisely because Koontz took great care to include as many audiences as possible. Those readers approaching it looking for horror will be gruesomely pleased by graphic, nauseating, *gooshy* details in passages such as the following:

Blisters formed, swelled, popped; ugly sores broke open and wept a watery yellow fluid. Within only a few seconds, at least a ton of the amorphous flesh had spewed out of the whole....The great oozing mass lapped across the rubble, formed pseudopods—shapeless, flailing arms—that rose into the air but quickly fell back in foaming spasming seizures. And then, from still other holes, there came a ghastly sound: the voices of a thousand men, women, children, and animals, all crying out in pain, horror, and bleak despair.

For those less interested in the visceral, there is the intellectual excitement as the characters systematically anatomize their enemy—literally and figuratively—struggling to place it within some knowable taxonomy of creatures. For others, there is a marriage and honeymoon at the end, and the promise of a restored family unit.

In short, there is something for everything...for every reader, for every interest.

That is, I think, one of the strengths of Dean Koontz' stories...and of King's, and McCammons', and great numbers of books by a great number of writers who are usually passed off as simply writing *horror*. By themselves, horror motifs may not be strong enough to carry the weight of a novel. Joined with elements of other kinds of fiction, horror becomes part of a deeper, richer texture that, by means of monsters-as-metaphors and horrors-as-emblems, come to reflect the parallel depth and richness of human experience.

Yet *cross-generic fiction* itself fails to encapsulate the essence of a kind of story telling that does have as its ultimate aim a physiological reaction, a *frisson* along the spine, a coldness in the blood, a hesitance to turn the lights off after reading late at night. Perhaps the term is too clinical, too objective to direct attention to one of the most passionate and in many ways the most subjective modes of storytelling. It almost demands an intellectualization that monster stories struggle to subjugate to visceral responses.

Is the term *horror* the best possible label? Perhaps not. Is it the most appropriate, given the alternatives? Perhaps not. But I think that until someone invents a shorter, crisper, more convenient and more appropriate label than *cross-generic fiction*, one that will indicate a similar interest in storytelling from numerous perspectives that *still* has the possibility to chill, it may have to serve by default.

⚜ ⚜ ⚜

1 **New York Times** Bestselling Author

Phantoms
Dean
Koontz

"First-rate suspense, scary and stylish."
—*Los Angeles Times*

With a new afterword by the author

TIM WAGGONER
DEEP LIKE THE RIVER
A NEW NOVELLA
05 27 2014
DARKREGIONS.COM

WHAT THE HELL EVER HAPPENED TO...?

An Interview with Jeffrey Sackett

By Robert Morrish

Like more than a few other horror writers, Jeffrey Sackett found a promising career cut short by the full-scale publisher withdrawal from the horror genre during the late 1980s and early 1990s. In Sackett's case, he'd published five horror novels through Bantam Books before Bantam put the broom to anything with "horror" on the spine.

Each of Sackett's five novels featured a traditional horror theme, but each was also marked by a significant historical context, an aspect that reflects the author's personal interests and his day job: the recipient of three Master's degrees (two in History and one in Education), a Doctorate in Philosophy and a Doctorate in Theology, Sackett spent 32 years teaching high school History and English before retiring in 2005 and becoming an adjunct associate professor in the History and Philosophy departments of Dowling College and Suffolk Community College. As Sackett, puts it, "other than part-time jobs, all I have done with my life has been to teach and write." Which, he points out, "is not a bad way to spend your life."

Sackett reemerged recently through Crossroads Press, with all five of his previously published titles now available as ebooks through Crossroads, along with three additional (non-horror) titles.

* * *

Robert Morrish: Your first book, *Stolen Souls*, was published by Bantam. How did you place your novel with them? Did you have an agent for that first book, or did you connect with the publisher through their slush pile?

Jeffrey Sackett: I had an agent named Jay Garon of the Garon-Brooke Agency in Manhattan, who liked one of my early efforts, and signed me up. He was unable to sell that ms., but in a serendipitous moment, Bantam Doubleday Dell, as it was then known, was looking to expand its horror output just as I completed *Stolen Souls*. Jay was able to sell it to them, and I was hooked up with a wonderful editor, Amy Stout, with whom I worked on my next four books. (At the time, incidentally, Amy was married to Alan Rogers, who you featured in a previous installment of this column.)

RM: You wound up publishing five books in five years with Bantam, and I believe you were working full-time as a high school teacher during that period. You must have had a very disciplined approach to writing in order to be so prolific while working a full-time job.

The five novels Sackett published through Bantam are:

Stolen Souls (1987), concerning seven Egyptian mummies and a curse

Candlemas Eve (1988), blending rock 'n' roll and witchcraft

Blood of the Impaler (1989), focusing on Dracula and the Harker family

Mark of the Werewolf (1990), involving a 3000-year-old werewolf

The Demon (1991), is a shapechanger story involving a former sideshow freak

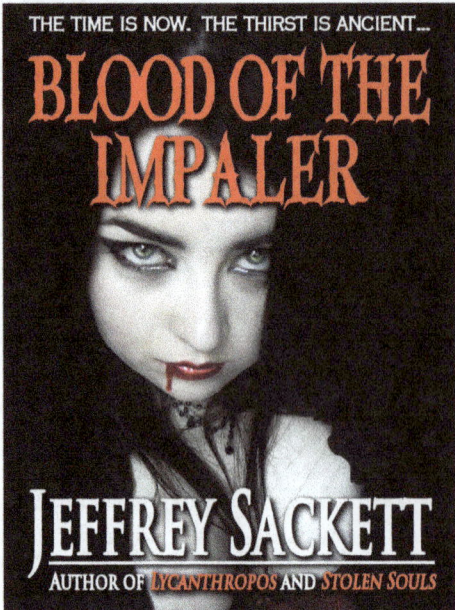

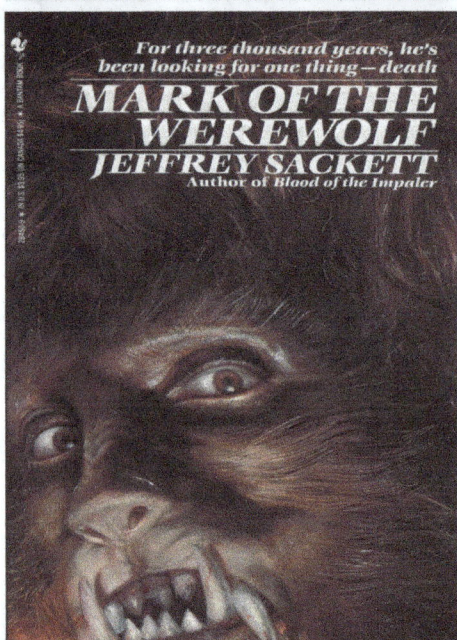

JS: I took a cue from the 19th-century British writer Anthony Trollope, who was a postmaster by trade. He also rose early each morning and wrote for one hour, no more, no less, seven days a week. (He was the author of *The Pallisers,* among other works.) Difficult to discipline one's self this way, but it works for me.

RM: Which of your titles sold the most copies?

JS: Not sure. I think it was *Blood of the Impaler,* but I'm not positive.

RM: I'm guessing that the end of your relationship with Bantam came about due to lower sales than the publisher was looking for, combined with the fact that the mid-1990s were not the best time to be peddling fiction with supernatural elements. Is that the case?

JS: Lower sales than desired was part of it, but Bantam was also moving away from the horror genre. They stopped buying books from a number of people at that time, not just me.

RM: You've recently re-published your five Bantam novels through Crossroads Press -- how did that relationship come about? I know that at least two of those five books are somewhat different in their Crossroads editions -- *Mark of the Werewolf* has been released under your original title, *Lycanthropos,* and with your original intended text, while *Demon* has been released as *Grogo the Goblin.* Are all five of the books at least somewhat different in their Crossroads editions?

JS: Regarding Crossroads Press: a gentleman named Hunter Goatley interviewed me for his publication *Lights Out* many years ago. He is now associated with Crossroads, and it was through him that I connected with that epublisher. As for *Lycanthropos:* the original story was about a werewolf captured by the S.S. in German-occupied Hungary during World War Two. Bantam liked the story but not the time and place, so at their behest I changed it to racist neo-Nazis capturing a werewolf in modern America. I did so reluctantly, but I didn't want to affect my relationship with Bantam adversely, so I complied. The book was published as *Mark of the Werewolf.* When Crossroads offered me the opportunity to publish the original manuscript, I jumped at it. I believe it to be my best work, both in concept and in execution. As for *Grogo the Goblin,* that was the original title of the book published as *The Demon.* Bantam didn't like the title. I did, and so the ebook restored it. Otherwise the books are identical.

RM: The story behind *Grogo the Goblin* is pretty fascinating -- tell us about that.

JS: Grogo the Goblin (Vernon Sweet) was a real person, a horribly deformed man who was a sideshow freak in a traveling circus some seventy years ago. He end up living in a cabin in the forest near a small town in rural upstate New York, close to a trailer where a friend of mine lived with his sister. They discovered Vernon's broken-down, abandoned old cabin, and a chest filled with his memorabilia. It was while hanging out in the ruin, drinking and smoking this and that back in the late '60s that the idea first came to me. It germinated for before it hatched. A good deal of the plot is something of a memoir. (It was a strange time to be in college.)

RM: In addition to re-publishing those five novels, Crossroads Press has published three other titles of yours: *Future History, the 2190 A.D. Edition; Uncle*

Adolph, and *The Warm and Witty Side of Attila the Hun.* Tell us more about those books. And will Crossroads be publishing additional titles?

JS: The other three books derive from my study and teaching of history. I have been teaching history in high school and (currently) college for over forty years, and I have been collecting amusing anecdotes on and off during that time. I collected them as *The Warm and Witty Side of Attila the Hun* (who, to all reports was neither warm nor witty.) My wife Paulette, an accomplished artist, illustrated the book. *Future History, the 2190 A.D. Edition,* is a dystopian fantasy about what America will be like in the future if we do not as a country change course. And *Uncle Adolf* is an historical novel dealing with the true story of Hitler's torrid love affair with his niece Geli Raubal in 1931. It is a fascinating tale.

RM: Do you have a personal favorite among your books?

JS: Two: *Lycanthropos* and *Blood of the Impaler.*

RM: Speaking of *Lycanthropos,* your website is titled Lycanthropos Enterprises...does that choice reflect your fondness for that book, or is there something more to it?

JS: The website is effectively closed now. It was just an experiment when I had time on my hands.

RM: Have you dabbled at all in short fiction?

JS: I have tried some short fiction, but I'm not comfortable with the limitations. I have never sold any short stories.

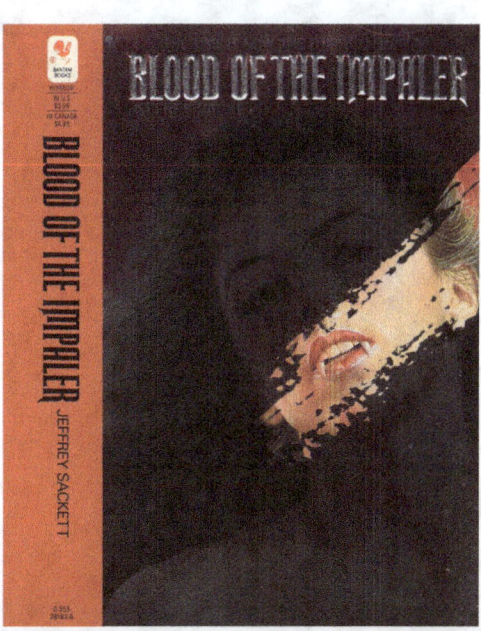

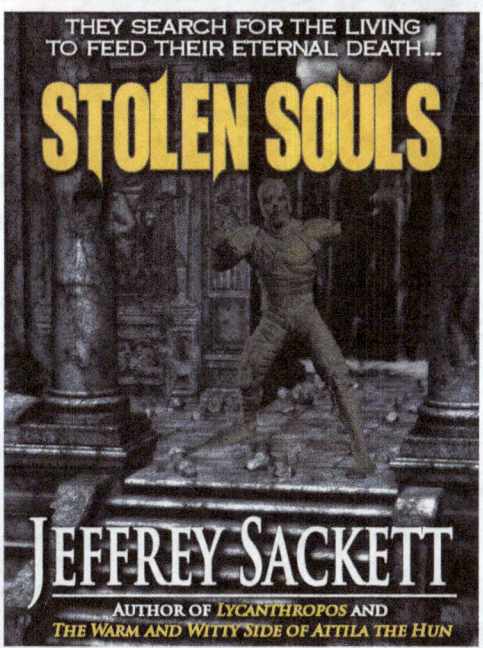

⚜ ⚜ ⚜

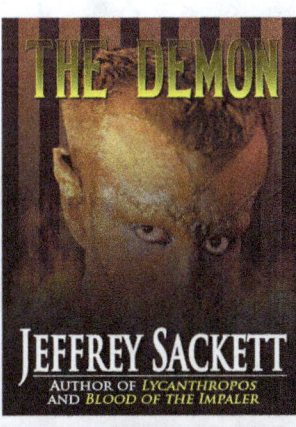

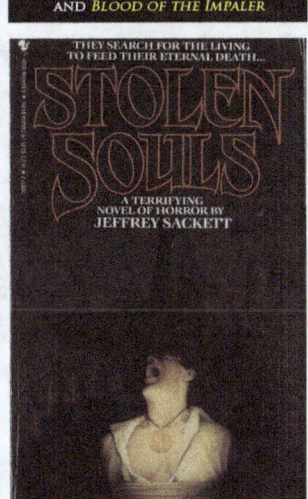

Photo courtesy of Jeffrey Sackett

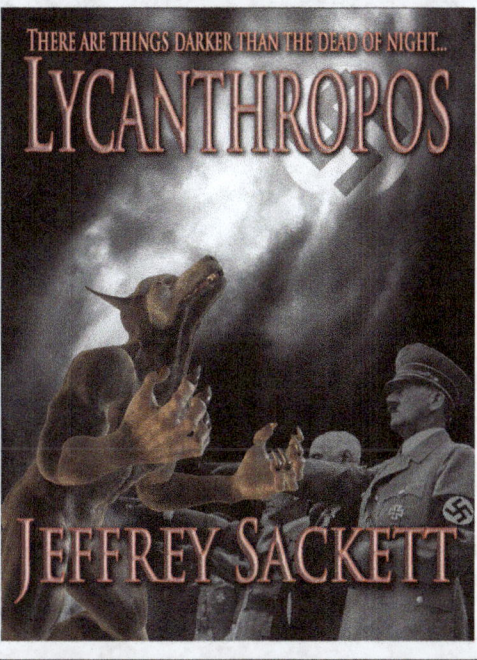

Communication

BREAKDOWN

By Maurice Broaddus

Unknown Number: Hey, what's going on?

Haley Cell: That depends. Who is this? I don't recognize the number.

Unknown Number: Ryan. I met you earlier. While we were talking, you took my phone and put your number into it earlier today.

Haley Cell: Sorry, dude. My name's Haley. I think whoever it was gave you a bogus number.

Unknown Number: Well … damn. That's embarrassing. Sorry to have bothered you.

The texting was a welcome distraction. On the monitor, Dylan looked suddenly small. A shock of unruly black hair over an unshaven face too gaunt for his own good. When they dated, it was a calculated look of unkempt cool. Now it came across as lazy and slovenly. He wore a blank glare. Haley had gotten used to his brand of constant disinterested anger, though she didn't quite meet his gaze as their marriage counselor encouraged them to stare into one another's eyes. Not even being able to be in the same room with him much these days, she peered directly into her webcam while trying to catch glimpses of the pair of them in her monitor. Silence had become the third partner in their marriage. It crawled into bed with them. Ate with them. Watched television with them. Back when they dated, silence was communion, the unspoken connection of comfort with one another. As they grew (apart), silence, too, grew; morphing into something awkward, tense, and seething. It bubbled underneath them like an angry undertow in the crashing waves of their marriage. Only a vestigial ember within her wanted to recapture what they once had. But she was so tired and no longer believed the effort would be worth it.

Even as words tumbled out of his mouth, Dylan wasn't even talking to her. Not really. His eyes fixed up and to the left, as if checking over her shoulder. He recounted his latest batch of sins, his inattentiveness, his distance. Aiming for the charm of self-knowledge and brooding revelation, he made another round of promises: that he'd realized what he'd done and where it stemmed from; that he'd work on it (whatever the "it" was this week); and that things would be better.

Haley toggled the panels on her screen so that Dylan and their counselor appeared next to one another. Truth be told, she no longer cared. Whatever Dylan blathered on about were just words. Angry at daddy words. Disappointed in mommy words. Secret shames and private pains words. Empty words. Stacked upon broken promises and countless disappointments. Their marriage was a continuous slow grind of passionless drudgery as they went through the motions of being together.

The counselor piped up, not quite interrupting him, as if reading Haley's body language. The counselor's office walls framed her in a pallid shade of mint green, a piece of art peeked from behind her like a halo in abstract as she suggested a *communication tool* for Haley and Dylan to learn and practice. One of them would say some truth about the marriage. The other would mirror the statement. Summarize it. Validate it. Empathize with it. Then they'd switch roles. The counselor promised it would stop the re-injuring process and begin to open the way for conscious healing. Haley and Dylan stared at each other across their Internet connection, neither daring to begin.

"*As I think about our marriage, I feel …,*" the counselor encouraged, her eyes soft and open, attempting to model the gaze each of them struggled to approximate.

"*As I think about our marriage, I feel,*" Haley read the first line from the set of notes the counselor e-mailed to both of them, "trapped."

"*I heard you say that you feel trapped. Did I get that so far? Is there more about that?*" A sharp stab of fresh pain registered on his face.

"*When I look at you, I feel … as if something died between us a long time ago and try as we might, we can't rekindle the feelings we once had. And when I see how you look at me these days, it makes me sad.*"

"Good job, Haley." The counselor leaned forward. "That was some brave sharing. Dylan, how do you respond to Haley's vulnerability?"

"*So to summarize, you feel … smothered by any attempts to love or be loved.*" Looking away from his notes, Dylan's eyes hardened into cold, cobalt flints. A bitter steeliness tinged his voice.

The counselor adjusted her webcam. "Dylan, I don't think …"

"I'm just following the script." Dylan muted her. "*Based on what you just said, that makes sense to me because … relationships for you have always been about you. When they are going well, it's great because your needs are being met. When things start to go badly, you get to whip up all of your friends and family to support you and ride high on their attention. You stay in the relationship not because you want to make it work, but because it allows you to play the victim. You get to run to your girlfriends, play 'woe is me,' they rally around you, and pick you up. You have a case of Marital Munchausen Syndrome. Is there more about that? Did I miss anything?*"

Haley bristled with electric hostility. He knew how to punch every one of her buttons. "Only that I have married the embodiment of my self-hate."

"*That must make you feel …*" Dylan pantomimed checking his sheet of *feeling words*. "Antagonistic. Castrating. Insecure. *Are any of those feelings correct?*"

"Fuck you." Haley's face reddened with anger.

"*Are there any other feelings you are feeling?*"

"Contempt. Loathing. Fatigue. And fuck you."

"I can't keep living like this, Haley." Dylan's face

filled her screen as he leered into the camera with disgust. Then he turned his camera off.

***

Haley had always been a bookish child, more comfortable with the inviting world of stories than the rough and tumble antics of classmates. She'd like to be able to point to some incident, that one moment of bullying or trauma that caused her to withdraw from the world, but there wasn't one. The world was simply a mean place, full of pain, and people who hurt, so she just played life safe, gradually sliding away from them. Unfettered by the complications of people, she came of age online. In her room, on her laptop, she was safe. Message boards. Xanga. Chat rooms.

SMOKINGHOTCHICK342246: I'm surprised you met Dylan at all.

HAYTHERELONELYGIRL: It was pure chance, Monica. Chat roulette.

SMOKINGHOTCHICK342246: How'd you get past all those guys with nothing better to do than hold their junk up to a web cam?

HAYTHERELONELYGIRL: LOL. Almost didn't, though I thought it was funny at first. Then I ran across Dylan and we started talking. It was wonderful. He was so easy to talk to. We'd chat constantly. Instant message while we were at work. It was great.

SMOKINGHOTCHICK342246: You guys were the first online wedding I went to.

HAYTHERELONELYGIRL: My mom almost disowned me over that. The idea of dressing up for a wedding but only virtually attending … she still reminds me how foolish she felt standing in front of a web cam.

SMOKINGHOTCHICK342246: You should've had a guy flash her his junk.

***

Unknown Number: Hey. What's going on?

Haley Cell: Is this my wrong number?

Unknown Number: Oh, my bad. Thought I'd try again.

Haley Cell: See if the number was right this time?

Unknown Number: It's magical thinking, I know. But you never know when you'll make the right connection.

Haley Cell: What if I was her? This woman you met for a moment, but left you with such an indelible impression, and a number to a stranger.

Unknown Number: Then I'd ask why you gave me a bogus number.

Haley Cell: Fear. Why does anyone do anything? Afraid to commit. Afraid to risk. Afraid to say 'no'.

Unknown Number: Fear is good. There's always risk in getting to know someone. But if we were always afraid of being hurt, none of us would ever get with anyone else. The fear reminds us that we're alive and still feeling. No shame in that. You know what I mean?

Haley Cell: I know exactly what you mean. It's funny, I've rarely met too many guys who get that. The fear, I mean.

Unknown Number: Well, I get you, anyway. The way I look at it, worst case scenario, you're guilty of being nice.

***

SMOKINGHOTCHICK342246: So what did you do?

HAYTHERELONELYGIRL: Nothing, Monica. I swear.

SMOKINGHOTCHICK342246: Nothing or *nothing* nothing?

HAYTHERELONELYGIRL: Nothing serious. I mean we talked.

SMOKINGHOTCHICK342246: I still don't believe you.

HAYTHERELONELYGIRL: What? I barely even know his name. We just talked.

SMOKINGHOTCHICK342246: Oh, *that* I believe. But I don't believe it was just nothing. Conversation is how it goes with you.

HAYTHERELONELYGIRL: Conversation is a lost art.

SMOKINGHOTCHICK342246: Exactly. And when someone does that with you, they *got you*. Mentally. You get so … connected. It's like you have an easier time opening up to words on a screen than you do the people in front of you. But I understand. Anonymous is the way to go. It adds to the excitement and that's what this is all about.

HAYTHERELONELYGIRL: So then what don't you believe?

SMOKINGHOTCHICK342246: That you wasted time texting with *this* dude. He was already blown off by a woman you don't even know. So he's a secondhand reject.

HAYTHERELONELYGIRL: Stop it. You make it sound so tawdry.

SMOKINGHOTCHICK342246: So why do it?

HAYTHERELONELYGIRL: It's just a little diversion. You know, from things going on around here.

SMOKINGHOTCHICK342246: Things bad?

HAYTHERELONELYGIRL: Things are the same. And I'm tired of it. Dylan's personal demons find some measure of comfort in making me as miserable as him. The sad part was, he doesn't even mean to. He flits through life making his messes as he goes along and he leaves it to others, mostly me, to clean up. It's exhausting. And it hurts. And it's hard.

SMOKINGHOTCHICK342246: And things are easy with Anonymous Ryan.

HAYTHERELONELYGIRL: I'm just saying that relationships shouldn't be reduced to … this.

***

Haley sat on the couch opposite from Dylan, knowing her husband as much as he did her: from the nose up. Laptop screens obscured the rest of their faces. The television played in the background and ostensibly the two of them watched it together. After their last session, their counselor encouraged them to spend time in the same room together, to allow that to be their first step in rekindling any sense of intimacy. She couldn't help but think they had retreated to neutral corners: Dylan sat up along his black, faux-leather couch, his papers spread before him like an offering to an easily displeased god. She curled along her micro suede couch. Small mementos of vacations past lined mantles and end tables. But no photos or anything *too* personal. The room, like all the rooms in the house, seemed incomplete and shabby. Forgotten. Not worth the effort to furnish or clean properly. They fell into utter hopelessness, hidden behind computer screens.

Haley had put on her favorite shirt, a black T-shirt with the words "This is not about being defined by others" emblazoned in white across it. With her red hair styled short—tapered at her neck—she brushed her long bangs to the side. Dylan loved long hair. She hadn't grown it out in years. Between her light pink lipstick and her shell-colored foundation, the residual glow of her screen drained her face of any vitality. She cocked her head to each side, popping her neck, then stood to arch her back.

"What are you working on?" Dylan asked.

"Just Facebook stalking a few friends."

"Chatting with anyone?" He lowered his laptop. To Haley's mind, he might as well have been peering over a pair of glasses sitting low on his nose.

"Not right now. Monica's out on a date," Haley said.

"Hmph. There's always someone." Dylan tried to hide the fear on his face, like she'd stumbled across his secret. His shame.

"What do you mean?"

"We're supposed to be watching TV, spending time together, but there you are, screen up, another wall between us for me to hurtle."

"Your screen suddenly invisible?"

"Mine's work related. And went up after yours. That's the first difference."

"And the second?" There was always a second. His mind worked like that, one unrelenting logical point after another. If she were a five bullet-point presentation, if he could somehow systematize her and lay her out in an eye-catching flow chart, he'd have an easier time talking to her. He'd get her intuitively.

Like Ryan.

"The second is that I'm not chatting with anyone. I'm not getting to know someone while ostensibly being with you. I'm not multi-tasking relationship with you. I'm not building a relationship, dividing my heart …"

"Dividing your heart?" It was an unusually poetic turn of phrase for Dylan, something else he'd lost over time. She almost felt bad for breaking his rhythm. There was the spark of passion to his cadence.

"My attention. All those people you chat with are more real to you than I am even though I'm in the same room as you. Right next to you. But you'd rather text or chat or anything else rather than be with me."

"Did you really mean what you said?" Haley dropped her screen partway.

"Which part?"

"About my … 'Marital Munchausen'."

"When folks ask you why you stay with such an 'obvious monster,'—since that's the impression of me you give—you get to claim that you're doing it because you don't want to give up on your marriage, because vows mean something to *you*, or because God, or whatever higher power you believe in this week, convinced you to or some other reason which makes you sound noble … and then you're lauded for that. You get to be a relationship martyr." Dylan paused. He didn't ask if she really meant what she said about marrying her self-hate.

"Go back to your spreadsheets."

"Fine. I don't want to keep you from your imaginary friends."

***

Haley Cell: I much prefer a friend that's comfortable with himself, is all I'm saying. People play too many games with each other. I'm too old to play games.

Unknown Number: I don't believe that.

Haley Cell: That I don't want to play games?

Unknown Number: That you're old.

Haley Cell: Flatterer. You know, I'm really happy to have connected with you. I spend so much of my time in front of the computer. Telecommute. Eat. Sleep. That is the rhythm of my life.

Unknown Number: It's because I'm not real. You don't even know me. Not really. You put on me the dreams of what you want me to be. I'm an ideal I can't live up to. The daily motion of your life has lulled you. You exist. You don't live. Opening up to a stranger doesn't seem wise, but sometimes it's easier. Anonymous. Without accountability.

Haley Cell: So if that's all there is to my life, then Dylan shouldn't begrudge me one of the few voices that make it interesting. And bearable.

Unknown Number: I can live with that.

Haley Cell: So Mr. Not Real, tell me something true about you.

Unknown Number: You first. The fear and all.

Haley Cell: I'm a chronic agoraphobe who can't help but be an irrepressible eternal optimist. What about you?

Unknown Number: I'm the devil.

Haley Cell: That's not funny.

Unknown Number: But I could be, you don't know. What am I but a signal transmission? I'm just a stream of ones and zeroes you are interacting with. I could be anyone. Anywhere. It's what we all are, signals broadcast into the universe.

Haley Cell: So once you're done being a philosophical man of mystery, are you ever going to tell me anything about you?

Unknown Number: We all have secrets.

Haley Cell: Some people are open books.

Unknown Number: Like you? You're right, you're easy. You live with the fear that if you expose yourself, show people who you really are, they will no longer like or outright abandon you. So you convince yourself that you would rather be alone and unhurt rather than risk others in your life.

Haley Cell: I think I've had enough honesty for one night.

***

SMOKINGHOTCHICK342246: He sounds creepy.

HAYTHERELONELYGIRL: That's not fair. You don't even know him.

SMOKINGHOTCHICK342246: Neither do you, that's the point. You're just drawn to the mystery and danger of new people.

HAYTHERELONELYGIRL: Danger? You don't think you're over-stating things?

SMOKINGHOTCHICK342246: You know how it goes. You choose to share something, make yourself vulnerable and you give people a choice: they can accept/love you or they can reject/destroy you.

HAYTHERELONELYGIRL: Dramatic much?

SMOKINGHOTCHICK342246: You know what I mean, don't try to deflect. Where's Dylan during all of this?

HAYTHERELONELYGIRL: Around, I guess.

SMOKINGHOTCHICK342246: I got an idea: see if you can get him on chat. Then you can just cut and paste the convo over to me without him knowing.

HAYTHERELONELYGIRL: Okay. That sounds a little … going with your girlfriend to spy on your boyfriend.

SMOKINGHOTCHICK342246: What are virtual friends for? Just be careful. The heart's a fragile thing. Especially yours.

***

Haley pecked at her keyboard, cloistered away in her small office. She could work anywhere in the house, but sometimes she needed a closed door to fully seal herself away. She always imagined that she would be braver away in her tower, she was a princess who didn't need rescuing she told herself. She was so guarded about her life. Where she was once so talkative about her life, her dreams, her passions, her affections, now she remained isolated, her joy withered and bled out through the wounds of relationships. A hermit of her heart. That was what allowed her to accept the measure of unrealness to her virtual relationships. She was little more than a digital pen pal, close but safe. Unable to see them. Unable to feel them. Unable to … fully experience them. She had the memory of them, the impression of them, though not fully formed. She caught herself and her unconscious smile as she typed. As she enjoyed the conversation, the repartee of it. Like a bantering couple in an old romantic comedy. And Dylan recognized the smile. She wondered if she smiled over him since they'd been married. She massaged the gooseflesh that dappled her arm as she typed.

***

MrNotReal99: I hate this.

HAYTHERELONELYGIRL: It's not so bad. And it's easier than typing on a phone.

MrNotReal99: Not really.

SMOKINGHOTCHICK342246: Creepy.

HAYTHERELONELYGIRL: Quiet, you.

HAYTHERELONELYGIRL: I still want to know something about you.

MrNotReal99: If you want to keep a secret, you don't have to tell anyone. It will just lie in you, festering as you carry it about like a cancer seeking release.

HAYTHERELONELYGIRL: Fine, then tell me a secret.

MrNotReal99: I'm going to kill someone tonight.

SMOKINGHOTCHICK342246: WTF? Girl, you need to run from him. Like now.

HAYTHERELONELYGIRL: Why?

SMOKINGHOTCHICK342246: Why? He just said he was going to kill someone.

HAYTHERELONELYGIRL: He wasn't serious. They are words on a screen. There's no tone. No inflection.

SMOKINGHOTCHICK342246: Scary ass words. Ain't a 'ha ha' included after that shit either. And if there was, it wouldn't make it any less …

HAYTHERELONELYGIRL: Creepy.

HAYTHERELONELYGIRL: Who would you kill?

MrNotReal99: Does it matter? Another set of ones and zeroes. A Facebook friend who you never met whose friendship you didn't think twice about accepting. A friend of a friend, not even rising to the level of acquaintance. She never existed to you outside of an avatar anyway.

HAYTHERELONELYGIRL: Just ones and zeroes.

MrNotReal99: Exactly. Besides, you ever just get a bad vibe from folks? Some people are just plain broken. Beyond repair. Tainted by their past, their character determined by their history. Some people are just monsters.

SMOKINGHOTCHICK342246: Seriously, girl, block his ass.

HAYTHERELONELYGIRL: Sometimes you have to not be so … you.

SMOKINGHOTCHICK342246: He's right though. Some people are monsters. He should know: he's one of them.

HAYTHERELONELYGIRL: There are no monsters.

MrNotReal99: We're all monsters. That's what you fear in your heart. That the moment you let down your guard and let someone in, they will rend your heart into ribbons and devour what's left.

HAYTHERELONELYGIRL: Maybe … something less graphic.

SMOKINGHOTCHICK342246: Block. His. Ass.

MrNotReal99: If nothing else, one less person means one less distraction. Good night.

***

Now, staring at her blank screen waiting for a message, she had her doubts. Nervously tapped at her keyboard, gooseflesh rippled along her back. And for some reason, she felt like crying.

Monica did not receive chat.
Monica did not receive chat.
Monica did not receive chat.

***

Haley couldn't sleep. The voices conflated in her head, little more than static white noise. She lay in bed comforted by the whir of the fan. It wasn't warm at all, but the noise drowned out the dread silence. The dream faded into bleak reality, old and dark. The king-size bed stretched out into the night. It didn't matter if she slept in the middle of it or on the edge of her side, she knew if she reached out she would find nothing but a cold empty space. Something less than a one or zero. What peace she had once had long gave way to depression, which pressed in on her like fingers digging into a vulnerable throat.

"As I look back on what we've been through, I feel … regret. As if I've never been truly present a moment with you during our marriage. Of all my relationships, it was the most virtual." Her words hung in the night.

How could she hear what was never said in the first place?

"What I need most from you right now is… your presence. I feel so alone, but now I think it's too late."

Her life was imaginary characters and fabricated torments, unreal projections of the mind. So preoccupied with herself, protecting her anguished heart and oh-so-troubled soul. So alone, so afraid to be alone, surrounding herself with voices. And they came to her, on her terms, where she could remain safe. Untouched. And forever alone.

"One thing I think about but don't tell you is that … I miss the sound of your voice most of all."

She no longer even recalled her husband's name. Her virtual husband.

Nameless. Unremembered. The Internet void filled with nonsense and dreams she perpetuated. The illusion of connection without consequence. Where she could hide behind screen names and avatars. More projections of ones and zeroes putting masks people called faces on their non-existence. Waiting for the final dissolution of the soul. An absolution of mirage.

She imagined Ryan's voice. Her virtual soul mate. So romantic an image, the mysterious knight who understood her in the most primal of ways. Whose connection seemed so … real. His words resonated in her mind like a familiar melody. His voice grew stronger, almost audible now, like the murmurs of sleep talking. She recognized his voice because he retained that cryptic way of speaking to her. With a knowing, reading the pages of her heart, laid out like sacred writ. His presence like a pervasive shadow in her life. A shifting darkness to stem the solitude. Alienation. Isolation.

"What are you?" Ryan asked, a bodiless voice emanating from the shadows.

"Alone?"

"You were created to be relational, but you turn relationships into extensions of your subconscious, your ego, thus they become altars of worship to yourself."

"Sometimes we need to be shielded from pain," she whispered.

"We grow pretty comfortable being safe and unknown."

"Where's Dylan?"

"Does it matter? You kept pushing people away, fighting against what you say you want. Ending up exactly where you truly want to be: alone."

"I don't want to be hurt again. I don't want to be alone."

"And you've become what you feared the most. Relationships end the way they always end: in pain. None of it making any difference. You don't exist. No one exists outside of relationship to another. You're not here. I'm not here. God is nowhere. All is shadow from which we all came, *ex nihilo*, in which we all dissolve into absolute nothing."

Haley shivered and she closed her eyes against the terror of the night. The fan keened, a high-pitched squeal as if the blades were in need of repair. A sound which she found soothing, even comforting.

"What's that sound?" Haley asked.

"It could be your husband's death rattle no more than a few meters away. Does it matter?"

"I suppose not."

The monitor froze. She didn't remember getting up or turning it on. Maybe it never shut off and she never left its side. The computer thrummed with renewed vigor, its memory resources demanded by some puzzling algorithmic loop. Haley stopped pretending, her fingers on keyboard, numb and cold. Only the glow of the monitor kept the full darkness at bay, like a flashlight beam penetrating the darkness. The monitor stared at her. She wheeled back a few feet, not too far, not wanting to get lost in the darkness. The screen beamed like a lone eye against the black backdrop. Seeing nothing, reflecting nothing, knowing everything. Things stirred in the dark. Things crawled in the dark. Things were buried in the dark. The void. The eternal dissolution of identity across the void. The final flicker. Extinguished. The room narrowed, as if the walls were closing in on her, bringing with them deeper, cloying darkness. The air remained silent and still, save for the tap-tap-tapping of her fingers on the keyboard.

"We're all ones and zeroes."

❦❦❦

NIGHTMARES ON MAIN STREET:
THE MAD SLASHER PULPS

By Frank M. Robinson & Lawrence Davidson

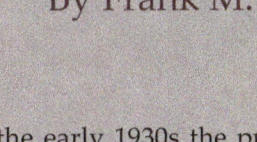

By the early 1930s the pulps were testing the limits of sensationalism in the mystery and detective magazines, some of which were quite sensational enough as it was. But Henry Steeger of Popular Publications decided to take the sensational a step further. He had just returned from Paris with visions of the Grand Guignol Theater and its graphic depictions of torture and murder dancing in his head.

At the time Popular's *Dime Mystery Book*, a companion to *Dime Detective*, was doing badly. The publisher responded quickly with changes. He shortened the title to simply *Dime Mystery*, and shrank the book-length novel to make room for short stories, which were a combination of gothic mystery, terror and sadism of a "heart-quickening" type.

Popular changed the covers as well. The new formula was to show a woman about to be butchered or in the process of being tortured or whipped. Sometimes her boyfriend was at hand, tied up and unable to help. The formula was unique, eyebrow-raising and successful.

Dime Mystery enjoyed an immediate spurt in circulation and soon was joined by Popular's *Terror Tales* and *Horror Stories*. The difference between the latter two was not always obvious to the reader (or author), but editor Rogers Terrill summed it up neatly: "Horror is what a girl would feel while watching a ghoul practice diabolical rites from a safe distance; terror is what she would feel if she knew she were going to be the next victim."

As usual with any successful genre, competition wasn't slow in developing. There was *Ace Mystery* ("Princess of Pain"); *Mystery Novels and Short Stories* ("Maidens of Bondage"); *Strange Detective Mysteries* ("Coming of the Boneless Men"); *Thrilling Mystery* ("Slaves of Dancing Death"); and *Marvel Tales* ("Lust Rides the Roller Coaster"). Among the genre's aficionados, "mystery" now had become a code word for stories of torture.

With time the girls on the front cover wore increasingly less, and the scenes of torture became more graphic. Inside the stories usually hewed to a consistent formula: no matter how outlandish and weird the circumstances, in the end everything had to have a natural, if not plausible, ending—frequently, though not always, involving a mad scientist. This distinguished the magazines from the more literate *Weird Tales* and *Strange Stories*, which tended to the supernatural in a story's resolution.

It's interesting to note that the formula for the 1930s terror tale, in its entirety, seemed to be the template for E.L. Doctorow's recent bestseller, *The Waterworks*.

Not all the magazines hewed to the relatively innocuous story formula of *Terror Tales* and *Horror Stories*. The Red Circle line of *Mystery Tales*, *Uncanny Tales* and *Real Mystery* were heavy on sexual

sadism and eroticism, with intriguing story titles such as "Debutantes for the Damned," "Dead Mates for the Devil's Devotees," and the all-time winner, appearing in Red Circle's *Marvel Tales*, "Fresh Fiancés for the Devil's Daughters" by "Russell Gray" (Bruno Fischer). The story concerns a beautiful woman who traps and tortures the men who spurned her, along with their wives. She then selects a lover from among her victims to bed down with before continuing the various tortures.

Hot stuff for the pulps back then—too hot. There were no feminist groups to urge the newsstands be cleaned up of publications that were obviously denigrating and insulting to women. But Mayor Fiorello LaGuardia of New York made all the appropriate noises, and the torture scenes disappeared from the covers; the women suddenly acquired more clothing; and some of the magazines switched to a less controversial mystery and detective format.

The "Shudder Pulps" featured some bylines that appeared in no other magazines. But there also were familiar names such as Arthur J. Burks, Frederick C. Davis, Wayne Rogers, Hugh B. Cave, Henry Kuttner, the ever-popular Robert Leslie Bellem and Donald Dale. Nor were the shudder pulps strictly a male preserve; "Donald Dale" was in actuality one Mary Dale Buckner.

By the early '40s the shudder pulps had reformed or disappeared from the newsstands. Martin Goodman, owner of the Red Circle group, ran afoul of the federal trade commission with *Real Mystery*, but it wasn't in regard to the salacious and sadistic content of the magazine. It seems *Real Mystery* used reprints from *Uncanny Tales* and *Mystery Tales*, retitled them and neglected to tell readers of the deception.

Goodman now largely retired from the pulp magazine business and spent his time developing a line of slick men's magazines and building his other business Marvel comic books.

Grace note: Years after the demise of the pulps, Hugh B. Cave, one of the major contributors to the "weird menace" magazines, moved to Haiti. He wrote a number of fine horror novels based on the voodoo culture of the island. *Legion of the Dead* and *The Cross and the Drum* are two of his best novels from this period.

With the advantage of moral hindsight, it's easy to criticize the shudder pulps and reflect that the sadism and denigration of women depicted on their covers couldn't possibly happen now.

Those who rush to judgment must never have seen *Halloween, Nightmare on Elm Street, Friday the 13th* or any of the other "slasher" movies so popular today.

(Chapter Excerpt from: Pulp Culture: The Art of Fiction Magazines – Collector's Press, 2001)

Check out the newly remastered DVD of The Power (1966) from Warner Brothers - adapted from Frank's classic Science Fiction novel:

http://www.amazon.com/Power-Remaster-George-Hamilton/dp/B0044LLO4M/ref=sr_1_1?s=movies-tv&ie=UTF8&qid=1395081403&sr=1-1&keywords=the+p ower+george+hamilton

❦❦❦

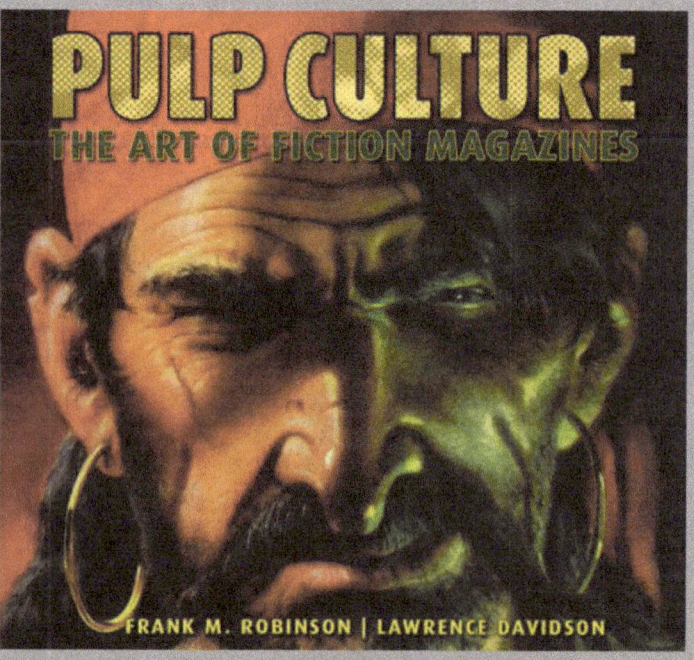

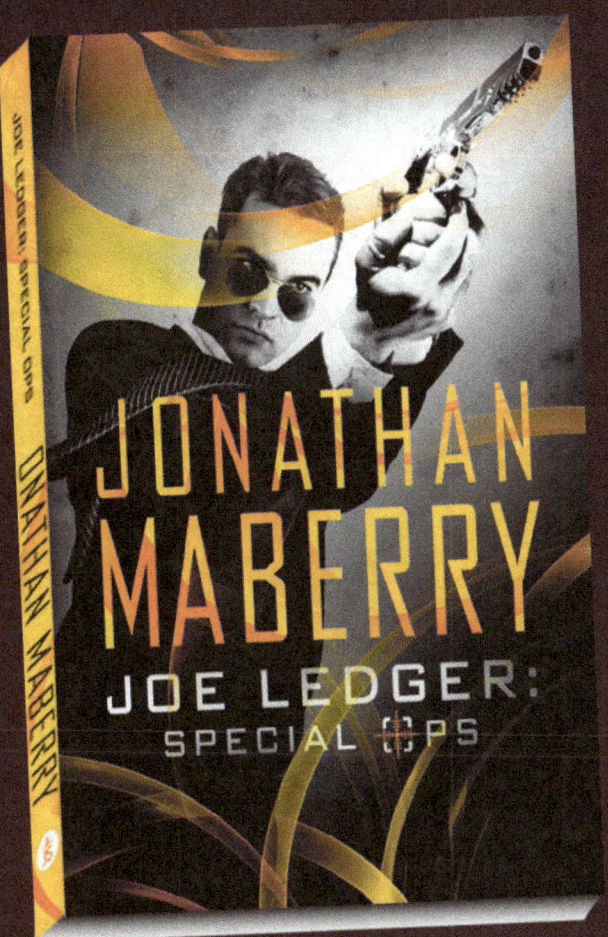

HANNIBAL LECTER'S REIGN OF TERROR

Aaron J. French

In looking at mystery-suspense-thrillers and horror genre fiction, we obviously find significant parallels, but we also find some glaring divergences. For instance, the theme of death is consistent in each, however the level of that death—the pitch of artistic fear and hysteria to which it rises—varies. While there usually *must* be a death or murder in any compelling mystery story (although a robbery would also suffice), that isn't the case with horror: sometimes the MC is slurped into another dimension of madness, disappearing from conventional space and time, to thereafter abide in some vast cosmic dread-o-mania. (Any Lovecraft fans out there? Fist bump.) The point is, there is a quality about the frequency of fear, uncertainty, killing, and violence that characterizes horror fiction, drawing it apart from its sleuthing companions. We here at the *Dark Discoveries* editorial department—fools that we are!—have nonetheless attempted to balance and equate the conflicting narrative elements in this issue.

One character who has strode this line between mystery and horror for years—defying the classical definitions—is Thomas Harris's Dr. Hannibal Lecter. Lecter has had a long career in fiction and film, and more recently with the NBC television series *Hannibal*, proving his longstanding intrigue and endurance.

I'm not going to summarize any of Harris's books or film adaptations here (they're all out there for you to enjoy, and I'd rather not spoil any of the plots if you haven't seen or read them), but rather try to penetrate into the cross-section (geometry!) of mystery and horror. Lecter is the blurred image of the two genres, a transparent mirror through which they meet and encounter one another: Lecter is a crafty murderer, essential for any well-told mystery, but he is also a cannibal, cooking up his victims and eating them—an element at home in any Jack Ketchum, Clive Barker, or Bentley Little novel. Just consider some of the ways in which Lecter disposes of his victims: decapitation by samurai sword (as well as by horse, rope, and tree); various instances of cannibalism (obviously); billy clubs, knives, hangings; and, of course, the infamous scene in which Lecter captures Justice Department agent Paul Krendler, lobotomizes him, and then he and Starling dine on his prefrontal cortex, sautéed with shallots, before Lecter finally kills him. That's getting a bit outside of your average crime scene investigation, I'd say!—and more into the high-pitched heights of violence for which horror reaches.

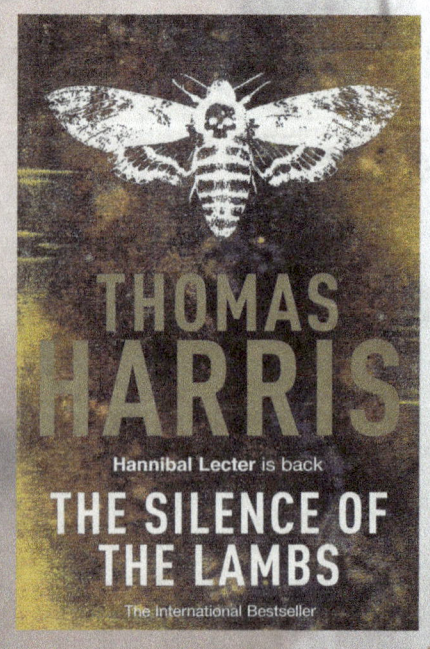

Thus, in Lecter the two genres are married. And this tends to confuse the fans and readers, especially the subsequent filmgoers, who remain unsure as to the type of imaginative story in which they are participating. These films and books draw a combination of fans from both genres, though it is arguable that the Lecter series attracts more of a horror crowd, but that's the topic of another article.

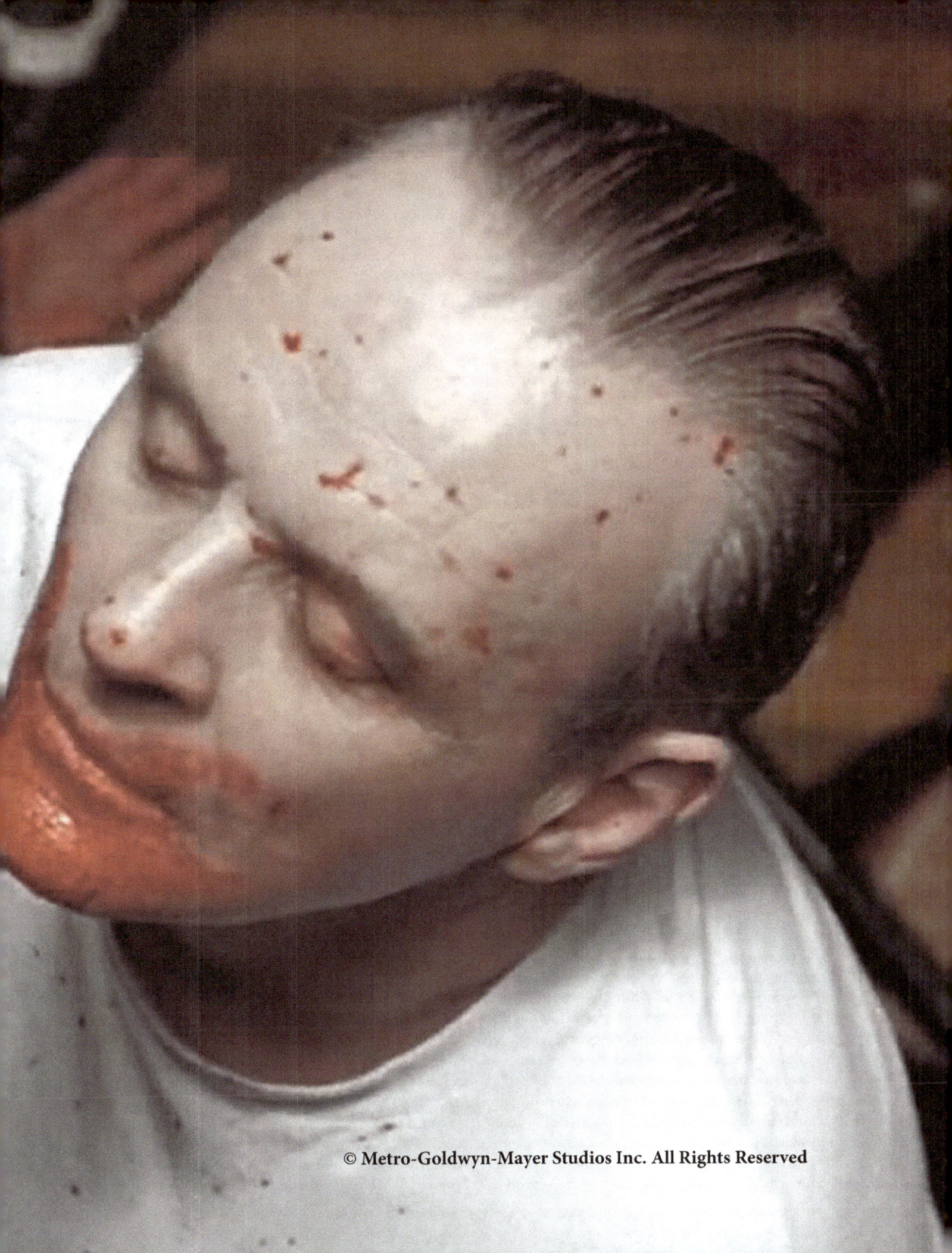

When I first saw *The Silence of the Lambs* film in 1991, I, like millions of other Americans, was shocked and horrified and elated. I immediately went out to buy the novel, thinking I was buying a horror book, but I soon realized the written version—though by no means any less horrifying—followed the style of a mystery or thriller novel, rather than the kind of horror fiction narration I was used to. That's not a point against Harris's writing, as I love the novel and have read all of his others in the series and enjoyed them, also I've probably seen *The Silence of the Lambs* film fifty times. I bring this up only to illustrate how, with reading the Lecter novels and watching the films, one gets caught in a crisis of genre, stuck between the tobacco-chuffing detective fiction world of Raymond Chandler, and that cannibalistic extreme horror world of Jack Ketchum. Again, this is not a criticism; in fact the blending of worlds is what has garnered the Lecter series so much notoriety and success.

I re-read Harris's *Red Dragon* (1981) novel—the first of the Lecter books, filmed initially as *Manhunter* (1986) and later remade with the same title as the book in 2002—as I was writing my own novella "The Order" for the *Dreaming in Darkness* project. It served as terrific inspiration. One difference is that I also introduced a Lovecraftian element into Raymond Chandler's plotline, as well as some extreme and occult horror which ultimately tipped the scales of my

work irrevocably toward *horror genre* whereas the Lecter books manage to straddle the fence between the two effortlessly—and are ultimately stronger, I feel, for doing so.

Perhaps the most distinctive quality of the Lecter series is its psychology, a theme common to both horror and mystery. What sets horror apart is that it follows the human psyche down the uttermost twistings and windings of the dark side of human nature, to such an extent that the darker aspects begin to feel *normal.* As the Lecter series progresses, we start to sympathize with him; by the final book *Hannibal Rising* (2006) he's actually become the good guy! This characterizes horror—where the most depraved darkness of reality becomes normal, accepted, and real. The artistic level of violence is still presented as

supposedly bad, but by HR we're clearly on Lecter's side. Oddly enough, HR is the least horror-like of the Lecter series, and my least favorite, speaking as a horror fan. But by the end of the series' journey, we've thoroughly probed the interior of Lecter's subconscious, as well as the subconscious levels of the rest of the characters *through Lecter's eyes.* We get to see that a) people are dark and deviant at bottom, tortured by immoral desires that come from an animal nature (thanks, Freud)—and, b) we have also learned to understand *why* these characters do the evil things they do, psychologically speaking. We've become psychologists ourselves (though technically Lecter is a *psychiatrist,* but it is human psychology we're discussing here).

In fact the series' analytical observations are so astute that I once erroneously believed the books' author Thomas Harris was also Thomas A. Harris, MD, the author who wrote the bestselling psychology self-help book in the '60s *I'm Okay, You're Okay.* Sadly, this is not the case, though I always sort of ~~wished wushed~~ wished that it were. I think you catch my drift, however; although an understanding of human psychology is apparent in mystery and horror fiction, an *acceptance* of the dark side of this psychology is key to horror. We find it manifestly in Hannibal Lecter.

To take it a step further, let us talk about body horror. Wikipedia describes body horror as "fiction in which the horror is principally derived from the graphic destruction or degeneration of the body… types of body horror include unnatural movements or the anatomically incorrect placement of limbs to create 'monsters' out of human body parts." We see a strong element of body horror in the Lecter books/films, such as the "becoming" of the Tooth Fairy in *Red Dragon* and his impressively Blakian tattoo; Buffalo Bill's second skin that he constructs out of female flesh (not to mention his fascination with transgender qualities); and Lecter's general carving on people, stringing them up, basting them, and endeavoring to shape them into works of art.

Body horror popularity has been increasing in the horror world, with anthologies such as *Zippered Flesh: Tales of Body Enhancements Gone Bad!* (2012) and *The Mammoth Book of Body Horror* (2012), and films like *The Human Centipede* (2009). For my story "Whirling Machine Man" in the *Zippered Flesh* anthology, the MC (also a detective) is brutalized and transformed by a deranged "scientist" in a cabin in the woods, who amputates his arm and replaces it with a curious Tesla-like antenna that conducts and controls the spiritual world. Like Lecter, his serial killer cohorts, and the crazed surgeon of *The Human Centipede* (whose forerunner is Herbert West, undoubtedly), body horror attempts to draw the ordinary to the artistic level by way of violence, disfigurement, and death, causing us, ultimately, to think of such achievements as being—what?—beautiful? Larger than the ordinary and higher than conventional reality, at any rate.

But whatever the case, whether Hannibal Lecter is a horror character or a mystery villain—or more likely both—it cannot be denied that the emotion evoked when living through Thomas Harris's world is one of terror; not only *fear*, but *terror*. And the terror becomes so amplified that it is elevated to a higher frequency, creating an atmosphere of *awe*. (This technique was incorporated into the later films *Se7en* (1995), *The Number 23* (2007), and the *Saw* series (2004-2010)—most effectively in *Se7en*). And yet there is, thankfully, a team of disgusted and appalled investigators in the Lecter series striving to reorder the world and set it aright, without whom we might lose ourselves into the darkness and accept if fully; maybe even embrace it. At that point we are no longer straddling the fence between the two genres…but have entered fully and irreversibly into the realm of horror… whence there is no escape…take it from me.

I would like to thank you for sitting through this mandatory, initial introduction. Time now for our definitive studies to begin.

Please, Dear Reader:

Tell me about your mother…

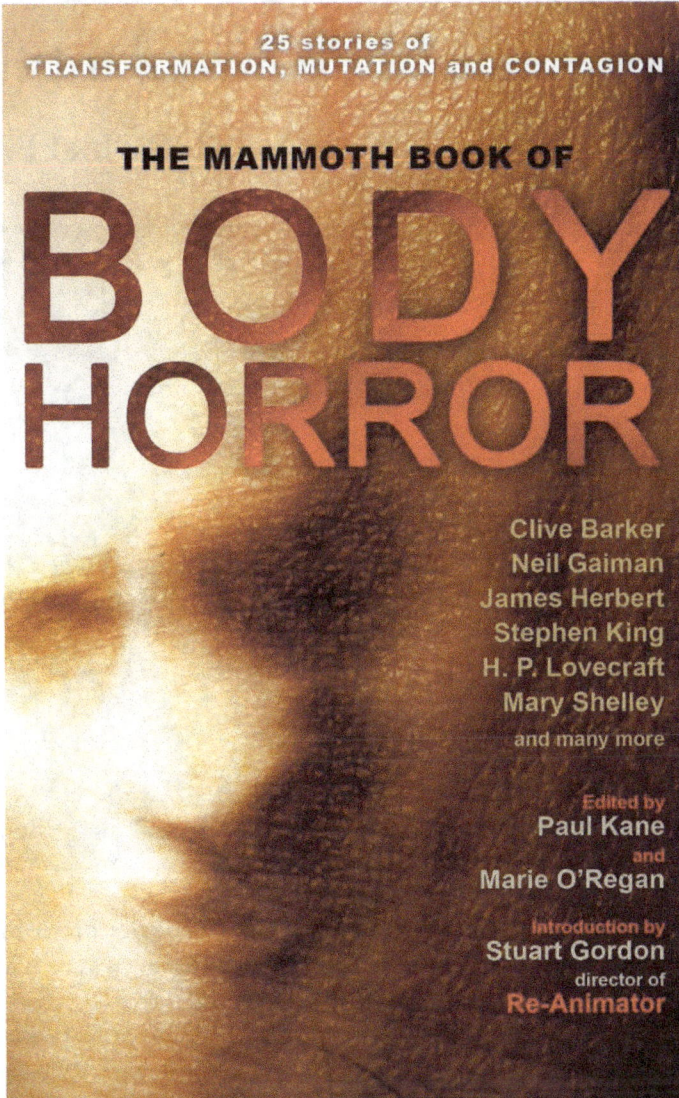

Meeting the Black: An Interview With Tom Piccirilli

By Joel B. Kirkpatrick

Photo courtesy of Tom Piccirilli

How do you best sum up more than twenty years of hard writing? Like this: four nominations for International Thriller Writers awards and two wins; eleven Bram Stoker Award nominations and four wins; hundreds of published works… etc.

He's fondly known as PIC, and there seems to be no end to his achievements. Yet after more than twenty years of brilliant story-craft, Tom Piccirilli could no longer see well; could no longer think clearly; could no longer stand up with confidence; and could no longer write. He could do none of those things without medical intervention to remove a tumor from his brain.

We still have him, and for that we are very thankful.

Joel B. Kirkpatrick: Your friends and fans will want to know how well you are doing, and if life is approaching normal again?

Tom Piccrilli: I've been in remission since the day of my brain surgery sixteen months ago. Not too bad considering my neurosurgeon gave me a 2-3% chance of lasting a year with this aggressive a cancer.

JBK: I read your post-op work Meeting the Black just last night. I was amazed how your words prompted such a vivid recall of my own similar experiences, even after twenty years. Yet I could not help but view your powerful seventeen pages as a bit of a test—some physical therapy for your healing brain. Am I close there? Were you concerned for your writing?

PIC: Very concerned. When you start having bits of your brain pulled out you never know what you might lose along the way. A memory, a skill, a dream. The whole essay is about living with the fear of potential loss.

JBK: Where do you believe is the spring for your talent and drive now? In your head, or in your heart? Is there any real difference in the two?

PIC: I don't think I can gauge the difference. Your emotions are as much a part of your head as your heart. I just hope I can keep telling my stories in my own way.

JBK: Writing for half your life into so many genres and themes, you have decidedly settled into noir, and speak so fondly of it. In an interview a few years ago, you offered: "For me, it feels as if the horror genre is a young man's game, whereas noir is for older men...." Can you explain for us how noir so closely fits your own experience now?

PIC: Noir is all about having a date with fate, and having cancer is certainly that. You run up against a powerful dark force and hope you can drag your ass out of the fight a winner rather than a loser.

JBK: Hardly a man of schedule when it came to writing, your habit was one of getting a thousand words a day any way you might—even between bouts

MEETING THE BLACK

TOM PICCIRILLI
AUTHOR OF THE LAST KIND WORDS

of trashy movies and reading loads of other great writers or just walking the dogs. Are you different today? Have you come back to writing slowly, or in some new rush?

PIC: It took a bit of time to shake the rust off, but when I did the stories began to flow pretty smoothly. I keep the same non-schedule, watch tons of shit movies, tons of classics, and read and reread a lot of favorites in between.

JBK: A common thread so powerful in your most recent novels, *family* positively jumps out at the reader in your first pages, your first paragraphs. I stopped counting the number of books that open directly into relationships between brothers. (Even the delicious description of one uncle in a cage…). I read that you felt you punished your own brother in your writing. Has he always been some sort of twisted, playful inspiration to you?

PIC: Yeah, some of it deservedly so, most of it probably not. But he or my father are usually there.

JBK: Let's look directly at your own definition of noir, as compared to horror. You've defined horror as more supernaturally based and noir as reality based. Some might think this question a bit rude, but isn't your battle against your cancer as noir as anything you've ever penned in a story, and isn't your recovery as supernatural as anything you've personally encountered? Doesn't your spirit play the more powerful role in your healing?

PIC: I don't consider positivity or spirit or support from friends and fans to be "supernatural" in any way. If anything it's the most natural thing in the world. You fight for your life in whatever way you can. In my own case with a brain operation, months of radiation therapy, and over a year of chemo. Hundreds of emails, letters, etc. only served to help. I am forever grateful to everyone who assisted me in whatever fashion. I learned that good thoughts have to go somewhere.

JBK: Please tell us: What is it with so many houses on the covers of Tom Piccirilli books? Are your publishers picking up something subliminal in your stories, or do you have input in the artwork chosen?

PIC: Even with the horror titles the idea of family as a backdrop theme was important, so I guess the houses are just a response to that. But I don't really know, I have no input. Or not much anyway.

JBK: Another theme, never subliminal in your text: we meet your characters just at the moment they would rather be somewhere else than in those first pages. Your style has always been to open right in the most uncomfortable situations.

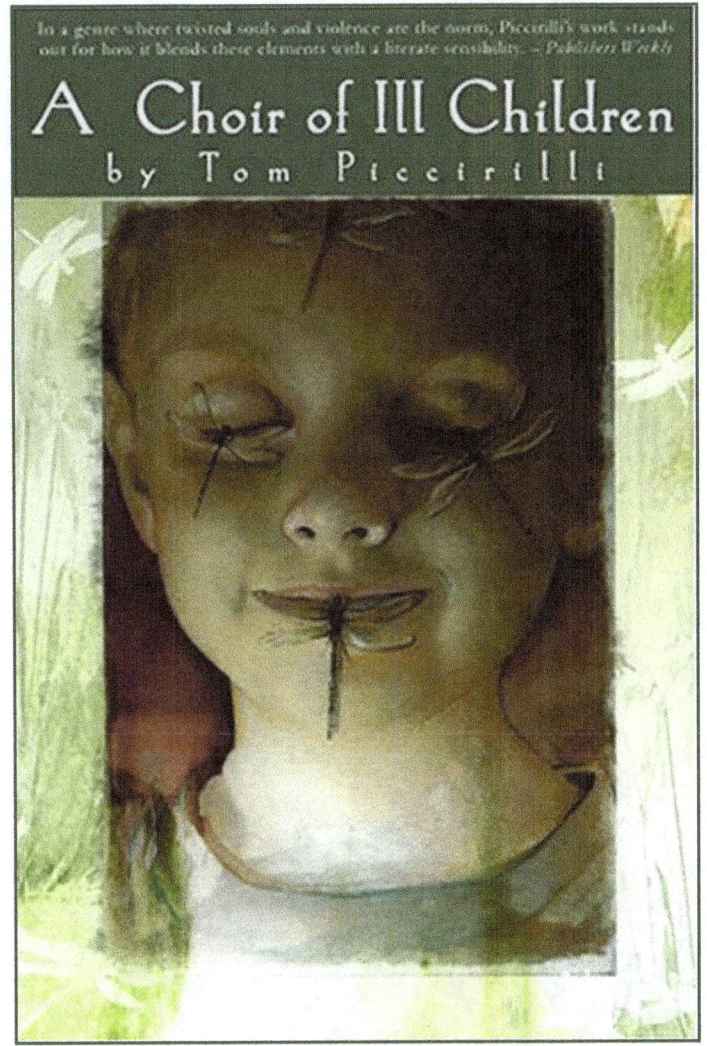

A Choir of Ill Children
by Tom Piccirilli

PIC: I'm a big believer in starting in the middle of action, as close to the ending of the story as possible. I don't have much patience and I think most readers feel similarly. Start a story thirty pages before the action or horror starts and the readers will tend to skip over a lot of those pages in search of some kind of hook or heat.

JBK: So often described in your text—asylums—were you brought up near any similarly sinister settings?

PIC: Pilgrim State Psych Hospital was across the street from Suffolk County Community College and about a half mile from my high school. A lot of property, a bunch of old spooky buildings, torn down fences, etc. It's the kind of place that just slithers into your imagination.

JBK: You expressed once in an interview that you wished you had more Hollywood attention, and then my mind wanders to Sebastian, Jonah, and Cole from *A Choir of Ill Children*. I cannot begin to imagine how any director could create that story on film. But it would be great to see them try. Don't you have a fear that Hollywood might mangle a Piccirilli story?

PIC: CHOIR would probably be the most difficult of my

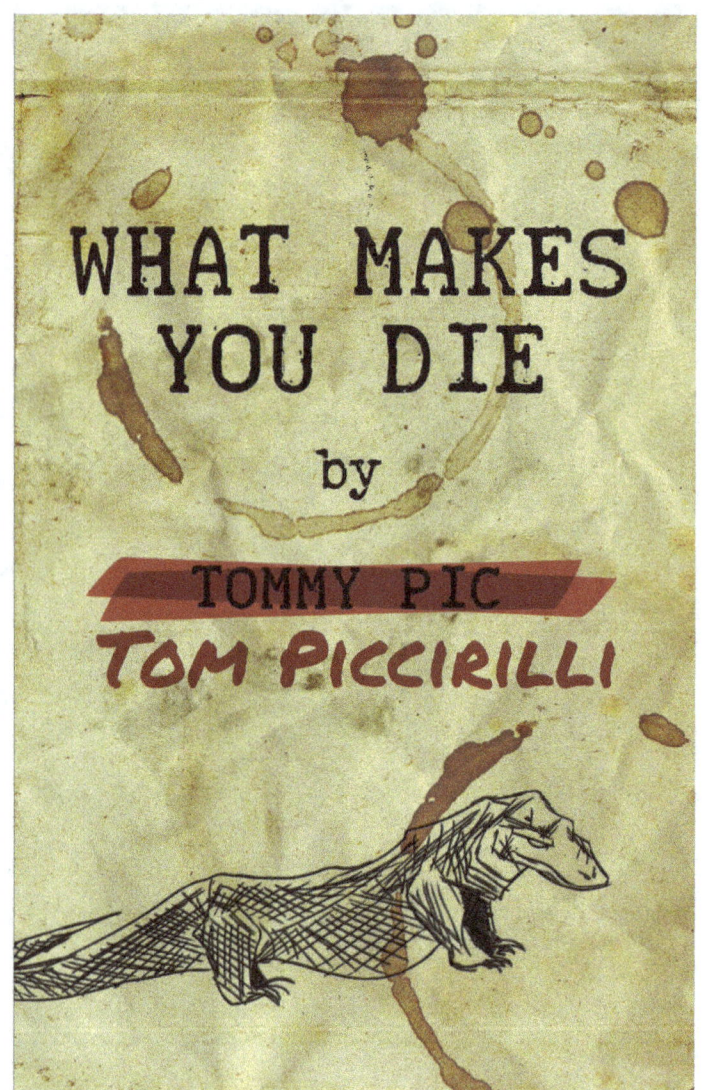

PIC: Creeping Hemlock has sadly shut down production. They cancelled all their projects and my two titles got the ax along with all the others. They're with my agent now, so we'll see where or if they land anywhere in the next year or so.

JBK: Your stories often contain ghosts. Terry Rand can't help but see the ones he and his family have made in *The Last Kind Words* and *The Last Whisper in the Dark*. Tommy Pic wakes in restraints surrounded by family who are both dead and alive in *What Makes You Die*…. Do you believe in ghosts?

PIC: I believe in hauntings. Hauntings by regret, by bad choices, by disappointment, by wasted time. I think it's an area that everyone can agree on, especially when they're flying into their mid-life crises.

JBK: Your early career is described, by you, as backward—busting out novels before you knew how to craft a story. You then began the earnest study of your own writing by concentrating on short stories. Are novels just not a

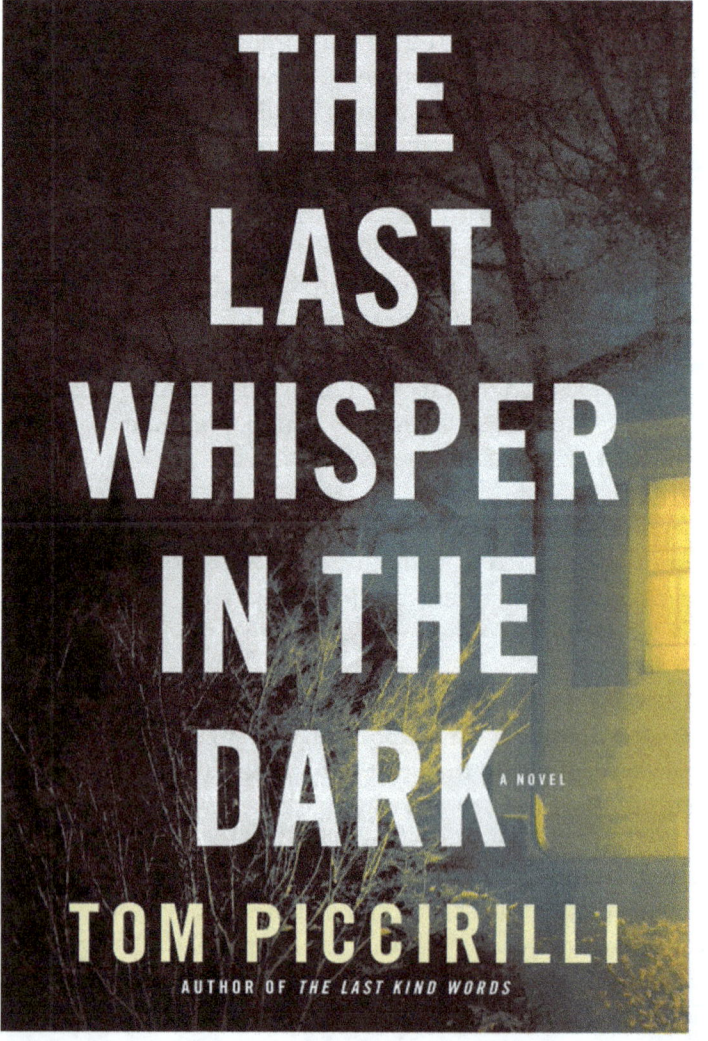

novels to bring to the big screen, although if somebody could make NAKED LUNCH they could probably make anything. And if they fuck it up, who cares, so long as they give it a go, cut me a check, and say what the hell.

JBK: As haunting as *A Choir of Ill Children* might be, you really claim that *What Makes You Die* is your only true journey into unhinged writing. Readers seem to agree: *What Makes You Die* is a Piccirilli story they never imagined they would get. You have claimed that all your books have been difficult to write. Was unhinging a bit any easier?

PIC: I do enjoy writing offbeat work, but I learned the hard way that you always have to be rooted in reality. Early on I was brimming with weird story ideas, but they weren't stabilized or informed enough with reality. I was young and immature and didn't have much life experience. That's why the strange and speculative meant more to me than realism.

JBK: Before your surgery you were busy getting the finishing touches on a novella, *Pale Preachers*, which was released just this year by Creeping Hemlock Press. And, natural place for your creative mind to be? What are your personal obstacles to getting a novel going?

PIC: Novels probably are my more natural comfort zone. You have miles to move around in. Short stories and novellas need precision. If anything, I dig writing novellas most of all. You can focus in on all of your strengths and worry less about your weaknesses.

JBK: A friend of yours, also a well known author, once cautioned you to never throw away any story notes or scribbles, that you might someday have the talent to craft stories from them. You have written hundreds of shorts and novella works over the years. How often does one of those shorts beg to become a longer tale?

PIC: I knock them out one by one. I don't leave much lying around for months or years. When I need an idea I just go around and start finishing the half-written stuff up.

JBK: You've had many relationships with editors, we are sure that there have been *noir* relationships and *horror* relationships. Is there one person, friend or editor, who is your best reader?

PIC: If you're talking about professionals I would think Ed Gorman gets me and I always listen to anything he has to assay about my work on bended knee.

JBK: How often have you ever encountered a problem getting a story concept across to an editor? Most of your books originate from an invitation and contract with a publisher, right? Aren't you required to come up with some outline of a story idea for them at the beginning? How can you do that with unusual plots, such as WMYD?

PIC: Well, I wouldn't say that WMYD is my only unhinged piece. All my books are bizarre in their own ways. But WMYD is one of my few pieces of meta-fiction where the reader can presuppose that the book is actually about me, Tom Piccirilli, the author, since the narrator is Tom Piccirilli the author. So long as it affects them strongly in some fashion.

JBK: There have been authors who were published and then could never get another book printed. You were published and then never seemed to run out of success. Have certain projects stood out as a sudden new direction, or has any certain book taken on a new life after reaching print?

PIC: Actually, it was a pretty long drought between my first and second novels, about five years' worth. I thought I might never get published again. I wasn't as proud of *Dark Father* (1990) as I'd hoped and the whole editing process proved to be pretty hellish. My original editor left and

someone who clearly didn't like the horror genre took over Pocket Books' paperback horror publishing arm and didn't know what to do with me. Not that I blame them. So I just kept my head down and kept writing novels, knowing they might never find a home or an outlet. After I had four or five books in the pipe, I decided to go back and learn my craft again. I worked on short stories for about a year, learned how to edit, continued to find my voice and my themes, and then started to sell short pieces consistently. I re-edited the books, figured out where they had gone astray, and when Leisure came along in the late 90s I had a bunch of stuff for them to wade through.

JBK: Few readers will really understand the importance of an award for writing, such as your numerous Stokers. Writing awards are not doled out for selling a certain number of books the way gold records are pasted up on walls by musicians. Awards for writing are peer-to-peer devices, aren't they?

PIC: They are generally given by peers, but really, considering what a lonely art/craft writing is, you need validation wherever you can find it. Whether it's success from sales, good reviews, or awards—wherever they may appear.

JBK: You once said that everything is about the writing, and never really about the social posing. How often, I wonder, do you get into your own Wikipedia entry to make sure they have your biography and bibliography correct? Have you ever bothered?

PIC: I may have updated it once or twice, but no more than that. I leave it to others to get all those facts straight.

JBK: There are legitimate reasons to be wary of self-published authors, and yet there are an equal number of misunderstandings about what self-publishing means. Without its technology and ease, many established authors might see some of their works disappear forever—and many are endeavoring to revive their older works by self-publishing. What do you think?

PIC: E-books are certainly the future. The trouble with self-publishing is that the bar is lowered to a personally accessible height. You don't have to get better because you don't have to make money for a publisher. You don't spend the years in the trenches any longer when you can just pay somebody a few hundred bucks to publish you or to do it yourself. It takes weeks to build a career instead of years.

JBK: The 70s witnessed a surge in remarkable fiction from authors in both horror and science fiction. Has crime fiction and your own favorite noir themes been steady over the years, or was there a golden age of those styles?

PIC: I think noir and dark mystery is making a comeback. When I first started working in the field all anybody wanted were cozies. But with the advent of Lee Child, Dennis Lehaane, Charlie Huston, Ken Bruen, Megan Abbott, Sara Gran, and dozens of others, there's a much richer landscape of literature.

JBK: How does your poetry equate in popularity to your fiction works?

PIC: Beats the shit out of me.

JBK: Can you describe your writing process in any detail for us? What prompts a poem from you, say?

PIC: Poetry is a distant fourth behind novels, novellas, and short stories. I'm not sure what prompts me down that road as opposed to the other formats. It's one of the endless mysteries of this wacky business.

JBK: You've called writing *"…a constant fight against the white."* Doesn't that fight ever end, when a story is clicking, and you just can't stay away from the keyboard?

PIC: Sure, once a story gets rolling along it's easier to work on it than not. But it's still a fight to fill the empty page (which is what I mean by "the white").

JBK: Years ago, before you forced yourself to use a keyboard, you wrote longhand on paper and then transcribed your stories. Have you embraced technology now so that you've become the writer who pauses on the sidewalk or in a grocery aisle to whisper a thought into a digital recorder?

PIC: No digital recorders but I don't write longhand any longer. The last time I did that was for Choir, which I wrote on a long yellow pad, which I still have around here someplace.

JBK: You wrote your first story at age eleven. Have you lived that kid's dream? What would you say to him at this moment, if you could?

PIC: It's not too late to become a plumber. Learn the mystic arts of plumbing.

JBK: Ha! So on that note, what's your next project? Is it already being written?

PIC: I have about 10k words of my next novel *Blue Autumn* finished. Also working on some novellas for various anthologies.

JBK: Has your experience mellowed you? Can you look back at any one of your characters and think, "…you know, I've been too hard on that guy?"

PIC: The characters suffer only as much as they have to in order to serve the stories. I never hurt anybody gratuitously.

Readers who want to help Tom with his recovery may do so easily by browsing on Amazon to Tom's book, *Meeting The Black,* or any of his Crossroad Press titles. Those proceeds will help his family defray the costs of his ordeal.

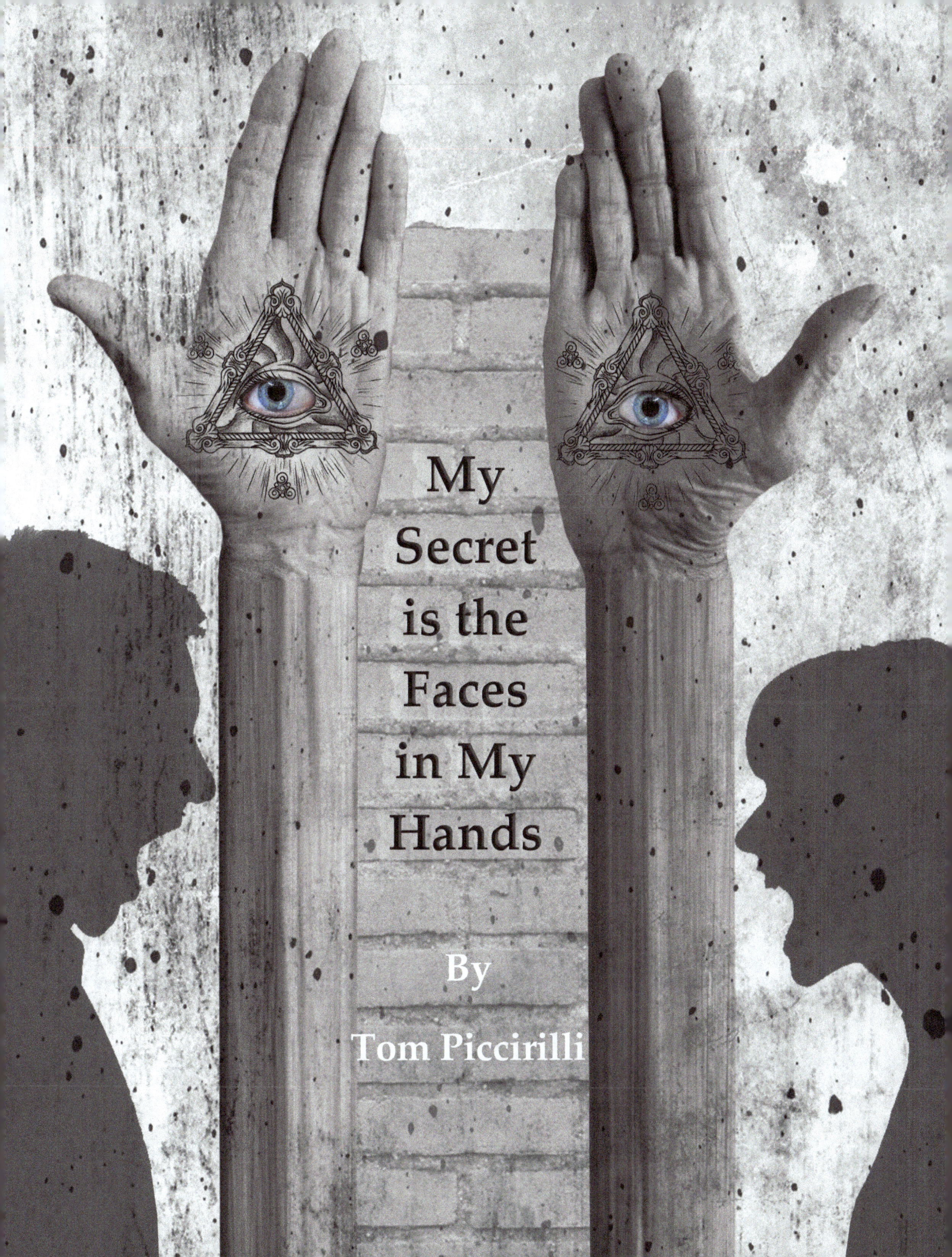

My Secret is the Faces in My Hands

By

Tom Piccirilli

Don't give your particular skill set away for free.

The old-time torpedoes always sang that song. There weren't many of them left around because they'd all done free jobs at one time or another, and the free ones got you caught.

I washed my face for the third time in a row and listened to the guy next door beating hell out of his wife again. She screamed and he argued and said he knew she was cheating on him with the guy upstairs, the truth was that the heat had him, he was behind in his rent, she was cheating with me, and he had to hit somebody and he couldn't hit a real man, because a real man would knock his teeth out and shatter his jaw. So he chose his wilted wife, Rosie.

He was also skunked on that yak juice he called whiskey. I could smell it from here. There was a thud, a slam, the sound of breaking glass, and Rosie screaming once more. I stared at the horrid wallpaper on our shared wall and after a minute it began to change into people and the people began to move and talk to me. My father told me to kill myself. He was still mad that I'd strangled him when I was fifteen.

I had strong hands. They'd only gotten stronger in prison. I stuck my fingers into the wallpaper and down into the sheetrock. I broke my father's neck again. Big Sal Moroni was there, smoking a cigar and growling my name. Smoke poured out the wedge-shaped wound in his throat, where I'd crushed his windpipe. He was playing cards with his lieutenants. I could see him very clearly cheating. So could the others. I figured Sal would have to do a lot of persuasive talking in hell to get out of this one.

The woman shouted for help. She banged on the other side of the wall, trying to reach me, or just reach help. He grabbed her by the hair and hurled her forward. I heard her head crash into the cheap framed mirror designed to look like an antique. She was lucky. It didn't shatter. She called my name, the name I was using. I thrust my fingers in deeper. The prison hack JoJo Martinez appeared in the wallpaper and laughed in my face with his lower jaw still torn off. I laughed right back.

"You hear me over there?" Buzz Talmedge shouted to me.

"I hear you."

"You fuckin' my wife too? If you're fuckin' my wife, you're dead. First I'm going upstairs to stab that piece of shit, then I'm coming to visit you."

"Come over here first," I said.

"Don't worry, you'll see me soon enough."

It wouldn't be soon enough, it was never soon enough. The muscles in my shoulders and back writhed with want. I heard him stomp out of the apartment, down the hall and up the stairs, heard Rosie crying for him to stop. I exerted myself and shoved up against the wall for all I was worth. It took about a minute before the whole thing caved in. I walked through the hole.

Her eyes were so bruised and swollen that she couldn't see me. Her mouth streamed blood and so did her nose. The nose was broken. Two teeth were missing.

She said, "What is that? What is that?"

"It's me, Rosie," I told her.

"What was that noise?"

"Nothing."

"You have to leave. Buzz can't find you here. He'll kill you."

"He's not going to kill anyone except you if you don't leave him as soon as possible."

"I can't go now."

"Yes, you can, and you will. I'll help you."

She said the name I had given her and opened her arms blindly. "Why?"

"It's the thing I do. Sort of."

"I thought you were a teacher."

"I am. I teach the hardest lesson to learn."

I got a dishtowel from the kitchen, ran cold water over it, and washed her face. My hands wanted blood, anyone's blood. The torn wallpaper kept talking. My hands started talking as well. They reminded me of secrets I had long forgotten. I had money stashed. I had bodies stashed. My hands hissed and whispered. The eyes in my hands winked at me. The faces in my hands began to assume familiarity. A scream erupted upstairs.

I knew the kid who lived above me. We had a few beers together on occasion. He was just an innocent punk with a nice smile, the kind of smile that would kill men like Buzz Talmedge by degrees of jealousy in their sleep. The kid shouted. He wasn't going to go out easy. He was fighting hard, throwing shit around. He was young and strong. Glass broke, what sounded like a lamp, furniture, a kitchen drawer full of utensils. Fifty forks ringing off the linoleum.

"I'm sorry, but this is going to hurt," I told her and snapped her nose cartilage back into place. She moaned briefly. "I've got to get you to the hospital."

I took her by the shoulders. She struggled almost gently, almost with love. I drew her into my arms and scooped her up. "No, no...I can't leave Buzz..."

"Of course you can."

"But I shouldn't. He's had it so rough these last couple of years."

"Everyone has."

"But—"

"He's currently slugging it out with the kid upstairs."

"Ronnie."

I carried her to the door just as Talmedge descended the stairs, covered in blood. He didn't care about forensic evidence. He didn't care about anything. He looked at me as I backed into his apartment with his wife. He wasn't holding a knife so he must've left it up there with his fingerprints. He snarled something and jumped the last few stairs. There wasn't going to be a way to reason with him, or him with me. I was past the point of return. My hands told me so. My muscles craved murder too much.

"What did you do to my wall?" Talmedge asked. Rosie started to reach for the sound of his voice. The rage rose up and sat in my brain like it was a velvet throne.

"It's my wall too," I told him.

"Now it's your turn."

"I've been waiting."

I held my hands up as if he was aiming a gun at me. The faces in my hands were his and Rosie's.

"What the hell is that?" he asked. "What kind of freak are you? What the hell is wrong with you?"

"This is what it looks like when I kill you."

He barreled forward. He was even dumber than I'd thought. He had a switchblade in his pocket and went for it. There was so much blood that when it snapped open the blood flew against the side of his face. Switchblades were the worst weapon ever designed. A thin piece of metal hinged on one side. Any real resistance and they'd break in half.

He ran at me. He didn't know how to wield the knife correctly. Almost nobody did. He brought the point down toward my chest and I caught his wrist.

"Buzz, no, please..."

I knew she was actually begging me not to hurt him. It was clear nothing would ever change until he murdered her. His face in my hand began to beg for his life. Rosie moved to me and wrapped herself around my arm. I tried to shrug loose but she was stronger than I expected. I wondered why she never fought back.

Talmedge started to argue with his face. "Shut up! Who are you? What are you?"

"I'm you," the hand said, "right before you die."

He stabbed at me again and I broke his wrist. The knife fell point-downward and stuck in the wood floor. Rosie mewled her love for him. The sound disgusted me. I reached around her and pulled her a little closer. I pressed my lips to her temple. The hand with her face in it said, "I hate this little gutless bitch. I want to kill her."

"Who said that?" Rosie asked, not recognizing her own voice.

Talmedge slashed and got lucky with the blade. It sliced against my chest and hurt like hell. The rage howled. One hand went for his throat, the other went for Rosie. It only took twenty seconds to crack their windpipes and only another thirty before they were dead on the floor. I had given my talents away for free but didn't feel too bad about it. She was going to let him kill her anyway, and he needed to be put down.

I stepped back through the hole in the wall and cleaned up the knife slash. I washed my hands and they were just my hands again. I wondered if I should check on the kid upstairs but that would be a waste and I had to get moving. My father continued laughing. Buzz continued snarling. Rosie continued to whimper her love. Big Sal kept cursing me. Things were back to normal already.

☙❀❧

JADE SKY

EPISODE ONE: OLD FLAMES

Original Story by Patrick Freivald
Adaptation by Patrick Freivald and Joe McKinney
Art and Lettering by Chris Bell

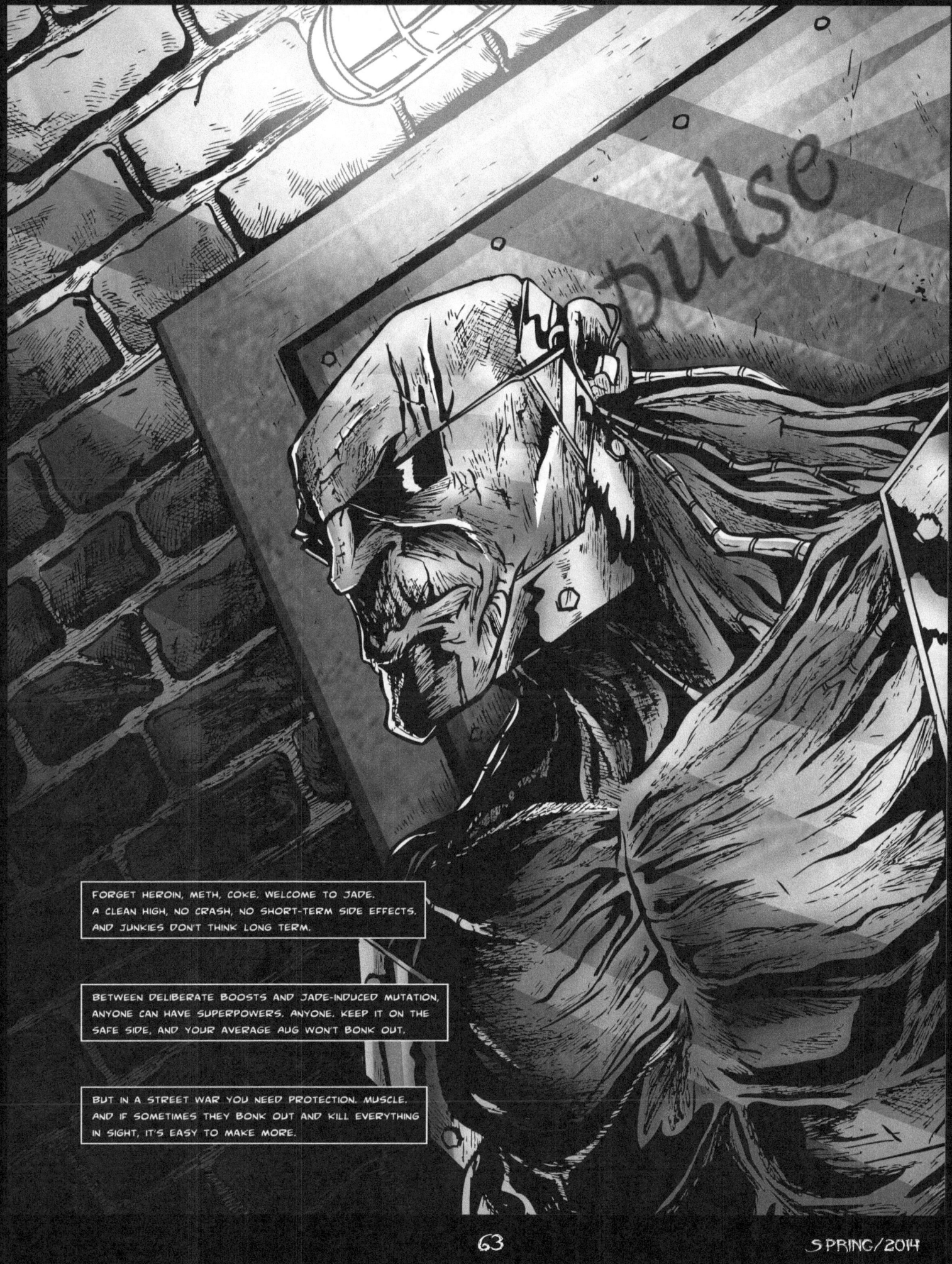

FORGET HEROIN, METH, COKE. WELCOME TO JADE.
A CLEAN HIGH, NO CRASH, NO SHORT-TERM SIDE EFFECTS.
AND JUNKIES DON'T THINK LONG TERM.

BETWEEN DELIBERATE BOOSTS AND JADE-INDUCED MUTATION,
ANYONE CAN HAVE SUPERPOWERS. ANYONE. KEEP IT ON THE
SAFE SIDE, AND YOUR AVERAGE AUG WON'T BONK OUT.

BUT IN A STREET WAR YOU NEED PROTECTION. MUSCLE.
AND IF SOMETIMES THEY BONK OUT AND KILL EVERYTHING
IN SIGHT, IT'S EASY TO MAKE MORE.

SPRING/2014

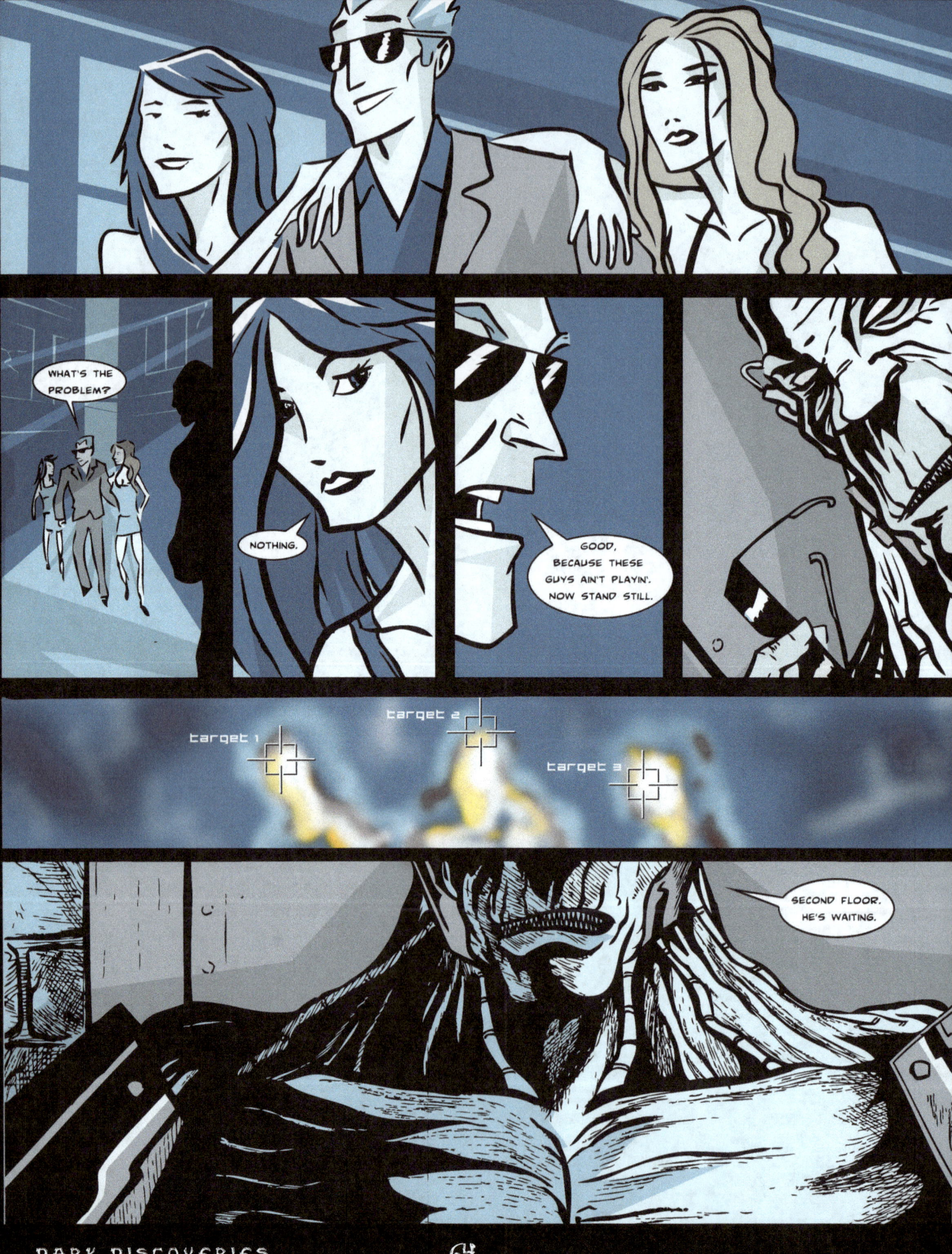

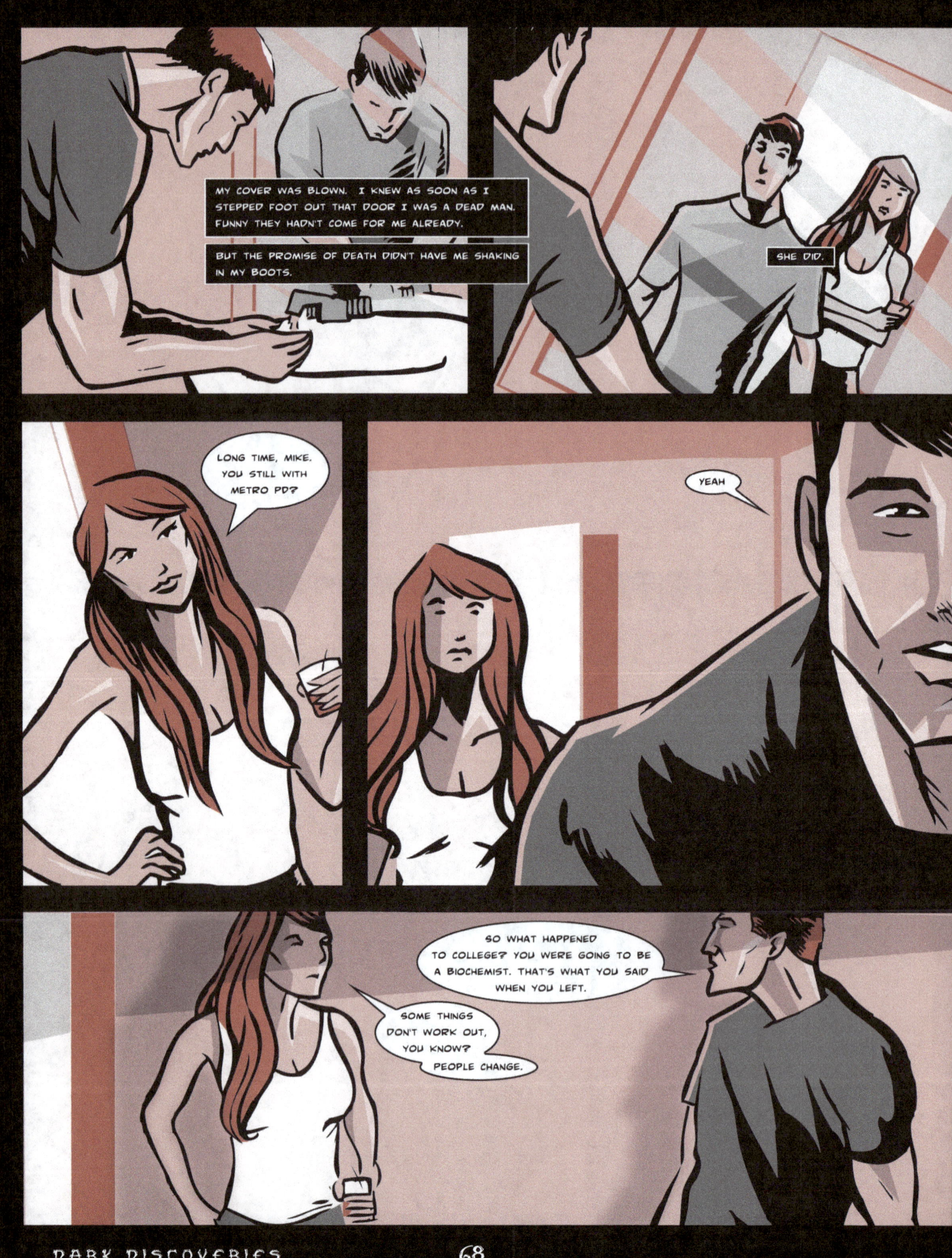

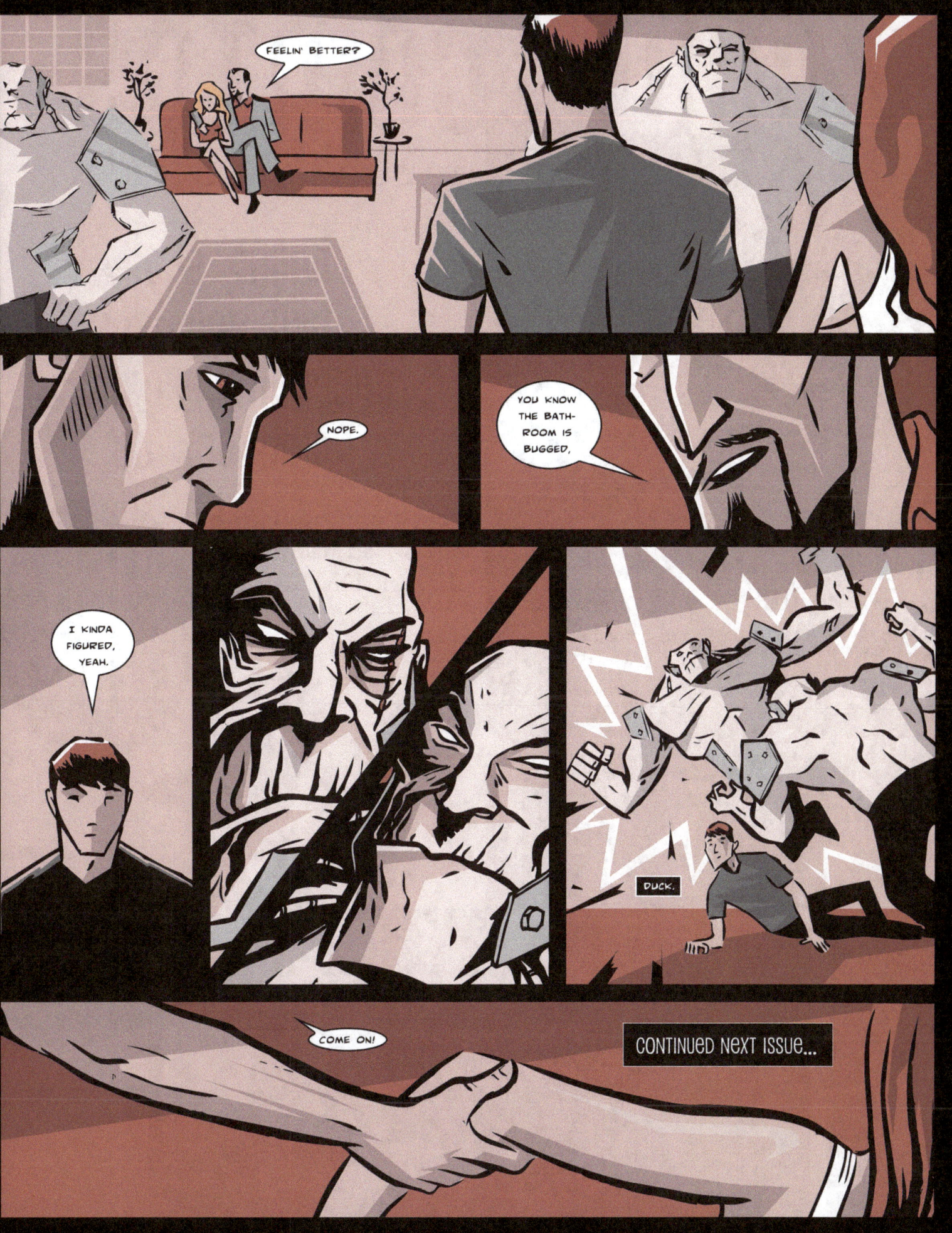

THINGS THAT BITE

Legends and Folklore of Supernatural Predators

By Jonathan Maberry and David F. Kramer
Bram Stoker Award-winning authors of THE CRYPTOPEDIA

CRYPTIDS AND THE SCIENCE OF CRYPTOZOOLOGY
Part Two of Three

More 'Maybe' Monsters

Last time we began our hunt for strange monsters that might be more real than imagined. Let's do a quick recap of the classifications of these creatures:

- UMA's (Unidentified Mysterious Animals) that, due to lack of physical evidence, spoor or DNA, resist scientific classification in the known biology.

- LEGENDARY CREATURES such as the Cyclops, Pegasus, Harpies and similar monsters from myth.

- RELICTS are surviving examples of species believed to be extinct or so close to extinction that living examples are rarely found.

- CRYPTIDS are animals that are believed, and sometimes observed, but which have not yet been proven to exist. The science of searching for and classifying them is called Cryptozoology.

Join me now as we continue our hunt for some of the strange creatures that people around the world believe are *real.*

EBU GOGO: In the mythology of the Flores people of Indonesia there is a long-standing series of tales of a race of diminutive humanoids known as the Ebu Gogo who were reported to be only a few feet high. The name 'Ebu Gogo' is rather chilling when translated from the Flores language. Ebu means 'grandmother', but Gogo means 'one who eats everything'. This combines to 'Grandmother Who Eats Everything", and refers to a creature of omnivorous tastes. The Ebu Gogo will eat plants, animals, fish and, in a pinch, human flesh.

In the folklore of the region the Ebu Gogo were given many of the same qualities as elves —magical natures, prankish personalities, a strange language, and so on—and any question of their reality was routinely dismissed as hogwash (at worst) or popular myth (at best). However in one of those all too rare moments of science and superstition

coming into agreement rather than colliding, scientists have begun to think that the Ebu Gogo are, in fact, real. When Professor Richard "Bert" Roberts of the University of Wollongong investigated reports of a race of diminutive people he was quoted as saying: "They are described as about a metre tall, with long hair, pot bellies, ears that slightly stick out, a slightly awkward gait, and longish arms and fingers - both confirmed by our further finds this year." Along with other scientists he searched for physical evidence and has, in fact, uncovered bits of hair and other artifacts in places where the Ebu Gogo are believed to have lived. Roberts does not, however, insist that the creatures still exist, though like many of his colleagues, he is leaving that open to the findings of continued investigation.

EL DIENTUDO: Throughout the rural areas of Argentina, especially in the dense forests surrounding Buenos Aires, there is the legend of a horrifying monster called El Dientudo, which translates as "The Big Teeth."

This aptly named creature is a flesh

eating and blood drinking predator. It is vaguely manlike in appearance, covered completely in thick matted hair, stands seven or eight feet tall, and reeks like rotting flesh.

EMELA-NTOUKA: One of the more fascinating cryptids, this monster has been sighted in and around the Likouala swamp regions in the Republic of the Congo. Emela-Ntouka is the Lingala phrase for "killer of elephants", which eloquently describes the ferocity of this hulking, amphibious monster described as being as large as an elephant but with an armored tail more reminiscent of a Nile crocodile. It has a snout ending into a hooked break and a single large horn sprouting from its forehead, and its huge footprints indicate sharp, clawed toes. Despite its fearsome appearance the Emela-Ntouka is said to be an herbivore, but when confronted it shows a far more aggressive side. There are eyewitnesses who claim to have seen the Emela-Ntouka disembowel a bull elephant and trample a lion to death.

ENNEDI TIGER (also Tigre de Montagne): This critter is a sabertooth cat reported in the lands east of Chad in Africa. Residents and travelers in the region have reported two distinctly different types: land cats who hunt in the mountains (called Hadjel, Gassingram, or Vossoko), and those who live in and around lakes (called Mourou N'gou, Mamaimé, or Dilali). Sabertooth cat species (such as the Megantereon and Afrosmilus) are believed to have become extinct 500,000 years ago, however sightings of the Ennedi Tiger persist.

FERLA MOHR (Also Brenin Llwyd, Big Gray Man, Grey King): A creature resembling King Kong is not the sort of thing you'd expect to find loitering around the mountain passes of the Scottish Highlands or the more remote forests of Wales, yet legends of a 20-foot tall gray-furred gorilla have persisted for centuries. Known as Ferla Mohr in Scotland, Brenin Llywd in Wales, and a number of other names throughout the British Isle, the creature's nature varies from legend to legend from an overgrown hominid to a supernatural king of some elder faerie race.

FOUKE MONSTER (Also Boggy Creek Monster): The Fouke Monster of the Texarkana region of Arkansas has often been described as Bigfoot's nasty cousin, and that's not that far from the truth. Unlike the shy and docile Bigfoot, the Fouke Monster is reputed to be vicious and predatory, and is anything but shy. In 1997 there were over 40 sightings of the creature, and at least a couple of dozen a year since.

The creature has been spotted hundreds of times since the first sightings back in the late 1860s, and several times over the years it has chased residents. Luckily there are no deaths reliably tied to the monster.

Like many of the larger hominids, the Fouke Monster stands about seven to nine feet tall, is covered with coarse wiry hair, and has a roughly simian face. At one point a good quality plaster cast had been made of the creature's footprint, but in the late '70s that useful piece of evidence was destroyed in a fire at the service station where it had been on display. Despite the frequent sightings, most cryptozoologists dismiss the Fouke Monster as an elaborate hoax. The residents of that region, however, beg to differ.

GARKAIN: The Aboriginal people of the Northern Territories of Australia have folktales about a variety of giant and smaller hominid races. Some of these creatures are considered to be leftovers from the days of the Neanderthal, and some of have a more supernatural origin. These creatures terrified the Aborigines in ages past. Legends tell of giants, pygmies, ape-men (similar to Homo erectus, or the Java Man), and the bloodthirsty vampiric creatures called the Garkain. Garkains lived in remote areas, inhabiting caves and rock shelters on higher plateaus. They hunted in the swamps, hiding in the rushes and feeding on reptiles and insects.

GIGLIOLI'S WHALE: This as yet unconfirmed species of whale was first reported by Enrico Hillyer Giglioli (1845 -1909), an Italian anthropologist and zoologist who spotted one twelve-hundred mils off the coast of Chile in

1870. He was not able to take specimens, however, and did not have ready access to camera equipment. The creature swam along side the ship for half an hour, while allowed Giglioli to record a great deal of information. Giglioli estimated the whale's length at sixty feet, with two large dorsal fins (each over six feet high), and long curved flippers. Of the known whales in the fossil record only the Rorqual comes close, but that species does not share the same fin and flipper design. A similar type of whale was spotted off of the coast of Scotland a year later; and in this century—in 1983- French Zoologist Jacques Maigret saw one of them in the waters between Corsica and the French mainland. Though these sparse sightings have not lead to a verifiable discovery, the whale has been provisionally named: Amphiptera pacifica.

GOATMAN: There is something very peculiar about in the backwoods of the United States—a creature that is part man and part goat. Unfortunately, witness accounts seem to differ as to which part is which. Spotted from Washington, D.C. all the way to west Texas, the Goatman has been described by some witnesses as a great brute of a man with a huge black goat head set on his muscular shoulders; while others claim that the head and upper torso are that of a man but that he walks around on a gnarled pair of hairy goat legs. The former image fits some artistic representations of The Horned God, Goat of Mendes, Baphomet, or the God of the Witches (take your pick), and suggests an earthly manifestation of a satanic creature. Most often referred to as Baphomet, this image first came to public awareness during the persecution and trials of the Knights Templar, when the once exalted knights had been brought down with accusations of devil worship and paganistic rituals. The latter image brings to mind the satyrs of Greek myth who were companions to both Pan and Dionysus. In either case, cryptozoologists have long wondered what they are doing in America. Most witnesses claim that the creature was the size of an ordinary man, though a few more hysterical reports claim that the thing was gigantic, towering twelve to fifteen feet high.

HIBAGON (also Hinagon): Japan has its own domestic version of Bigfoot, with sightings beginning in the early 1970s. Known as the Hibagon, this apelike hominid is of the shorter variety, barely topping five feet, with a face that is more human than simian (though not much). It has bulky shoulders and a slumped posture, but walks upright. Castings of Hibagon footprints have been taken and these are grossly out of proportion to its stature: the prints are six inches wide and ten inches long!

ILIMU: Among the Kikuyu tribe of Kenya there is an enduring legend of a shape-shifting monster called the Ilimu. It is not a human being cursed to be a monster,

like the European werewolf, but a demon that possesses animals and shapeshifts into the likeness of a man. This creature appears in one form or another in legends from many African nations, including Ghana and Uganda. In 1898, two lions in Uganda were suspected of being Ilimu, and were responsible for the deaths of over 130 people involved in the building of a bridge across the river Tsavo. The lions hunted together using deceptive tactics and trickery uncommon to animals, and over the course of their two month reign of terror everyone—even the Europeans supervising the construction—came to believe that there was something supernatural about them. Big game hunters eventually brought the lions down, but only after the lions had foiled their traps time and again. The incident was made into a movie The Ghost and the Darkness (1996), starring Michael Douglas and Val Kilmer.

INCANYAMBA (Also Howie): In South Africa there is an ancient legend of a lake monster called the Incanyamba, and the descriptions suggest a beast startlingly similar to a plesiosaur—the group of aquatic dinosaurs that generally have long necks and flippers. The plesiosaurs were a very hardy group and their tenure on earth began at the beginning of the Jurassic Era and ended, as far as we know, during the Cretaceous, with the big K-T Extinction.

JERSEY DEVIL: One of the most enduring of American legends, with thousands of sightings dating back more than two and a half centuries and more occurring every year. Stories of the Devil's origins vary dramatically, but there are two versions of the story that are told most often. In the first version, a woman called Mrs. Shrouds of Leeds Point, N.J., had twelve children and was so frustrated by her hard life she swore that if God wouldn't help her provide for a dozen hungry kids, if she ever got pregnant again that child would fathered by the Devil himself. That is, apparently,

one of those things a person shouldn't say, because she certainly got pregnant again and shortly after she gave birth the child transformed into a misshapen monstrosity with goat-like legs, a human torso, bat wings, and an elongated snout variously described as similar to that of a wolf, horse, fox, or crocodile. When Mrs. Shrouds tried to suckle the infant, it spread its wings and escaped up the chimney.

In the second most common story a young girl from Leeds Point supposedly fell in love with a British soldier during the Revolutionary War. Naturally the local townsfolk felt that she betrayed her country and laid a curse on her that any child that came from that union would be a devil. This too, ended badly. Since the birth of the Jersey Devil is has been spotted by politicians, dignitaries, forest rangers, police officers and thousands of travelers. Even Joseph Bonaparte (brother of Napoleon) saw it while living in exile in America. In the 19th Century, a naval officer, Commodore Stephen Decatur, who was engaged in artillery testing at the Hanover Iron Works in Hanover, N.J. fired at and hit it, but the creature flew away, apparently uninjured. The commodore claimed that the creature he saw was at least nine feet long from head to tail.

KILLER BADGER (The Beast of Basra): Though this sounds like a Monty Python skit, the Killer badger is an enduring myth the region around Basra in Iraq. Local legend has it that a yard-long carnivore with a gray and black pelt and a face like a lemur that has boldly attacked both livestock and animals. The locals accused the occupying U.S. Military of having released a strange mutant creature, and though you wouldn't think such a claim would even be acknowledged, the level of outrage was so high that UK military spokesman Major Mike Shearer had to issue an official statement: "We can categorically state that we have not released man-eating badgers into the area." He managed to keep a straight face, too. As it turns out, reflooding of marshland originally drained by Saddam Hussein drove various animals into Basra, including The Ratel, a particularly vicious animal also known as a Honey

Badger. So...this is one of those cases where a cryptid just turns out to be a little-known animal. Even so...killer badgers?

KINGSTIE: Since 1817 fishermen on Lake Ontario have been reporting the presence of a 30 to 40 foot long serpent, black or dark brown in color, with a fierce head and glaring eyes. One witness was so adamant that he swore to his account under oath and before a magistrate. Since many of the sightings have been near Kingston, Ontario the creature has been dubbed "Kingstie." The most significant recent sighting, reported in 2001, was by two men diving the wreck of the George A. Marsh, a coal ship that sank in 1917. They said that the creature was gliding along the bottom near the ship, and at first they thought it was some kind of cable, but then it turned toward them, swam to within thirty feet, and then turned and swam away very fast. Because the serpent was between them and the ship they were able to approximate its length and put it at 25 feet. They reported that it appeared to be curious but not aggressive.

KONGAMATO: Though the register of world cryptids includes plenty of lake and land monsters that appear (at least according to witnesses) to be holdovers from the age of the dinosaurs, there are only a few reports of flying dinosaurs. One of these rarities is the Kongamato, a probable pterosaur that has been variously described as a gigantic bat, a great vulture or a creature closely resembling a pterodactyl. The Kongamato has been seen throughout the sub-Saharan region of Africa, where the Kaonde tribe of Zambia claim that it attacks humans. Its name even means "overwhelmer of boats."

In his 1923 book, *Witchbound Africa*, author and adventurer Frank H. Melland conducted interviews with Kaonde natives and recorded their descriptions of the beast.

KUNG-LU: Whereas the vast Himalayas are home to

the docile Yeti (see entry later in this chapter), the lower mountain passes are the hunting grounds of a similar race of giant hulking monsters, the Kung-Lu. Both are gigantic manlike creatures covered in fur, but the similarities end there. The name Kung-Lu means "great hulking thing." There are ancient tales of wild tribes of Kung-Lu sweeping down on villages and slaughtering everyone before drinking their victims' blood and eating their flesh. Also known as Dsu-The, Ggin-Sung, or Tok, the Kung-Lu sometimes hunt solo, often stealing a human child for their meal.

LAKE VAN MONSTER: A monster found in Turkey's Van Lake, which stands as the most frequently sighted sea monster in the world, and also one of the most recent. First spotted in 1995, the creature was caught on film in 1997 by 26-year-old local man, Unal Kozak. The video footage shows what is believed to be the creature's head, partly submerged, and a single piercing black eye glaring out of the water. The footage was shown on CNN and other news services and has become something of a classic for Cryptozoologists. Since 1995 there have been well over one thousand sightings of this monster.

LEVIATHAN: Like Behemoth, the Leviathan is a gigantic fire-breathing monster from Biblical legend that was so vast and dreadful that is "teeth are terrible" and "out of its mouth go burning lamps, and sparks of fire leap out." Leviathan has impervious armor and even if peppered by arrows it would not so much as twitch to acknowledge it. Some Biblical scholars assert that Behemoth is male and Leviathan is female, but God ordained that they were not able to reproduce. At the end of time the Leviathan is destined to battle Behemoth to the death, and the loser's flesh would be fed to the righteous.

LEECH MONSTERS OF THE GREAT BLUE HOLE: Belize, a favored diving spot in Central America, has a culture built around the sea. Aside from sport fishing, island tours, and diving, there is also active trading in folktales of monsters from the deep that prey on unwary swimmers and fishermen. Most of these tales center around an offshore atoll called the Great Blue Hole, just off Lighthouse Reef. Seen from the air it looks just like: a vast blue hole in the ocean floor that was formed about 15,000 years ago, during the last Ice Age, when glaciers from the north trapped so much water in their vast frozen expanses that the sea level in these areas was lowered by more than 350 feet. Over the centuries fresh water Fresh flowed through the limestone deposits forming huge caverns, and the collapse of the roof of one of these formed the Great Blue Hole. The result is a creepy sinkhole full of dark blue shadows that is considerably deeper than the surrounding shallow waters.

© MACLAURIN COMM LTD

LOCH NESS MONSTER (also Nessie, Niseag): Nessie, the Loch Ness Monster of Scotland, is the world's most famous lake monster is also the one with the longest track record of sightings, with glimpses of Niseag (Nessie's Celtic name) going back as far as 565 C.E. when Saint Columba saw the creature shortly after attending a funeral for a man purported to have been killed by it. The most famous encounter, though, took place in 1933, when a couple, Mr. and Mrs. Spicer, saw the creature cross the road right in front of them. The creature had an animal carcass clutched in its jaws and paused to look at them before taking its meal and slipping back into the chilly waters of the loch. There have been hundreds of sightings as well as very well organized scientific investigations, but despite some rather questionable photos and some curious sonar readings, no hard evidence has yet been found. Even so, belief in the existence of Nessie is very strong, and not just among Cryptozoologists—quite a few scientists, oceanographers and biologists have stepped up to defend the possibility that the monster could really be there.

LOFA: Many of the blood drinking or flesh-eating monsters of North America, especially those whose sightings continue into modern day, seem to be variations of what most people would refer to as Bigfoot. Among the Chickasaw of Oklahoma (the reservation to which they were transplanted), and their ancestors in what is now Mississippi, there is a story of a race of intelligent beast men called the Lofa.

LOVELAND FROG (also Loveland Lizard): Since 1955 there have been a number of sightings of strange batrachian cryptids in and around the back roads of Loveland, Ohio. In the initial sightings the creatures were described as being about as big as a medium-sized dog, and were able to stand erect on their hind legs. At full height they stood about four feet high, and probably weighed about sixty pounds. The beasts appear to be amphibious, with froglike faces and glistening, leathery skin. It's doubtful that kissing this frog will turn it into a fairytale prince.

Next time we'll conclude our hunt for Cryptids, UMAs and other beasties of the unknown!

ABOUT THE AUTHORS

Jonathan Maberry is a NY Times bestselling author, four-time Bram Stoker Award winner, and comic book writer. He writes the Joe Ledger thrillers, the Rot & Ruin series, the Nightsiders series, the Dead of Night series, and the Watch Over Me series. He also writes the monthly comics V-WARS and ROT & RUIN, and has written extensively for Marvel Comics and Dark Horse. Two of his novels (Rot & Ruin and Dead of Night) are in development for film, and another (V-Wars) has been optioned for TV. He teaches Experimental Writing for Teens, is the founder of the Writers Coffeehouse, and the co-founder of The Liars Club. Prior to becoming a full-time novelist, Jonathan spent twenty-five years as a magazine feature writer, martial arts instructor and playwright. Jonathan lives in Del Mar, California with his wife, Sara Jo.

www.jonathanmaberry.com

David F. Kramer is the Bram Stoker Award winning co-author (with Jonathan Maberry) of *They Bite Supernatural Predators in Folklore, Fiction and Film* and *The Cryptopedia: A Dictionary of the Weird, Strange and Downright Bizarre*. He is a long-time newspaper and magazine writer, editor and web designer. He has written horror fact, fiction comics, and on dark music of all persuasions. He is vice-president of the Pennsylvania-New Jersey Chapter of the Horror Writers Association. He lives in Philadelphia.

✿✿✿

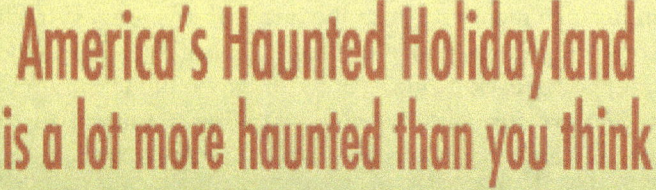

THE EXCHANGE

By John R. Little

"What would make you steal ten thousand dollars?"

"What? Who is this?"

"That's not important. Tell me, what would it take?"

"Don't be ridiculous."

"What would it take, Barry? What would turn you into a criminal?"

"I'm going to hang up now."

"Don't do it, Barry. You *really* don't want to do that."

"Who the hell is this?"

"Everyone has a pain point, my friend. Everyone. Tell me what yours is. Tell me what you wouldn't want to lose. What's so important to you that you'd commit a crime to keep it safe?"

Barry Holder hesitated. He really wanted to just hang up. The call display on his phone just said Private Caller so that was no help. He didn't recognize the voice, but it had a hint of a Brooklyn accent, so it was likely somebody local. Barry lived in an apartment in Manhattan, the Dakota, famous for being the place John Lennon once lived and where he was murdered.

"Let me be clear. Nothing could make me steal any money. There's nothing you can say that would make me do that. Our conversation is over."

He hung up the phone without waiting for a reply.

Stupid crank call, he thought.

Barry took off his glasses and dropped them on the kitchen counter and swept his sparse white hair back with his hands.

"Nobody knows who I am," he whispered. "It was just a freak call."

Although Barry hated to admit it, whoever it was had gotten to him and he was feeling a little rattled. He put his glasses back on and went back to check on the steak he was broiling in the oven. He poured himself a glass of white wine (a Sauvignon Blanc he'd picked up the weekend before) and drank half of it in one gulp.

Without thinking much about it, he walked to the apartment door and made sure it was locked. He couldn't help glancing out the peephole, but there was nobody there.

Of course nobody's there. Get hold of yourself, Holder.

He picked up his phone and checked again, but there was no way to find out who had called. His phone was a state-of-the-art smartphone with all the gizmos any technophile would love, but it had no way to trace the call.

"Just a stupid asshole." Barry knew he was trying to convince himself, but deep down he knew it wasn't going to be so easy. He expected the phone to ring again at any moment, yet it stayed silent.

He clicked on his television and switched to a channel that played continuous soft classical music, hoping it would soothe his nerves.

Before he knew it, the bottle of wine was empty and the sun had set, casting darkness throughout his apartment. He clicked the light on in his bedroom and almost considered popping the cork on another bottle, but he knew he'd regret that in the morning.

9:30 p.m.

He yawned and decided to check his e-mail one last time before bed. There were several pieces of spam that his filter hadn't funneled directly to the trash can, and other than that, there was only one new message.

To: Barry Holder, Director of The Switch
From:
Re: My Phone Call

Barry, the next time I call, do not *hang up. That would be a big mistake. To help you understand how serious I am, you should check on Jake's welfare. In particular, his* friend, Aaron. I suggest you do that right now . . .

❋❋❋❋

"Sarah?"

"Dad?"

"Is everything okay?"

"Umm, what do you mean? It's been quite a night, but . . ."

"Is my little grandson okay?"

Sarah hesitated and sighed. "Jake's okay now. It took him a long time to calm down. He— Dad, how do you know?"

"What happened?"

"His friend, Aaron. It looks like somebody strangled him. Jake was the one who found him. God, he screamed so loud and so long. Aaron's mom ran out, but—"

"He strangled an eight-year-old boy? Who in God's name would do such a thing?"

"The police don't have a clue so far. It's still early, though. It just happened a couple of hours ago."

Silence hung on the phone between them.

"Dad, I've got to go. I don't want Jake to be alone right now."

"Sure, sure, honey. I'll call you tomorrow. Or soon."

"Bye, Dad. Love you."

"Love you, too."

Barry didn't sleep well that night, expecting his phone to ring at any time, but it never did. He stared at the ceiling and tried to imagine who could be trying to blackmail him, and more importantly, what he was going to have to do to call him off.

Hopefully, it really *was* only about money.

At a little after four o'clock, he finally drifted off to a sleep filled with sleazy little nightmares.

❋❋❋❋

The clock radio burst alive at 6:15 a.m. as it did every morning, seven days a week, 365 days a year. Barry Holder had no weekends, no vacation, no Christmas or Thanksgiving, and sick days were considered only in extreme cases. He'd been the Director of the Exchange for fourteen years and nine months, and in three more months, he'd be retired. His retirement would consist of full salary for the rest of his life, and that could be a very long time, indeed, due to the fringe benefits of his job.

He never regretted the grind, because there was always that carrot dangling out there, reminding him that he would be a very wealthy man and potentially live forever.

This morning he was dead tired after the lack of sleep, but he still climbed out of bed without hesitation and staggered over to check both his cell phone and his e-mail. There was nothing unusual at either.

The shower felt unusually cold, but Barry knew it was just his imagination. He dressed in one of his dark blue suits and picked out a lighter blue tie to go with it. He had a massive closet that held several dozen suits. Once a month, The Exchange sent a shopper in to replace any suits that were no longer in fashion or were wrinkled. They wanted the Director to always look his best, and of course he had no time himself to take care of such things.

His normal limousine was waiting at the front of the Dakota. Frank Chambers had been his driver for his entire tenure at The Exchange, and Barry breathed a sigh of relief when he saw Frank behind the wheel.

The Exchange's official name was *The New York Time and Life Exchange*, but nobody ever called it that. The most important commodities market on the planet was always just called by its two word nickname.

The limo was customized with bulletproof glass and was reinforced with an extra-thick body and floor, so that even explosives wouldn't cause any damage. The security Barry commanded was similar to the president's, but to many people his job was even more important. He traded people's lives every day.

The next phone call came that evening, only a few minutes after he got back from work.

"What would make you steal ten thousand dollars?"

"Leave Jake alone."

"Would you steal ten thousand dollars to keep him safe?"

"Listen, you son of a bitch. I can have you thrown in jail for threatening me."

"You try any such thing and Jake is dead. I swear to God I'll kill him the same way I killed his rotten little friend. Don't push me, Barry. *Don't fuckin' push me!*"

Barry hesitated, not knowing how to react. He'd thought of calling the FBI throughout the day but had always backed down. The thought of Jake being killed was too big a risk to take.

The voice on the other end of the phone was dead serious. Of that, Barry had no doubt. He could hear it in his voice, and he'd proven his point by murdering Jake's friend the night before.

"What do you want? I know it's not about money."

"You know damned well what I want."

"I can't. There's too many controls in place."

"I don't give a rat's ass about the controls. I just want you to get me five years. Just five. You do that and your little shit of a grandson lives to see another day."

Barry squeezed his eyes shut, wishing for some magical solution to appear.

The voice continued, "You do anything stupid and Jake is dead. It can happen in minutes, Barry. You can't protect him, so just fuckin' concentrate on what you need to do."

"When?"

"You tell me the best time. This week, though. No screwing around."

Barry tried to think but his mind felt cloudy, as if all the neurons in his brain were just running around in circles.

"I'll have to think about it. I just can't come up with anything right now."

"I'll call again tomorrow." Barry heard the Brooklyn accent again, stronger than the night before. "Remember, Barry, don't do anything stupid. I'll know."

Barry believed him.

That night, he felt every one of his 53 years. Muscles throughout his body ached from being so tired after having so little sleep the night before. He thought of opening another bottle of wine, but somehow the thought didn't appeal to him very much.

His couch seemed to call to him and he sat and put his legs up on his glass coffee table. His own face stared back from the three-month-old issue of *Time* magazine that he kept there. It was a bit of vanity that he hadn't been able to keep in check.

On the magazine cover, he smiled broadly with his arms folded in front of him. The Exchange was behind him. He remembered the security concerns of having the photo taken outside on Wall Street, but really, until that issue of the magazine was published, not many people would have been able to put a face to his name.

The caption on the cover was blood colored and read "The Most Trusted Man In America?"

The focus of the article was about his upcoming retirement and who might take his place. Of course the article implied nobody could, but in his heart Barry knew that almost anybody had the skills. His career had been built on trust, but the actual work was minimal. America didn't know much about that. They just knew he was the king of Telomeric Stasis Transfer. Most people assumed he'd invented it, which was nonsense.

He picked up the magazine and flipped to his favorite page, which had an old photo of him and his wife, Kathy, on their wedding day. They were young and full of hope.

Kathy died of leukemia when Sarah was just two years old. After a year of grieving, Barry decided to devote his life to stopping such unnecessary deaths, joining a DARPA project looking at the biochemical reactions of telomeres, the tiny ends of DNA strands that looked like the little plastic things on the ends of shoelaces. As DNA replicated, the telomeres grew shorter with each copy, and that gradually weakened the person built from that DNA, allowing disease to creep in.

Private industry hoped to find ways to capitalize on telomeres, but the Defence Advanced Research Projects Agency beat them to it.

Barry had wanted to find a way to stop telomeres from shrinking, but instead, his team found out how to use nanotechnology to mine enzymes that controlled the telomeres.

They found how to move them from one host to another, taking time from the end of one person's life and transferring it to another.

"I miss you so much, Kathy . . ." He rubbed his thumb on the photo, as if he were caressing her cheek. "I wish you could tell me what to do."

The phone rang. He wanted it to stop, wanted more than anything for it to be silent again. He knew it was the man who wanted him to cheat the system, but he felt paralyzed to do anything.

After three rings, Barry finally moved and grabbed the phone. Then he could see it was Sarah calling.

"Sarah? Is everything okay?"

"Oh, God, Dad. He's gone. Somebody took him." She broke into a long crying session. Barry's heart sank.

"Sarah! Tell me what happened!"

She cried a moment longer and then was able to compose herself. For the first time in many years, he wished he lived in Boston with her.

"Somebody took Jake. It was at the playground. We were there and I was reading a novel and Jake was playing on the swings. Oh, God, I didn't take my eyes off him for more than a minute, but then I heard him scream and a man was running and carrying him in his arms and they got to a dark car and the man got inside with Jake and they drove off. Somebody else had the car ready to go and there was no time. They stole him, Dad!"

Sarah started crying again, but softer this time.

Barry was stricken silent. Everything was more real now.

"Did you call the police?"

"Of course I called the police. They're looking but they don't have much yet. The car didn't have any license plates. I don't really know what kind it was . . . a big black car with tinted windows. I don't know cars, Dad. Oh, God, they have to let him go. They can't—"

She bit off the end of the sentence but Barry heard it in his mind. "They can't strangle him like they did Aaron."

"God . . ."

"What am I going to do?"

"Is Pete there?"

"He's coming home now. He was in San Francisco on a business trip. He got the first plane."

Barry didn't know what to say. He couldn't say, "It's because of me. They're using Jake to blackmail me." And he couldn't tell the police. That would seal Jake's doom.

"I'm going to try to come down to see you on the weekend, sweetie."

Unexpectedly, Sarah laughed. "Yeah, right. Like you'd miss time so close to your retirement. Don't patronize me, Dad. I just need you to listen, not make commitments you can't keep."

Maybe I can, he thought.

Sarah had to get off the phone a few minutes later, as the police lieutenant had more questions for her. She'd only been able to take a quick break to call him.

There was one thing she hadn't asked: "Yesterday, when you called, you seemed to know something was wrong. How'd you know that, Dad? How'd you know something was very wrong? What are you hiding?"

She hadn't asked, and part of him wondered if she really had forgotten, but he knew better. Sarah was a smart cookie who noticed everything. That was really why she'd called tonight—to see if he'd volunteer anything he might know. He felt like he'd let her down.

It took an hour for the kidnapper to call him.

"What would make you steal ten thousand dollars?"

He didn't answer at first. He felt a million years old. He just wanted to curl up and cry, and he was surprised that tears were actually leaking from his eyes.

"Are you there, Barry? Don't fuck around."

"I'm here," he whispered. He grabbed a tissue to wipe his eyes.

"Jake's asleep. He was crying a long time so I drugged him. He's going to stay drugged until he's either tossed back safely to his dear old mama or I strangle him and toss his useless body in the dump. What's it going to be, Director?"

"I'll do it."

"Tomorrow."

"Yes, tomorrow. Come at 3:00. Trading is over then, and that's when I do the transfers. I only have two scheduled. I'll cancel one of the recipients."

"Five years, Barry. You understand?"

"Yes. It'll be five years. But I need Jake free."

"Not until after we're done. He's been blindfolded the whole time, so he can go free. You just have to do your part."

Barry Holder nodded, not sure he could speak. The most trusted man in America was about to commit first-degree murder.

✸✸✸✸

The clock radio woke him at his normal time, 6:15 a.m. No surprise there, no magical awakening to find that the whole mess was just a fanciful nightmare. It was all just as real as the night before.

Barry wondered if Jake was still drugged. He wondered if he'd ever see his wonderful grandson alive again or if the next time they were together would be for the funeral. He wondered how Sarah was doing and whether she'd mentioned anything to the police about Barry calling out of the blue the night that Aaron was brutally murdered. He wondered if he could just go back to sleep and pretend the whole awful mess had never happened.

But he couldn't.

He showered and got dressed in a light brown suit with a tan shirt and a matching striped tie.

He tried to eat some toast for breakfast, but he had no appetite.

Soon, he climbed into the limousine and said good morning to Frank Chambers, who talked about the Yankees game the night before. Barry didn't follow baseball, but he always let Frank talk.

The Exchange started trading at 10:00 a.m. Barry was in his office, where several computer monitors huddled in a semi-circle on his desk. He could see the bid and ask prices change through the day.

At the opening, the lowest ask for a year's worth of time was $3,000,000. As always, he wondered who would want to sell a year of his own life for any amount of money. Most of his sellers ended up being young, under thirty, and he supposed it was the standard belief of the young that they would never die. What's one year off a life that would be stretching far into the future?

Except it wasn't always the future. Kathy proved that. She died when she was twenty-six, and Barry would have given any amount of money for one more year with her.

The highest bid was $2,950,000. That was the most anybody was currently willing to spend to buy a year that would be added to their normal life span.

It didn't seem like that much to Barry, but then, he couldn't have afforded it. Only the obscenely rich could afford to buy time.

America didn't care. America was proud that they'd found a way to extend life, even if the vast majority of the population would never be offered the chance.

As he watched, a match was made. A new buyer agreed to pay the $3 million fee and the buyer/seller combination was filed away in the central computer system. Later that day, Barry would contact them both to start working out the arrangements of the transfer.

The money left the buyer's bank account immediately, of course. There was never a chance that the deal could go south. As both parties understood, five percent of the fee would go to the government as their commission, while the remaining 95% would stay in escrow until the transfer was complete.

Five percent of the time would also be stored away for Government use, so the buyer was really only adding 347 days to his life, not a full 365.

The buyer wasn't guaranteed to live that extra year, of course. Just guaranteed he wouldn't die of natural causes. He could still die in an accident or other un-natural way.

Barry continued to watch the monitor as trades were completed during the day. By the time The Exchange closed trading for the day, sixteen deals had been consummated. The final year was sold for $3,675,000.

It was 3:00.

One of the computers (the one on the right, which was used for non-essential everyday administration purposes) listed four people in his waiting room.

Two donors, one legitimate receiver, and the blackmailer. Barry clicked an icon on the computer and saw the image from the camera mounted in the waiting room. All four were men, but it was easy to tell which was the blackmailer. He was older than the other men, late forties, and he clenched his teeth and kept looking furtively around the room. The others were more relaxed, not fearing anything. After all, they knew they were in perfect hands.

He clicked on two names and watched the receptionist send the two patients into the operations room. He deliberately wanted to get the evil deed out of the way first, so he left the legitimate couple waiting.

After several minutes, Barry took a deep breath and went into the clinical room to join them. The support staff had gotten the donor and recipient stripped to the waist and the two men were lying on comfortable raised cots.

"Mr. Joseph Brown?"

The donor smiled and nodded. "That's me."

Barry turned to the other man. "You'd be John Smith?"

"I would."

The blackmailer stared up at Barry, with eyes that looked like beacons of evil. Barry could almost read his mind: *You only have one chance to save Jake, pal.*

He locked eyes with his enemy and nodded. A lump formed in his throat. His breathing felt heavy and he could feel his own heartbeat.

He told them both, "It's really a very straightforward procedure, as you know."

"Then get on with it," said Smith.

Ahh, there's that Brooklyn accent.

Barry wanted to hear him say one more time that he would let Jake go when they were finished, but he knew he couldn't say anything like that, not with Joseph Brown there to listen.

The procedure was very simple and Barry had performed it tens of thousands of times. He'd never had a mishap, and every single customer had left satisfied, either because they'd had a year added to their life or they had just turned into a millionaire.

The most trusted man in America.

First, he would inject the donor with a solution containing billions of atomic-sized nano-machines. They had only one purpose: to search out telomeres and attach themselves to the enzymes nearby, essentially forcing the telomere to contract in size by a tiny fraction.

Second, Barry would extract as many of the tiny machines as he could and inject them into the recipient. The machines worked slower with the recipient, taking several days to go through the entire body, lengthening the telomeres with the stolen enzymes.

Once that was done, the job was complete. It looked as if Barry was just extracting a magical life force from one person and giving it to the other.

"This won't hurt," he said.

And it didn't. Both men stayed resting for a few minutes after the transfer, but they were then able to leave. They didn't experience any side effects.

After they left, Barry completed the transfer on the other two patients, and then closed up for the night. As always, Frank Chambers drove him back to the Dakota.

❋❋❋❋

"Dad! Jake is home!"

"Oh, thank God! Is he hurt?"

"No, he's fine! Oh, I'm so relieved. He says he doesn't know who took him or why, but it doesn't matter. He's home now and I'm never going to let him out of my sight again."

"What a relief!"

"Dad?"

"Yes, Sarah?"

"You didn't have anything to do with this, did you?"

Barry stared at the phone, not wanting to lie to his daughter. But, then, he realized, he'd done much worse today.

"No, of course not. Why in the world would you ask that?"

Sarah didn't say anything for a moment. "Forget I said anything."

They talked a bit longer and then said their good-byes.

Barry wondered how "John Smith" was feeling tonight. He likely felt on top of the world, having had an extra five years of life surging through his body. Everyone felt that way at first, even though research had shown it was purely a placebo effect. There was nothing in the transfer itself that would cause euphoria, but they all felt it.

He popped the cork on a bottle of Merlot, feeling like celebrating. A smile crept across his face as he took the first sip and he toasted the empty room.

He opened the *Time* magazine one more time to see his beautiful wife.

"Here's to you, Kathy. You're still my inspiration."

He wished he could tell Joseph Brown the truth. The man had come to The Exchange expecting to lose a year of his life in exchange for a lot of cash.

Instead, he got the cash, and five years was added to his own life instead of any being subtracted.

John Smith, who was likely out celebrating his newfound youth, would never know his life expectancy had actually been decreased by the same five years.

After all, nobody knew when the grim reaper would come calling for them. It was the business of The Exchange to move time and life around, but in the end, nobody really knew when their time would be up.

Not even Barry Holder. He finished his glass of wine and yawned, knowing he'd be able to sleep soundly tonight. As he walked into his bedroom, he clicked the alarm on his clock radio off. For once, he planned on being late to work.

As he fell asleep, he decided he really was overdue to take a few days off and go visit Sarah and Jake.

Life's too short, he thought as his eyelids drooped.

❋❋❋

FUNERARY RITES

1. What Ruby Said

When the foreigners first came, they rented the old Dunwoody place with its rundown barn at the back.

"Coppery people," is how Ruby began her description of them. "The women wear these yellow and blue robes draped like this," she drew her hand over and across her shoulder, "and they set everything in straw baskets gently, like putting babies down to sleep. You should have seen the look I got from Jean-Marie when I helped them. My *goodness,* you'd have thought I was passing nuclear secrets to the Rosenbergs."

We walked home from her father's store where my wife took afternoon shift three days a week while our son spent time with his aunt. It was one of those warm, unhurried summer evenings from which we stole ten trouble-free minutes together, headaches calmed, hand-in-hand like kids.

"They say much?"

She shook her head. "Just pointed at things. Held out cash for me to pick and choose from. They've got a smell." Realizing how ugly this sounded, she added, "Not unpleasant at all. But unlike anything I've smelled before. Wonder what it is?"

Ruby, whose family went back two hundred years in our village, had never seen three women who looked so different from anyone else in her world.

My wife, a relative innocent, had grown up within the village terrarium. In some ways, it's why I loved her, particularly after the war, when everything else changed so much. Ruby had retreated in some respects and become more of a small town, old-fashioned girl than she'd been when we met.

This is not to say she was ignorant or backward—or even shy. She got her education—a good one—having studied history and art in a local college of pastoral setting, with an ambition of moving *to New York City or even Paris and working in a little gallery or maybe the Metropolitan Museum of Art,* she said within the first twenty minutes of our inaugural conversation, surrounded by a dome of chatter and music.

Who could not fall in love with her?

What a momentous night that was for me:

Imagine if that busload of college girls had not arrived from the state's outer reaches to crash the October tri-collegiate party at Oyster River where dancing went all night and lights were strung like the Milky Way from beam to beam in a barn-sized boathouse.

There, I—morose and undone by my first full month away from home—approached this most compelling girl who stood alone at the edge of everything. She, of soft dark hair and narrow brown eyes hidden beneath the kind of glasses you'd draw off just before you'd kiss her.

She was dressed in what looked like her grandmother's cocktail dress with the pelt of a long blue cardigan draped across one shoulder, a magnificent misfit, clutching a bottle of Coca-Cola in one hand as if ready to crack heads with it, a permanently unlit cigarette in the other, not giving a damn about dancing or drinking or whether she looked foolish or not.

"Look around, the world's coming apart at the seams but in here it's all fun and games—and I'd avoid the punch if I were you," Ruby said to me. "I had to be dragged here. What's your excuse?"

"I think I came here to meet you," I said.

Ruby probably would have left with me after college—and headed off for New York, Paris, or just plain old Boston—had not history both large and small cut short the path.

War intervened the following winter, during which I mainly saw the inside of safe, dusty corridors packed with bespectacled and exacting old men nearly as boring as the work. Flat-footed, four-eyed, color-blind, with a slight hand tremor from birth and an aptitude for numbers and memorization, I was deemed fit more for paperwork than for fighting; I cataloged the missing and the dead.

It became my unenviable job to connect names with numbers and home addresses so that—eventually—a doorbell would be rung and some family stateside given the bad news.

I ran across the names of college friends who had fallen, neighborhood sons who'd been lost in the Pacific, and those possibly dead in the rubble of Europe. I grew to hate the larger world and dream of the kind of village where nobody knew much about what went on out there.

During the first year or two of the war, Ruby and I wrote constantly to each other. The news came from the Pacific that her beloved brother died in combat. In fact, I saw his name on the lists and felt a jab in my heart when I thought of how Ruby would take the news.

Later, when her mother grew sick the letters trickled and then stopped entirely.

She had become moored to her home by that point. Her father needed her, she wrote in her last letter, her sisters couldn't keep the store running, it looked grim for her mother, and Ruby couldn't shake the thought of her older brother dying like that.

And then, the silence.

As soon as I could, I returned, terrified I'd lost my girl to someone else. After I'd located her and spent days in her company, I proposed marriage, imposed pregnancy, and then there was no getting her to up-and-go anywhere else.

For me to be with Ruby, I had to give up the outside world.

At the time, it was how I wanted it. Her hometown

remained locked in a dream of what a New England village had always been. The milk was fresh, the air clean, the trees thick with leaf, the streams ice-cold in summer, the neighbors a bit dull, distant yet companionable, friendly in an untrusting way.

After several months, the long lists of the dead vanished from my dreams. I loved my wife and child, I disagreed affably with my father-in-law; we worked, we loved, we played, we ignored; we kept shutters closed in winter and opened our doors wide when spring finally came.

We nestled into village life.

There we were, fairly typical among the locals, more than a decade after our wedding, me at the bank counting other peoples' money and her at the afternoon shift, not ten minutes' walk from where she'd been born, our only child—named for her dead brother—eleven years old the summer that the Smiths arrived.

On that particular walk home, within the first few days of our foreign invasion, I grew inordinately happy.

My wife glimpsed a new horizon in the foreigners and hadn't shrunk from it. In fact, she'd become curious about the newcomers, because "sometimes I feel like a stranger here, too. I don't really think like my father, do I?"

"No," I said. "Not your sisters, either. Or anyone we know. Thank god."

"I think maybe we should travel more," Ruby said on that particular evening, "now that Caleb's older. Aren't you a little bored with things the way they are? I know I am. We could use a breath of fresh air, maybe a change of scenery."

The time had come. We'd hidden too long. Perhaps we'd buy a Chevrolet and drive out west; or do a southern trip; maybe go see Manhattan and tour around a little.

I welcomed the arrival of outside influence in our lives in the form of the Smiths.

At least, I did for a while.

2. About the Smiths

The general scuttlebutt went that they were a pack of gypsies, then Hindu, Amazonian tribesmen, possibly deposed Mongolian royalty, exiles from Borneo or the Sudan or Burma, terrible Barbary Coast people, islanders of some ruined South Sea paradise—and finally something else entirely that most of us had never heard of.

You might assume we were not the friendliest of villages, but many in town were worried based on the news reports. Immigrants packed Boston, Portsmouth bulged with foreigners, and Manhattan to the far south became a different country entirely.

We never thought outsiders would make it so far inland.

First there were maybe six of them.

Within a week or three, we could count at least fourteen on Main Street on a morning so bright you had to shield your eyes from the sun to make out their crowd hanging around the butcher shop.

Tom Raleigh, who worked the register, told us the foreigners always asked for cuts of meat that nobody ever ate.

"You mean like marrow bones?" Ruby asked.

"Heads," I guessed. "Or hooves."

"No," he said. "I'm not even sure these parts got names. We usually throw that stuff out."

I looked at my wife and she at me, with a crooked, slight smile breaking the calm of her face.

In the pause, Tom added, "It's a little disturbing."

"Well, it's not exactly the end of the world," I said. "I mean, these people seem okay, don't they?"

"Sure," Tom said as he weighed and wrapped up the pork loin we'd have for supper. "I got nothing against them. Nothing at all. I just don't think it's normal. But what do I know? I mean, to each his own."

"I'm going to be up all night wondering what those cuts are," Ruby said on the way out as I held the door open. "It's not like they're cannibals or anything."

"He made it up," I said when we got to our car.

"Now, why would Tom do that?"

I opened the car door for her; she slid in. Once I'd gotten in on the other side, I said, "He's like everyone else. He's got to put his two cents in, have a story about them, spread a little dirt. This town's too damn small."

After that, other strange and unsavory Smith stories began cropping up. Lois Abbott, who ran the library, said Smiths had been stealing books. Paul Lockwood said he caught some of their men peeping through windows at night when most people were asleep. May Peters, at the coffee shop, swore on her father's grave that they went through the trash early in the morning "like a gang of raccoons." Even Helen Cooper—usually less gossipy than most—told my wife she didn't like the way the Smith men eyed teenage girls in town—"like they're sizing up which ones to kidnap as brides."

The Smiths, it was said, held strange celebrations out in the autumn woods accompanied by ghostly chanting and drumbeats "like in *Tarzan*." Two Smith women were seen bare-breasted down at the stream, washing sheets against the rocks.

And then some idiot spread the rumor that some Smiths had been caught out at the cemetery "doing voodoo."

You could attach any cockamamie story you wanted to the name Smith, and nine times out of ten, it would stick.

We called our foreigners the Smiths because nobody could pronounce their names. "Smith" became a joke that we'd never in a million years mention to their faces. Little Smith, Smith Junior, Uncle Smith, Big Smith, Old Smith, Pretty Smith, Ancient Smith—that kind of thing.

Most of their clan grabbed the lowest-rung mill jobs. They never complained these were beneath them or that they were made for better things. They took them happily, and by all accounts, turned the mills around.

We'd see Smiths wandering around on weekends or sometimes early Monday morning. They'd arrive to town in packs of four and five to pick up sundries and fabric or when a big brown trunk arrived from the old country to our post office.

The Smiths didn't drive cars. They used ox-drawn wagons and bicycles. The older ones walked into town clutching hand-carved staffs like Biblical shepherds. The elder Smith ladies carried groceries on wooden crossbars at their shoulders or in baskets balanced perfectly on their heads. They'd slowly trudge back—barefoot in summer—to their rented rundown farm, a two-mile walk on a blistery afternoon.

You couldn't even offer them rides—I tried once or twice but just got nods and dismissals from the Smith crowd, along with that chattering sound they made when trying to be polite.

At first, we were all proper with the Smiths and respected their customs. You could say—despite the gossip about them—that there existed peace in the land.

But then there was that incident at the cider mill.

3. The Battle of Dunwoody Farm

The rowdier boys in the village claimed a Smith started it.

The boys who raised the flag and ran up the hill mainly came from the Crocker family, six tawny-haired scoundrels between the ages of 12 and 17, all of them destined for prisons in some distant future, all of them getting away with their crimes (stealing a few sawbucks from a till, spying on a local Venus in her bath, egg-fights along Main Street, a window shot through, the murdered parakeet incident, the famous joyride in a jalopy ending in a crash and tumble, whisperings of girls-in-trouble leaving town under mysterious circumstances).

There were others, too, the sheep-boys who followed the bad ones. These little disciples were as guilty; and yes, I counted my own son in that. Caleb had turned twelve at the time with just enough rambunctiousness in his blood to do the wrong thing.

The boys of the village first threw hard, green apples like grenades; then the warm pies sitting out along cooling shelves; finally rocks and marbles and anything that could gain velocity between fist and back-of-head.

The Smith boys—most of them under the age of fifteen—fought back, of course, but with less dumb luck.

A skirmish ensued, war declared. What began at the cider mill ended with a chase out to the Dunwoody farm. Cows fled their pen, chickens flew, windows smashed, a threshold trespassed.

A flaming arrow made it into a barn window and someone—I suspected Paul Lockwood's kid—dumped manure in the well.

After the whuppings—and there were several—we all made our sons apologize.

It was quite a spectacle: twenty boys of varying shape and size, prodded forward by their fathers in a kind of Death March through town, out along the little bridge over the stream that went to the Dunwoody place.

Their heads hung low, they scratched at imagined itches, some hands clasped in droopy prayer or slow hand-wringings, some (mainly those Crocker boys) cast sidelong glances to the fields beyond the stone walls as if plotting escape routes.

My boy Caleb bowed his head and said he was sorry to every single Smith, though he only marginally participated in the fracas and received not a single belt to his behind. Still, I gave him a good talking to and there'd be no privileges for a good long while.

He had, I told him, better damn straighten up before he ended up like a Crocker.

The kids cleaned up their mess. An offering of cash for repairs. A calf given as a gift. A fence mended. We—of the Selectmen—got out and repaired the barn.

The Smiths themselves quickly offered the olive branch, spoke slowly and formally in a language none of us understood but I guessed was their way of telling us to put it in the past and leave them alone and please—in their eyes a sliver of fear—*don't ever bother us again.*

A cloud came over our town that day and remained.

We felt ashamed of our sons' behaviors. We didn't like the idea that we'd become the bad neighbors. We preferred to think of foreigners as a kind of benign tumor to be watched for signs of malignancy.

We were not arrogant people. We liked to live in peace. We didn't nurture disagreements, though they existed. We didn't want to get involved in conflicts with any foreigners. We'd heard that some towns created battle lines with their own versions of the Smiths and sometimes this ended in terrible consequence for everybody.

Turns out, in their exuberant and uncalled-for attack, our boys managed to desecrate some sacred cow or other.

Young Smith—one of the eldest of their boys—explained the whole thing to me in halting English without actually naming our sacrilege.

A blasphemy had occurred. Our boys had no idea what they'd really done. Young Smith told us that their women stopped eating because of it. Two middle-aged

Smiths had to leave at once—at great expense—for the journey to the motherland to offer propitiation. Offerings were being burnt even as we were informed of this.

We had crossed into the territory of taboo and Young Smith warned us that the older men of his tribe wept with this injustice, a strong-hearted young man lost his left hand in a mill accident and a young wife miscarried twins with misshapen limbs, among other signs of tribal apocalypse.

"This house is no longer holy," Young Smith told us. "It is a place of darkness to us now. We must avoid a war."

A war?

Foreigners! Invaders! War!

All the things we didn't want in our little off-the-beaten-track borough.

Later, at our town meeting, we scratched our heads and came up with possibilities of which line had been crossed. Was it the hay that burned in the barn? The well? The escaped cow? Someone even suggested it might be that apples were sacred to whatever hundred gods and goddesses the heathens worshipped.

Or the pies?

We never figured it out, but nobody wanted to start a war—"their word not ours"—with the Smiths because "nobody knows where that'll end."

The lowest of our minds—and we had more than our share—imagined machetes, spears, little knives, or shrunken heads all in a row.

The Smiths moved a little further out of town.

For their new tribal home, the Smiths grabbed the big house at the edge of the marsh.

Malvern House—enormous and colonial and crumbly—was somewhat hidden from an untrammeled dirt road behind high stone walls and jagged trees. The marsh stench was impossible to avoid. Who else would choose to live there but outsiders?

My friend, Cormac Danielson, their landlord and a man who owned several dilapidated properties in the deep woods, took some heat over this rental, a few nasty looks by the harsher folk in the village, but most of us didn't care. Few ever traveled that road, no one hunted at the marshes anymore, it was a dead end off an out-of-the-way half-past a nowhere. The place came surprisingly cheap and held a good twelve bedrooms—perfect for the Smiths—and not a single indoor toilet.

By then, there were at least twenty of them living at Malvern, all loosely related, most coming down the matriarchal side from the old lady we called Ancient Smith.

Twenty became forty. More Smiths arrived over a two-year period.

One winter, they bought Malvern House for what was reportedly a tidy sum. Well of course, some people

said, they could buy it and the damn marsh and even the fields around it when they lived forty to a house and they all took the mill jobs away from more deserving people. They'd been moving up in their jobs, and rumor went that one of them was about to make an offer on the paper mill.

"They're going to own us all soon enough, just watch," Paul Lockwood said, though we all laughed at the time.

Local boys—expressly warned to never bother the Smiths again—reported strange goings-on out there. Wild animal cries. Smells of strange spice and odd bonfires along the marsh. Music played on weird drums, screechy fiddles that sounded like mating cats and odd-shaped clarinets that produced even odder whines. Lights in the sky. Bizarre sounds of strangulation that might pass for singing.

Paul Lockwood began calling Malvern House the city of foreign relations by the time my boy turned fifteen. People eventually forgot that it was ever called Malvern House and instead, it became known as Smithville.

By then, they owned the paper mill and had bought one hundred fifty acres of woodland along the river, including the old Shalcross farm. A much larger Smith settlement arose, and the boundaries of Smithville continued nudging out along the county line.

We pretty much stayed away from them, and they—in turn—kept their distance.

Until something happened to change it all.

4. The Coffee Shop Debate

One summer morning, the oldest Smith boy came riding his bicycle to town.

He was tall and scrawny and wore only a cloth at his waist. He dropped the bike in the street and went running up to Dr. Knowles' office, across from the bank where I worked. The kid shouted so much that we all went to the windows to watch as the doctor stepped out and exchanged a few words with the boy. Then, Dr. Knowles went back inside.

The boy paced, striking the air with his fists. He glanced over at those of us watching. The look on his face was devastating—tears streamed down his face, his mouth open and sagging, his eyes pleading.

"Something bad's happened with those people," one of the bank tellers said.

Dr. Knowles came out to the street, spoke with the boy, put his hand on the boy's shoulder. They left together in the doctor's sleek Chrysler.

It was the first time—to any of our knowledge—that a Smith sat in a car seat.

This became a topic of interest down at the coffee shop where several of us watched the Chrysler return and park across the street, just after the workday had ended.

Dr. Knowles, noticing our stares as he got out of his car, came striding over.

Once inside the coffee shop, he called an informal meeting of the Selectmen.

This was easily accomplished because we were all sitting around with half-drunk cups of coffee in our hands.

"The old lady's so sick, I wanted to put her out of her misery," Dr. Knowles told our group when we'd pushed tables together and gathered with our lemonades and coffees and pastries. "They don't believe in hospitals. And it doesn't matter—she won't make it to one. I got her as comfortable as anyone can be in that condition."

He stirred his coffee and looked down into it as if it were a crystal ball. "She'll be dead by tomorrow."

"Terrible," I said.

Ruby sat opposite me, next to Helen Cooper, whose husband Josh—my closest friend in town—was to my left. Paul Lockwood sat to my right, while Dr. Knowles had squeezed in between Willie Crocker and Dave Neary at table's end.

"Awful," Ruby said. "I feel as if I just saw her at the store last Wednesday. She's old but I didn't think…"

"As weepy as this is," Paul Lockwood said. "What's it got to do with any of us?"

"They need to perform funerary rites," Dr. Knowles said.

"Sounds heathen," Paul grumbled.

"Well, everybody has customs," the doctor said. "And they have a particular way they bury their dead in that country."

"But they're not in that country."

Dr. Knowles laid out the basics:

"The boy told me his family fasts for three days. There's some holy man of theirs in Manhattan who will come up. Preparations may take a full week. The body stays above ground. They say prayers night and day. The women cover themselves in ash and the men will wear nothing but a plain cloth around their waists. No one washes until after a customary period. The children won't speak during sunlit hours. There are a few less-savory aspects to the customs, but there's no need to talk about it here. By week's end, they'll have a feast—and even games."

"I assume this won't be like the Olympics," Willie Crocker joked.

"Sounds heathen," Paul Lockwood groaned. "I mean, I'm not saying it's wrong. I hate to judge people, but it sounds so damn heathen."

We all looked across the table at him.

"Never seen you in church," I said.

"Church is for hypocrites and sinners," Paul said.

Dr. Knowles continued. "The son took off

immediately. There's a larger community of his mother's relatives over in Boston. They have a whole process to this. It's very regulated, I suppose. Now, I may not agree with it but I know these people. I know how hurt—and angry—they'll be if we can't accommodate this one night."

I shrugged. "Let them do whatever they want out there."

The doctor offered an inscrutable look. "It's more involved than that."

A few among us muttered things, but I kept my eyes on Dr. Knowles' face.

"Drop the other shoe," I said.

He rubbed his eyes. The man was exhausted.

"They need to parade her through our streets," he said.

Paul Lockwood jumped in. "That's necessary? A *parade*?"

"This was their matriarch," the doctor said. "She's sort of—well, I suppose you'd call her a queen of their tribe. She gets a royal procession."

"Like Fourth of July?" Dave Neary said.

"Maybe we should roll out a red carpet," Paul Lockwood said. "Bow down. Pray to their gods."

"Damn Smiths," Willie Crocker said. "They should just take the boat back to where they come from."

Dr. Knowles sighed. "This is no different than our funerals. You go along the streets, the hearse, all that. If this were our President, or even the Governor…" He looked around at the rest of us. Then at me, as if I might help convince the others.

"Sure," I said to our group. "It's a little unusual. But it's not like we didn't go all out when Vernon Browne kicked off a few years back."

"Not the same thing," Willie Crocker said. "He was an American war hero."

"I don't see why we need to let them bring their customs here," Helen said, avoiding all our looks.

"We were here first," Willie Crocker said. "When those Smiths have lived here for two hundred years, then they can have some say in this."

"I have nothing against them. Honestly," Helen said. "But they don't live in the village."

"They buy from us," Ruby said. "They bank here. I mean, I'd hate to lose their business, Helen. Wouldn't you? The store's grown because of them. They could just as easily go to Remington or Hazelford if they had to, and I'd hate to think of the money we'd lose, if nothing else."

"I'm telling you, it's heathen," Paul Lockwood said for the umpteenth time, and on went the arguments.

"Here's the part that'll be a tough sell for our neighbors, I'm sure," Dr. Knowles said, interrupting our debate. "They have rules to this procession. No one can look at them. We have to draw curtains, close shutters. Not a single person in town—man, woman, child or dog—can be on the street. It's that sacred."

We all took this in.

"How long's this shindig going to last?" I asked.

"It'll start right at sundown and run until dawn I think. He told me it's involved. It'll be noisy, too."

"Primitives," Paul Lockwood said. "Wailing, caterwauling, no doubt chanting."

"It's a cult," Josh Cooper said. "I don't mind them, but I don't really like the idea of this." He leaned in to me. "I mean, do you? Why do they even need to come through our village? Can't they stay out on their own land?"

The table went silent.

May Peters brought the coffee pot over and refilled our cups. She apologized for eavesdropping, but added, "Whenever I hear about the Smiths, I just can't help it."

"May?" I asked.

"I've never liked them," she said.

"You ain't alone, sister," Willie said.

"They're not so bad," Ruby said. "If you give them a chance."

Truth was, they weren't bad at all; and yet, in my deepest self, I had to admit that I'd never been quite comfortable around the Smiths. They'd kept themselves so separate over the years that it was as if our own culture had been rejected by them as not worthy. I wasn't smart enough to explore why this bothered me, but it *did* bother me. This seemed at the root of all our unease.

They had never quite accepted *us*.

As if we hadn't heard her the first time, May repeated, "I've just never liked them and I'm not afraid to say it out loud."

Dr. Knowles looked up at her. "It's not a matter of 'like'. They're part of our town. They've hurt no one. They deserve our respect—and compassion—in this situation."

"They smell different," May said. "They cook strange stuff, too."

"My wife cooks strange stuff," I said, and Ruby reached over to swat the air in front of my face in mock anger.

"Close our curtains? That's ridiculous. I won't do it," May said as she receded into the coffee shop while her voice grew louder. "What are we supposed to do? Not go outside, not even look at the stars? Skip any kind of night out we might have planned? Who does that? Is everything supposed to shut down at nine o'clock for them? For those people?"

After May mumbled away, Dr. Knowles lowered his voice. "A lot of people are going to feel like that. Look, we must convince everyone to do this. The Smiths believe that if even one outsider sees the funeral parade, terrible things will happen. World-changing things, he said. For all of us."

"Like what?" Willie asked, a kind of backwoods challenge in his voice.

Dr. Knowles shrugged. "We really want to find out?"

"Maybe they'll set us on fire," Paul muttered. "They like their fires, those heathens."

"This *is* their Queen. And frankly," Dr. Knowles tilted his head slightly as if convincing himself, "they outnumber us."

There, someone had finally said it. More than three hundred Smiths occupied farmland and woodland, and our little village didn't quite hit that number. If you needed any kind of factory job, you probably worked *with* or *for* at least one of the Smith clan. If you worked over in Hazelford, where the great jobs tended to be, you had to drive twenty miles across Smith land to get there.

Dr. Knowles had said the one thing that none of the rest of us wanted to examine:

We didn't really run things in quite the same way as we once had. Oh, we ran the village, no doubt, and we were like the villages in all directions, but population-wise, the Smiths had us beat.

At the table, we chewed the subject a bit more, but agreed with Dr. Knowles in the final minutes before heading home.

We'd call an emergency town meeting to make this happen.

Then, after a night of shouting matches in the old meeting hall that went late into the night, we exhausted opponents of this proposal into offering just this one summer night to the Smith family and to no one else.

It was in the town's best interest.

One night we heard the sound of a strange horn— deep and sonorous—and knew that the funeral had begun.

5. The Funeral Parade

Sunset brushed the trees with a rusty haze. Within an hour or two, we all should've been heading to bed anyway but…well, who could sleep once they thought of the entire Smith clan and some strange priest of their cult walking down Main Street?

We anticipated some unavoidable indecency in the request to close our eyes to their dark celebration. It gave a little thrill to the quiet summer night.

Before drawing the final curtain in the front hall, I glanced out into the shadowed street and saw that all the neighboring homes were shuttered.

The village—from what I could see—shut down tight as a clam.

I closed the curtain.

The inside of our home became toasty to the point where we'd all stripped down to shorts and undershirts and my wife wore only a slip once we'd sent Caleb up to his room.

Josh Cooper kept calling me: had they come 'round yet? Did anyone see them?

And I kept telling him to forget it and just go to bed.

I sat in the living room watching Ruby pace back and forth as if expecting a guest at the door. Now and then, she'd look over and say, "I don't know why I'm so keyed up," or "You'd think I'd just read a book and go to bed, but I'm almost afraid."

"It's the heat," I said. "Look, if you'd just sit. Drink some lemonade. You'll cool down."

"It's not the heat," she said, "although my god, these fans do nothing without the windows open."

I pointed out the three windows that were in fact open, particularly the ones facing the garden. "And we have six fans going. It's not that bad."

"And the noise. Someone should invent a quiet fan. It's like living inside a beehive," she said. "I'm hoping they come through fast. I can maybe take an hour of this. Maybe not even an hour."

"Take a cool shower," I said.

"It is *not* the heat," Ruby said. "And I don't need a shower."

Caleb, expressly forbidden to look out his shuttered window, had gone to bed—reluctantly—early, with a book he'd been supposed to read all summer, although my wife and I heard his radio on upstairs playing rock 'n' roll over the hum of fans.

"Any other night, I'd yell for him to turn it down," I said.

Ruby ignored my comment.

"You think anyone will look?" Ruby asked. "I mean, how will they not? You're told not to do something, you do it. It's human nature."

"God, I hope not."

"It's not as if the Smiths'll notice," she said. "Jeanne-Marie told me she was going to peek. But only a little. There's that dormer window with a little bit of the shutter missing and she said she and Bill would sit up just for a looky-loo."

"They shouldn't risk it," I said. Then I swore. "Everybody promised they wouldn't look. I hope Jeanne-Marie was just pulling your leg."

"Well it's not as if the Smiths'll see them. And that's all we need to do. Make sure they don't see us looking."

"Is it so hard to just not look outside for one night? How often do we come home, have supper and then not even glance out the open window?"

"This is different."

"How so?"

"It's like being in prison," she said. "Or a coffin."

Ruby stopped pacing. She went and sat on the rug by the coffee table. She picked up a copy of *Reader's Digest* and read off all the article titles in a droning voice and then put it down again. She drew her knees to her chin, reminding me of a girl I once knew. Her long tan legs, the silky slip, the way her shoulders shrugged and her hair swept across half her face. She had never looked more appealing to me. Where was that girl with the Coke bottle in one hand, the cigarette in the other, the glasses and old-fashioned dress that I'd first met? Replaced now by this siren, a dream of slip and girl and desperation.

"Come here, you," she said.

"Honey?"

"Come here." She held her arms out. I went over and crouched down in front of her.

She drew me into the cradle of her body. We were sweaty and there was something filthy about her wanting me like that. I felt as if I were taking advantage of her.

I pulled back, and we sat there staring at each other.

"I know, I know," she moaned. "I just wanted to get away from all this. Can't we get away?"

I felt confused by this state she was in.

"It's okay," I said. "We can go upstairs if you want."

"No," she said. "It's like I want a pill or a drink."

"What a compliment."

"You know what I mean. I just want to block it out."

I returned to the chair and she stood up and began pacing again.

"I didn't think I'd feel like this," she said. "All jittery. It's like the world's going to end or something."

"I promise you the world won't end."

"I mean, they could've picked Hazelford. They've got that farm by the river. Why us? It's strange. It's just too strange."

She stomped her feet, just a little, a spoiled girl instead of a woman in her thirties.

"What's gotten into you?"

"I don't know," she said. "I don't know. But all I think is, you go along in life the way you're supposed to, you do all the right things, all the things that make a good life. You marry, start a family, raise your kid, work a job, go to church, honor your father, be nice to everybody, and then one night you're in a closed-up house with every door locked up and you can't even look outside because you're somehow not good enough. It's how I feel right now, and I know it sounds crazy, but when I think of my brother Caleb dying on some foreign island and my mother dying in her bed and thinking I'd lost you until you came back and then how things changed so quickly here and how I've been afraid to…"

I had to catch my breath as she went on and on. I'd never heard my wife talk like this. She dug up tales from her childhood, from our own past, some argument we had, the miscarriage after Caleb, the fact that I hadn't fought in the war but pushed papers while her brother had given the ultimate sacrifice, the idea of wifedom and what it meant, and sisterdom and daughterdom and motherhood and how fathers expected so much and how she'd given up chances because of the stupid war and all these women in town who made comments about your house and wallpaper and how much your husband made and how you dressed and all the stupid things she'd had to do because it was like following a rule book.

Her nose ran and spit flew in the middle of this rough waterfall of words and she stood over me flailing her arms around. I felt somehow responsible. She didn't shout, she just let this stream flow from her. She grew all teary-eyed. Sweat burst along her forehead. She went off on me and the world and everything she'd never mentioned before in her life.

I honestly wondered if she might be having a nervous breakdown.

Only then did I notice that our son's radio had gone silent upstairs.

My wife and I stared at each other in the buzz of many fans. I patted my lap. Calming, perhaps exhausted, she sat down and we cuddled, but I could tell that this wasn't enough. We were sweaty, uncomfortable, dissatisfied.

Just get through this one night, I thought. *She feels boxed in. It's the heat. It's the idea that we're not as free as we thought we were. That's all. She'll be fine in the morning.*

"You do everything right," she whispered as if in a confessional. "But it doesn't matter. You give up dreams. You do things so other people will think you're fine. You don't take risks because if you risk things, you lose. People you love might die. The world might fall apart. But nothing you do adds up. None of it makes sense."

I thought about how maybe we should've taken those trips we'd planned—to the Grand Canyon or to St. Augustine or even just to Manhattan to see the museums.

We'd let life get in the way.

The phone rang. She got out of my lap.

"Where you headed?"

Ruby glanced back at me and for a second I thought she wouldn't answer.

"Honey?" I said.

"I think I'll take that shower."

I reached for the phone.

"That you?" It was Josh.

"Who else?"

"Hear the music yet?"

"No."

"It'll get louder when it gets to your side. Believe me."

A pause on the line.

"You better not be looking," I said.

"I just snuck a peek out the attic window. Over the rooftops to where the road veers into town. And you wouldn't believe it."

"I don't want to hear about it. Just shut the curtains, go to bed, or go work in your basement or something."

"Hell with that. You should see it. Torches lighting everything up like it's the middle of the day practically. And Elephants! Camels! A wagon—no, more like a golden chariot, drawn by tigers! It's like the circus—or Cleopatra—coming to town. There must be a hundred or more of them—not all of them Smiths, either—waving incense around, twirling sabers and dancing. The men in robes, the women wrapped up like mummies but some of them—hold on to your hat—don't got nothin' on from the waist up."

"Quit looking," I said.

"All of 'em moving this way and that, a big guy blowing this bull's horn and a bunch of women playing some kind of flute. Bunch of little boys running around smashing cymbals together. Two guys wearing big antlers, some of them painted all in gold and silver. And then there's Mr. and Mr. Smith…"

"Wait, you're *still* watching?"

"Pretty much."

"Stop it."

"Look, you've got to see this—they have crowns on. Golden crowns with glittering jewels. Like it's the sultan and his queen or something. And that oldest boy of theirs? He's got this big pole and at its top it looks like a golden snake all wrapped around it. He has flowers all over him, head to toe, and maybe a dozen half-nekkid pretty girls following after him like he's the catch of the day."

"Shut it," I said.

"You've just got to look out a window. Wait, they're going around, over near your place," he said. "I'm telling you, you have never in all your days seen something like this and I'm guessing you never will again. You miss this, you miss everything."

I hung up the phone.

I argued with my better nature: we promised, this is their ritual, this is their custom, honor them, they're good neighbors, Josh exaggerated anyway, how could camels and elephants and tigers be all together here? They weren't even from a country of camels and elephants and tigers after all, why would they have them? Had they raided a zoo? Rented from Ringling Brothers?

But it drove me a bit crazy.

I went over to the living room window. I might just move the curtain slightly. Just a quarter inch. Just enough to see out.

I began to hear the music. The cymbals, the flutes, the beat of the drums, the strange string instruments that whined and screeched. If I stepped away from the curtains, our fans drowned the sounds out. But right up next to the window…

The Smith noise grew louder in my head.

My fingers brushed the curtain's edge.

Don't do it, I thought. *What if they see you?*

Josh Cooper already had risked a possible skirmish

by spying from his attic. How many more in town would break their promise?

"You're lying. Or joking," I said when I called Josh back.

"No," he said. "You need to look out there. They'll never see you. They're too involved in their…well, their spectacle. I saw three little girls riding some kind of large wild pig. I've never seen anything like it. And all these banners. And colored paper. And blankets with spirals and things all over them. And lights, these amazing lights."

"What about the coffin?"

"Coffin? What? Oh, no, it's not like that. They must not believe in that. Ancient Smith. The Queen. You should see. It's as if she's still alive. They have her raised up in this silver chair of some kind and she's dressed like she's going to a wedding, all bright scarves and bracelets. It really is something to see, you should just look, just for a second."

I went silent. I'd heard a noise from upstairs.

"Got to go." I hung up. I bounded up the stairs, thinking I'd check on Ruby in the shower. Halfway up, I saw Caleb crouched in the hall by the narrow window, his head beneath the shade.

"What do you think you're doing?"

He bumped his head on the glass. The paper shade slapped him as he ducked back from under it.

When Caleb turned around he couldn't look me in the eye.

"Sorry, Dad."

"Go to your room."

"But Dad, you got to see it. There's this—"

"Stop right there young man." I pointed at him as if throwing a lightning bolt. "You know the rules tonight."

"They'll never see me," he said. "And there's this bird—I think it's a bird—it's huge and clomping around. And one of the Smith kids is riding it just like a horse."

"Really?" I asked, losing my fatherly power for a moment.

"Just look for a second," my boy said.

"We promised we wouldn't."

"They'll never know."

"It's *honor*, Caleb," I said and then shooed him to his room at the back of the house.

I wanted to peer under the shade, but resisted.

Instead, I went to check on Ruby. I knocked on the bathroom door and heard her say, "Just a minute." I waited on the landing. I kept glancing over at the shade, wondering if my sense of duty was getting in the way of seeing something truly remarkable.

After a while, the water still running—Ruby loved her long showers—I went to our bedroom. I lay down in the dark and listened to the strange music outside.

I closed my eyes.

At some point in the night, I heard our front door slam shut and I got up and went downstairs, thinking someone might be breaking in.

The door wasn't completely closed.

Someone had gone outside.

Who?

I peered out the front window, nearly trembling, thinking that I was doing something awful.

The parade was still going but the drums had stopped their incessant beating. I saw flashes of it: large bears walking on hind legs, a woman riding a chariot drawn by tigers, several children carrying sparklers, wide hoops being tossed in the air and caught again as they landed effortlessly in young men's hands, the colorful robes, the elephants, the dancing women, the children playing cymbals and flutes, a long chain of dancers as the Smiths performed their rites all night through our village.

Among them, I caught a glimpse of my son.

Caleb was shirtless and had painted his chest in bright colors as he danced around with various young Smiths. Helen Cooper—with silk of various shades drawn over her—rode atop the elephant with others from our village, and there was Young Smith and Child Smith and Girl Smith and Middle-Age Smith, and then wonder of wonders, Paul Lockwood, too, part of this strange procession. Running after them, grabbing the hand of one of the Smith uncles, May Peters leapt up to a platform carried by several Smiths and began dancing. I worried about the idea of feuds and bad blood and thought of terrible futures for us, for the Smiths, for our village and its relative placid surface.

I felt a sudden urge to join in the festivities, but I remained worried: what would become of us? Would the Smiths forgive those who did?

Or would we pay a heavy price for breaking this rule?

World-changing things, Dr. Knowles had said.

I couldn't run out there. I couldn't just go grab Caleb. I'd cause more of a problem, create a greater sacrilege.

Better just to leave it. Pretend you saw nothing.

These are the things I considered in my three a.m. weariness.

I wasn't even sure if I might actually still be in bed dreaming; I had that half-awake, half-somewhere-else feeling the whole time.

When I went back to bed, I noticed that Ruby was not there, on the other side. There wasn't even an indent in the pillow where her head would have rested.

Probably sleeping downstairs in the den, I thought. Sometimes she did. Sometimes I snored. Sometimes, she told me, she couldn't stand my heat when we lay there together in the middle of the night.

I woke up later than usual.

I checked Caleb's room. My unease turned to panic when I went downstairs and could not find my wife.

Still-damp footprints went from the bathroom to the

front door, which was open wide to the street.

When I stepped out onto the front porch, I noticed several of the other houses across from us with their doors open wide, too.

By the end of the day, those left in town could only guess what happened.

"Dr. Knowles said we'd been warned," Josh said, when I stopped by his hardware store. "And they shouldn't have looked."

"I doubt that's all that happened," I said. "I mean, we both looked. We didn't join in."

"I didn't even think Helen so much as peeked," he said. "She was going a little crazy last night. It was so hot. She got angry that any of us agreed to their terms. But I didn't think…"

"Yeah, Ruby was sort of like that, too," I said.

I imagined Ruby, watching from the bathroom window.

The long cold shower, walking out, dancing, being lifted up onto one of their chariots.

"Why *them* and not us?" Josh said on another day when we'd gotten used to what happened the night of the parade. "Why'd Helen run out there like a kid heading for the ice cream truck? I mean, I saw it happen and I knew—I just *knew*—that if I stepped outside the door, I'd end up with the Smiths, too."

"Maybe they were missing something over here," I said, looking down into my hands. "Who knows?"

And another afternoon, workday done, in the coffee shop:

"Don't worry. They'll come back," Josh said, patting me on the shoulder. "I mean, living in Smithville? It's not what they're used to. The weather'll turn. It won't seem so exciting. They'll miss comforts. They'll wake up and wonder, *what the hell was I thinking?* I mean, I can't even imagine Helen without modern plumbing. I doubt she'll make it to October. And then they'll return home, tails between legs, the village'll get back to its business and we'll forgive and forget. We'll all look back on this summer as one of those odd things, like when the Crash happened, or when Pearl Harbor got hit, like we think it'll never be normal again, but you know, after a while, it just goes back to being what it always was."

"Sure," I said. "They'll come back."

6. Ruby Sightings

A new fear of the Smiths overtook our village. What else might they take? What further revenge would they exact? How much did we really know about them and what they were capable of?

We had weapons—some of us said—we can go free our children and husbands and wives at gunpoint; but no one picked up a gun because on some deep level we feared that the Smiths held a power greater than even bullets.

Or worse, that our loved ones wouldn't want to return to the lives they'd had. They might prefer instead the many hearths of Smithville.

Now and then, those of us who remained behind would drive out to their settlements to catch a glimpse of someone we'd lost.

I saw my boy Caleb—by then, seventeen—standing at a window at the old Malvern place. His face was painted in streaks of whitewash and blue. He wore a mottled blue and green robe wrapped over his shoulder like a toga. He held a little baby in his arms.

When I waved, he didn't seem to recognize me.

Caleb had their look—that Smith gaze, a strangely placid expression, a kind of flat affect as if he were living in a different world beneath his skin.

I tried to trap my son once or twice. He became docile when I locked him up. He wouldn't eat. He'd start chanting in that foreign language—a doleful bleating.

I had to let him go. What was the use? I didn't want to take the risk that he'd starve to death in his father's house or that I'd end up causing something worse to happen.

I watched as he rode his old bicycle back to Smithville.

I began to stay indoors, mostly. I shuttered the windows every night, stopped listening to the news, went to bed early, woke up late, did my job, said the expected things, and hoped for the best.

Others ran into Ruby now and then.

I'd ask them not to speak of her so much, not to me, not anymore. "She's not who she was," I'd say or else, "She's made her choice," or "I guess I never really knew her at all. How well do we really know anyone?"

If only, I'd think. If she'd just stayed inside, just kept the curtain closed, just done what was asked.

Friends told me about how good Ruby looked, but also how strange, how different, how similar, as if Ruby had been copied by the Smiths and the real Ruby no longer existed, not the Ruby they'd known their whole life, anyway.

How she didn't seem to recognize them at all when they tried talking to her. How she refused their offers of lifts or escorts or their whispered pleas to come back to town.

How Ruby would move past them, after a Saturday morning's errand, her hair long again, sometimes braided, her skin a deep rich summer tan, a crossbar yolk on her shoulders, carrying baskets of groceries or piles of colored fabric.

She walked barefoot—they said—and not too far behind a few of the other Smith ladies.

༖ ༖ ༖

GENRE CROSSOVER:
THE ALAN WAKE GAME SERIES

By Richard Dansky

Photo courtesy of Mikko Rautalahti

As HBO's *True Detective* aptly demonstrated, the line between detective fiction and supernatural horror can often blur into nonexistence. Folks on the literary side were well aware of this; one can point to Poe's "Murders in the Rue Morgue" as patient zero for this sort of crossover, predating even genre definitions.

But what about in video games, where genre is almost exclusively defined by play style, as opposed to content? Can there be a successful marriage of horror and noir in an interactive medium? Fans will point to David Cage's *Indigo Prophecy* and *Heavy Rain* as examples. But beyond them, the cupboard is relatively bare, and the gaming industry's highest profile dive into dark crime narrative, Rockstar's *L.A. Noire*, was regarded in some quarters as a disappointment.

I put the question to two writers who've explored this liminal terrain in their work. Anna Megill was the narrative designer on the highly anticipated upcoming title *Murdered: Soul Suspect*, wherein players take the part of a ghostly detective trying to solve his own murder. Mikko Rautalahti is the Story Team Manager at Remedy Entertainment, with credits including the critically praised *Alan Wake* games. They shared their take on what makes for good horror, the boundaries of genre crossover, and the very real horror that is recycling clichés…

What makes for a good horror game?

MIKKO RAUTALAHTI: That's a hard question to answer, not least because the game we made isn't something we thought of as a horror game—for us, *Alan Wake* was always more of a psychological thriller. Of course, a lot of the people who played it insist that it's horror. So maybe I don't know what makes a good horror game, maybe we made one by accident.

But let's pretend I do. If I had to distill it into one thing, though, I suppose I'd have to say "atmosphere." I mean, on one level, scaring people is pretty easy—you get some tense music going, then suddenly spike the volume and have something come at me really fast, I'll jump and scream. I'm entirely dependable that way. But that's more about being startled than actually experiencing horror—for horror, you need a build-up.

Where does that intersect with other genres like mystery?

ANNA MEGILL: Mystery drives horror stories. Ultimately, horror is a quest to understand that mystery. What's happening? Why is it happening? Can it be stopped? Who can stop it? How? Such questions are especially rewarding when the answers are clever or mess with your sense of reality. One of the first games I ever played was *Sanitarium*, whose protagonist is (of course) insane. The

Photo courtesy of Anna Megill

levels were a combination of reality and hallucinations; players couldn't trust the PC's senses or judgment. That inability to define reality kept players constantly off-kilter, and made for a powerful gaming experience. I think that uncertainty is the key to a good horror game.

How do you write horror specifically for a game? Is it different than writing it in another medium?

MR: Writing horror—or anything, really—for a game is profoundly different simply because games are interactive. In a novel, or a film, the pacing is exact—not a moment goes by that isn't accounted for. In a video game, the player can stop and look around, or even backtrack; depending on the game in question, sometimes they can even skip scenes, or approach them from a completely different direction.

It allows for a very rich experience, but it also means that you don't have as much control over the experience as you might like—and in case of horror, the atmosphere tends to be fragile. One moment of inappropriate laughter, or an instant of distraction, will take the wind out of your sails. On the other hand, you can also have the game react to what the player is doing in unexpected ways.

AM: How do you establish linear narrative within unpredictable gameplay? The best games use a lot of environmental clues to relate backstory, to fill in character histories, and nudge players toward the next step. Instead of telling you that a character has a troubled past, they direct players to explore an environment rich in clues. As players discover notes, personal items, recordings, and flashbacks, the story emerges organically. All these little bits of information fit together like a mosaic to form a complete picture, but they don't need to be experienced in a particular order. You can still build in jump-scares, and make sure players can't progress until they've discovered all the critical story elements, but the fun in writing horror for games is letting players stumble across compelling moments of narrative on their own. That NPC rocking in the corner of a dark house might have a terrifying story to tell, but only players who choose to interact with her will hear it.

Let's talk about Murdered: Soul Suspect for a moment. How did you integrate the horror elements with an interactive noir narrative?

AM: I'll be honest, *Murdered: Soul Suspect* is the closest thing to horror I've ever written, and it's more of a supernatural detective story with some horror elements mixed in. But I can see where there would be differences. In movies or novels, the writer has control all the time. You know exactly what the reader will see and do and in what order those events will happen. In games, unpredictability is built into the medium. Once you're outside of a cutscene, players can (and will) play the game out of its designed order, skip crucial content, and go the wrong way through

an environment as a natural part of gameplay. That's the main difference between games and other media: game writing must be instructive as well as entertaining. You must constantly provide guidance for players so that they know where to go next, what to do next, what's expected of them, understand the resources at their disposal, and what their options are. And you have to convey all of this information as unobtrusively as possible, or it sinks any emotion you're building to a climax.

And there's not a lot of what some people consider "traditional" gameplay in *Murdered*, where you blast your way through every level?

AM: There's been a lot of press about *Murdered*'s gameplay and how Ronan doesn't have a "ghost gun," so you're not just shooting your way through the afterlife. Because that's what a lot of horror games do and do really well: combat. But there's a different kind of suspense in being recently dead and not understanding the rules. It's not even that you find yourself in a strange place with terrifying creatures; it's that added element of being a stranger to yourself. You don't even know you.

MR: A classic example of this [approach] would be the *Silent Hill* games, where the combat is difficult and dangerous, and the enemies are creepy and disturbing. They look like something you wouldn't want touching you. So fighting is something you want to avoid, but even

so, it's not the combat that creates the feeling of horror in these games—it's the creepy feeling that everything in the world is completely fucked, and there's no way around that. There's that creeping awareness that whatever it is that has infected the world has its roots deep in you. You get to thinking that perhaps it's not the world that's fucked, maybe it's just you. You can't fight that. All you can do is keep going and hope that there's a way to get clean by the time you reach the end. That's not really about the gameplay—you start to feel like the gameplay is a symptom of the sickness that permeates the town and everything in it, including you. *Especially* you.

Anna, you raise an interesting point: Part of horror is learning the rules that the supernatural elements obey through deduction and observation. Mystery is often about unraveling a particular horror through those same techniques.

AM: That's part of the attraction behind stories where people transform into vampires or werewolves, etc. It's like becoming a superhero, because you get all these great new powers. But as you're learning what those powers are and what you're capable of, you're incredibly vulnerable. You don't know what can hurt you (As a ghost, can you even be hurt?), and you have to run away a lot in the beginning before you level up and get a better understanding of your capabilities. In fact, leveling up allows players to experience—immersively and measurably—the journey of self-discovery, that "digging deep" that most horror story survivors go through.

Gameplay is all about agency. Horror is often about loss of agency—possession, the unkillable monster, the unstoppable prophecy. How do you reconcile the two?

MR: Monsters are not that great as a source of horror in video games. They tend to be full of monsters, many of them extremely gruesome and imaginative. They don't really make much of an impact by themselves—they're usually more of a violent thrill than something that induces fear. You either kill them by the bushel, which always runs the risk of being boring, or they're unkillable, which makes the player feel vaguely cheated. Monsters tend to be about the moment-to-moment gameplay, and if you feel a lack of agency in that, it's not a particularly engaging experience.

I think the special kind of horror that comes from a sense of inevitability usually works best in a video game. Gameplay elements can help—restricting resources the player has at their disposal, forcing you to make difficult decisions that you have no way of avoiding—but mostly, I think this goes back to atmosphere.

How do you collaborate with other disciplines to maximize the horror in your games?

AM: Games are collaboration. All disciplines have to work together to make a successful game. But in horror games, environment and character art are especially helpful for creating the necessary atmosphere. If you consider the Suspension Bridge Theory, there must be terrifying visuals for players to absorb as a source of—to blame for—their agitation. And I've already mentioned how environmental hints allow the narrative to unfold in a modular way while directing the player through the game. Instead of putting up a sign that says "Cemetery This Way" or burdening players with a wall of text, environment can build a dark path, with a single light at the far end. Players will understand that they need to head toward the light and will have a nerve-wracking trip down the path. A far more elegant solution than exposition.

MR: If I had to pick one discipline that's particularly important to me as a writer, I would probably have to go with level designers. They are largely in charge of creating the moment-to-moment experience, and I firmly believe that in the end, it doesn't matter how excellent my writing is if the level designers don't know what I'm going for. They're the ones who make me look good.

AM: Sound design is also critical for a good horror game. When you're in dark areas and you're dulling the player's vision, strange noises can make it a terrifying experience. It's the door creaking down the hall, or the sound of breathing in a room where you can't see anything. Or the faint scrape of something moving…right…behind…you.

Those moments give you that spike of terror and populate the darkness with your nightmares.

What's the one horror cliché you always want to avoid in your game writing?

AM: Oh man. The one cliché? Writers want to avoid clichés whenever possible, not just the horror clichés.

MR: Gore. Gore isn't scary, or very interesting in itself. I'm not opposed to it, per se; a lot of very good games have a lot of very gruesome content and I love it—I like a good decapitation as much as the next guy, probably more—but it's a very poor substitute for fear. I'm not sure people always get that; often you just see people turn on the hose and spray the area with chunky bits and pretend it's scary. It isn't.

AM: *Murdered* was tough because it combines two genre that are riddled with tropes: the detective story and

the ghost story. I can't speak for the other writers, but I was most concerned with all aspects of the Unfinished Business trope. Just from watching the *Murdered* trailer, you can see why I'd be concerned. I didn't want Ronan's story to follow a predictable path. Even though we're already defying convention to a certain extent by telling the other side of the cliché story, I wanted it to feel fresh. I wanted the path the protagonist follows while resolving his business to be unexpected. I wanted his interactions with both worlds—the lost living world and the new supernatural realm—to be surprising. The challenge of telling a story from a ghost's perspective is that he can gather information in ways the living can't (like the touch-induced murder flashback in the trailer), but he also has limitations the living don't (he can't pick anything up to inspect it). Players engage with the game-world in very different ways than they're used to. I hope the resulting gameplay feels fresh and fun.

MR: The abattoir of a room with streaks of old blood coating the walls and rotting human body parts hanging off rusty meat hooks…it just doesn't do much for me by itself. Throwing that in my face won't even make me shrug. I've seen that a thousand times.

On the other hand, if that room is unexpectedly in the basement of my player character's childhood home, that's a different thing. If I care about my character, you can bet I'll feel that. That's context.

Context is everything.

❦ ❦ ❦

Once Upon A Nightmare
YA Horror: The Black Dahlia

By Amy Shane

Instead of my usual Young Adult Column this time, I am focusing on the famous Black Dahlia murder case—in honor of the Dark Mystery theme.

The Black Dahlia

It was one of those macabre cases that seemed straight out of a noir mystery—with classic themes of damsels in distress, mob ties and movie stars. Yet it was real life. A character defined by her mysterious and seductive ways, whose charms entrapped her lovers and led them to harmful or deadly situations. Although this time it was leading her down her own compromising and deadly path: a path so dark and mysterious that almost 70 years later the outcome still haunts and baffles people today.

In the days of Rita Hayworth, Betty Grable, Ava Gardner and other Hollywood starlets, the newspapers flashed a news headline that would instantly make a young woman a star. Teenage girls would flock to Hollywood for the chance to have their names displayed among the marquee lights, cops wore hats with their suits and smoking was considered proper etiquette. It was during this time that a murder was splayed among the headlines, a case so shocking that it would make or break the local authorities' careers.

As color fades to black and white and cryptic music is the cinematic interlude, the background is set for a legendary crime drama. Darkness falls and a woman's singing fills the atmosphere, a low piano and trumpets play as the fog rolls in. Opening the scene for a story which, at no time, would mislead you into thinking there's going to be a happy ending. A crime filled with so much doom, ill fate, fear and betrayal, that not even a Hollywood writer could produce such a script. This is the Golden Age of Hollywood's most notorious murder case—The Black Dahlia.

The case of the Black Dahlia was a grim, horrible, gruesome crime—emulating fear at its deepest level. Falling within the parameters of a true crime noir, it was one with an overwhelming sense of terror.

Elizabeth Short was a young woman who set out to break the mold of what was expected of women at that time, swapping the role of the career housewife for Hollywood fame and glamour. Ironically, it was her gruesome death that finally granted her that fame.

Known to enjoy the Hollywood nightlife, Elizabeth always put forth the effort to place herself in the right places to be discovered. A true *femme fatale*, Elizabeth Short was described as using her feminine wiles of beauty, charm, and sexual allure to obtain what she wanted. Known for her penchant for service men, she was described as living a careless, tawdry lifestyle. Elizabeth had the propensity for dressing in all black, with sheer black undergarments and a black ring. Along with her jet-black hair, red lipstick and nail polish, and constant talk of her dream of being a movie star, her glamorous persona earned her the nickname "Black Dahlia."

However her American Dream quickly became an American Nightmare when Elizabeth became the star of her own horror noir. Instead of a shadow-filled back alley lit by a lone street lamp, the horror was placed among the tall grass. On January 15, 1947, what was thought to be a broken store mannequin laying in a vacant lot in South Hollywood turned out to be the

image from: www.gadailynews.com

nude dismembered body of Elizabeth Short. Lying on her back, with arms over head, her torso was cut cleanly in half at the waist, with the severed sections placed in a line. A joker smile was grotesquely carved into her face, exposing a morbid and horrific picture. Her death was caused by hemorrhage and shock from the Glasgow smile cut upon her cheeks (echoing the maniacal, freak-like grin reminiscent of the classic 1928 silent horror film *The Man Who Laughs*, where the character Gwynplaine was disfigured with a permanent smile to teach a lesson of treachery to his father), as well as the contusions on the brain from blunt force trauma. Rope burns flanked her wrists and ankles, while a large triangle of skin was cut out of her thigh removing her rose tattoo, along with her body drained of all its blood.

But it was the haunting discovery of the precise and meticulous way her body was cut in half and organs removed that baffled detectives. The body and hair had been washed and shampooed and then displayed for passersby to see.

The reference to the Chaney film draws a deeper meaning into The Black Dahlia's permanent smile. Being an aspiring movie starlet, the Glasgow smile carved on her face and giving her an eternal expression, is an act that taints even the memory of her former gorgeous beauty. Imagine a woman's last image of her heinously disfigured face, horrifically condemned to smile up at her murderer for all of eternity. Elizabeth Short's tragic death captured the public's imagination, while the media quickly painted a romantic image of the beautiful starlet, romanticizing the image, making her a household name.

The crime was officially declared unsolved, possibly due to the media's overzealous needs for headline material, or the fact that there was just too many details and leads for the time. A dramatic story that, if solved, very well could have lost some of its allure. The newspaper headlines at the time were utilized for teaching young adults lessons—like grim fairytales of horrific proportions—using fear to teach against disobedience, promiscuousness and even over independence. All that remained was the shell of a person that once was a beautiful young woman, stripped of everything that had made her feminine and female.

Chasing dreams of stardom still resonates among the young adults today. However, lucky for us, we now have avenues such as "American Idol," "The Voice," or "America s Next Top Model," all focused on discovering young stars. Differing from those of the 1940s, where young starlets grabbed their trunks and jumped on a train to follow the dreams to the golden Hollywood lights.

There will always be crimes that remain legendary. Victims' stories that are so compelling they transcend the test of time. Sixty-seven years later the Black Dahlia case still haunts us.

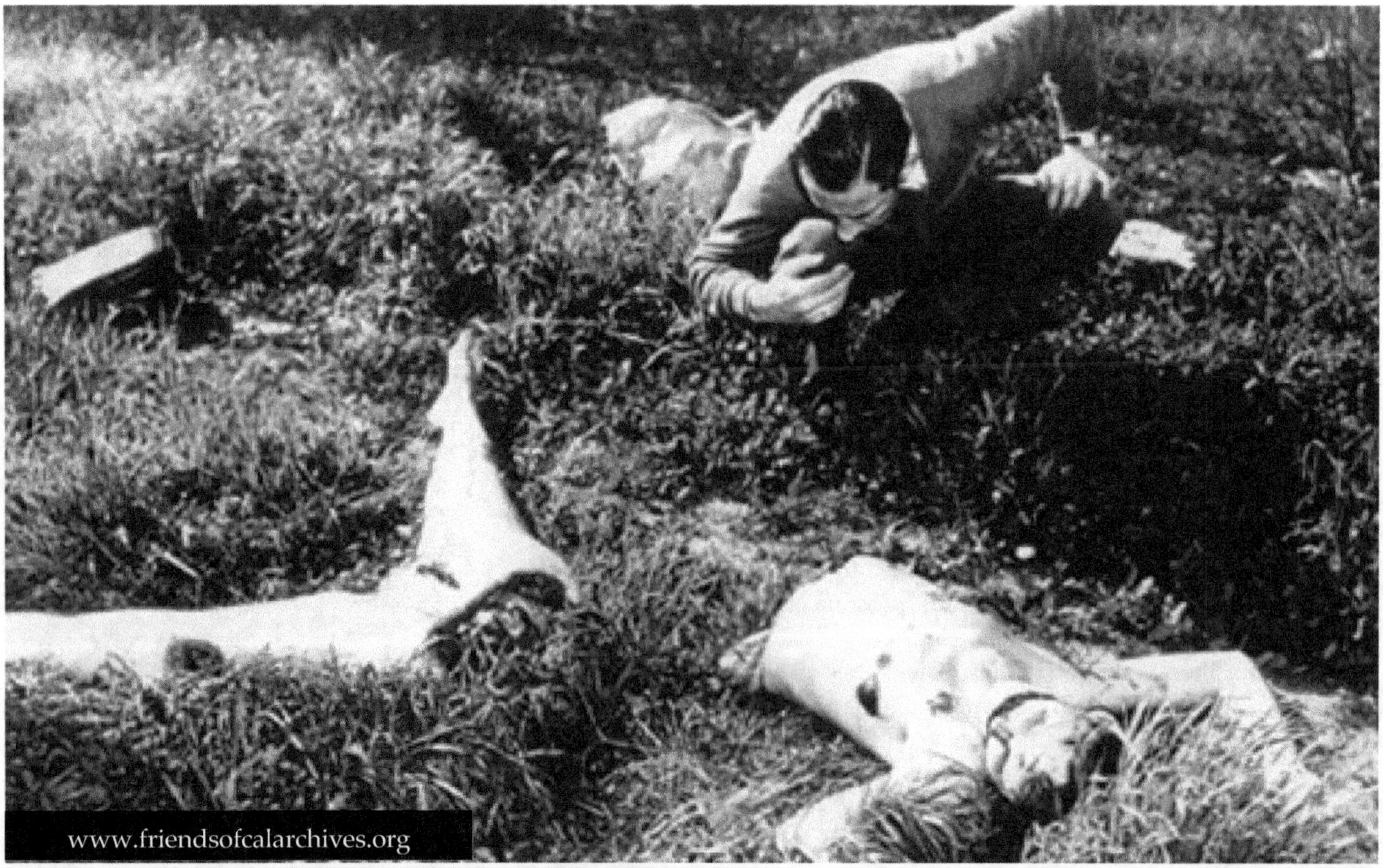
www.friendsofcalarchives.org

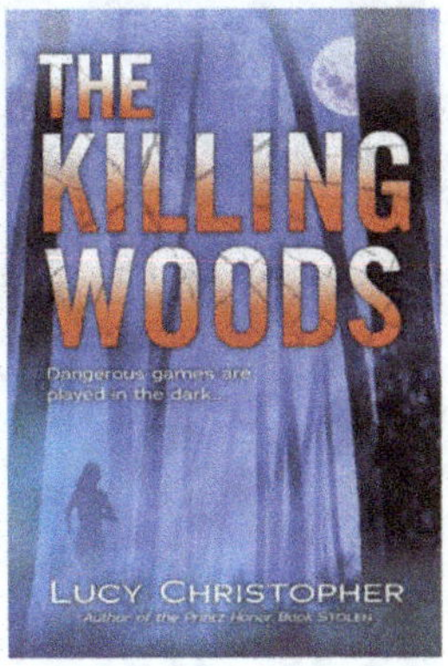

The Killing Woods
by Lucy Christopher
Publisher- Scholastic/Chicken House
hardback, 232 pages. Young adult

The Killing Woods starts off like a shot in the dark, bringing with it mystery, death and murder... In the dark, shadowed forest of Darkwood, night falls and a secret game begins. In the still of night, death falls upon the forest floor, burying with it memories, secrets and the truth, thus beginning the psychological thrilling chase of who's done it, and who really is capable of murder.

The story is narrated by Emily and Damon, two of the unlikeliest of characters to team up, who enter into a silent resolve to solve the murder for themselves. Emily is the daughter of the ex-combat soldier who is accused of the murder, and Damon is the last one to see his girlfriend alive.

Heartfelt and raw, the emotional angst surfaces as new and unanswered questions are brought forth, and the suspect list builds along with the mystery. As equally as Emily believes in her father's innocence, Damon protests.

For Emily, dealing with a combat veteran father, coping with PTSD seemed hard enough, until that night when she saw her father emerge from the woods with a girl draped across his shoulders like an injured deer. More shocking than the pale gray skin and blue tinted lips of the dead body was the fact that Emily's dad can't remember where he found her or why he has her. Charges of manslaughter fall upon him, leaving Emily as the only one trying to discover what truly happened to Ashlee.

For Damon, more questions arise as time passes. He can't keep silent the regret and fear that lurks deep in his subconscious. The nagging truth lays just below the drug-induced fog of that evening. Damon knows he should hate Emily for what her father did but he just can't understand why he feels compelled to speak to her.

Fractured memories are like the fractured light that seeps through the forest trees. Truth lies in the depths of their minds, and the only way to heal is through discovery of the truth, awakening a part in all of them that must discover what really happened that night.

Like a howl piercing the dead of night, Lucy Christopher takes you on a vivid, wild, imaginative ride. She musters the courage to shed light on the issues of drugs sexuality and dangerous games. Her writing is hauntingly realistic as she unearths the dark side of PTSD and the lasting effects that it has on the families that survive with it. With her dark and murky mystery, Lucy Christopher teaches us that truth is not always as it first appears, highlighting the dangerous consequences of a new epidemic among teens.

The Killing Woods hunts you down like a beast in the forest stalking its prey, baiting you with each chapter to continue along the path, keeping you from looking away even for a moment, and asking the question, Can the *mind* be the ultimate killer?

—Reviewed by Amy Shane

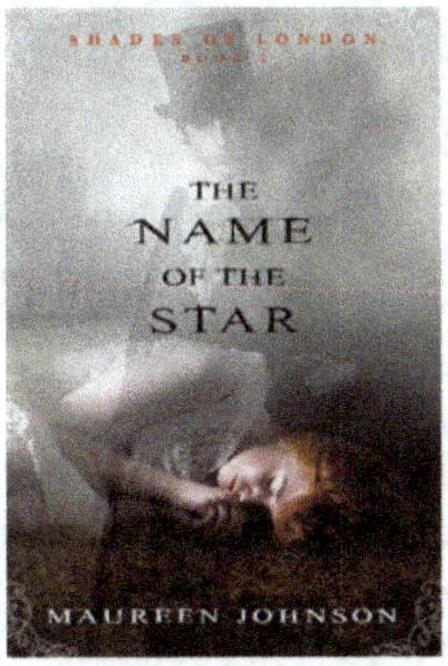

The Name of the Star-
Maureen Johnson
Putnam publishing
Paperback/hardback, 372 pages

It all started with a woman lying on the ground in a pool of blood with an open slash where her neck used to be. The news flashes the banner "Ripper-Like Murder in the East End," and that's where it all began—with the return.

Rory Deveaux is a small town Louisiana girl who loves her sweet tea, extra sweet, with every meal. A small town where oddities are its charm. So arriving to study at Wexford Academy in London should have been a welcome break from her crazy, freezer-collecting uncle and angel-communicating aunt.

Just trying to settle in at Wexford Academy, Rory arrives into a world of school uniforms, roommates and a heavy course curriculum, all while trying to make new friends. Instead she signaled the beginning of a string of murders echoing those of the 1888 Ripper murders.

Not long after she adjusts to her routine, the legendary killings of Jack the Ripper begin to haunt her, as she soon discovers that she is living right in the middle of the serial killer's playground. But everything changes for Rory when she sees a man on campus that her roommate can't, just before another murder is committed in the middle of campus. Did she just see the Ripper copycat? Details start to mount as the victims start to fall all around her, corresponding with the same dates as the Ripper's victims of 1888.

All too quickly "Ripper-Mania" sieges London, with the media giving people a countdown calendar to death. The people become more frantic, as fear begins to build in the streets in the days leading up to the next murder, where threats of a copycat loom on every street corner. CCTV cameras are mounted on every street corner, yet they still haven't caught any sign of the killer. Posing the question, Is this the work of a copycat killer or evidence that it is something more?

This opens up 100 years of fear and fanatics behind the case, with the allure of Jack the Ripper's notorious and signature slashes across the throats and displays of internal organs on all of the killings.

The real mystery for Rory is: What is she really seeing? Spinning in a paranormal twist to the plot, could the ghost of Jack the Ripper be responsible for the current crimes? All throwing Rory into a secret paranormal investigation with the elusive Scotland Yard team.

The Name of the Star lands itself as an on-the-edge-of-your-seat thriller. Mixing present day murders and London Academy life with bloodshed, murder, and the paranormal, set with historical accuracy of the famed Jack the Ripper killings, including vivid descriptions of London, and mixing the dark and horrific with charming characters, this book represents more than just the unknown, but rather fear itself.

—Reviewed by Amy Shane

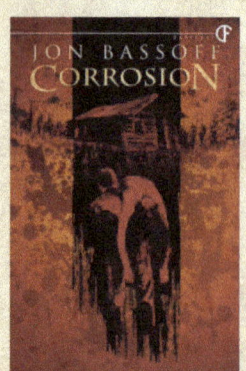

Corrosion
By Jon Bassoff
DarkFuse October, 2013,
ISBN: 978-1937771805
$15.99 PB, $4.99 Kindle

Independent press DarkFuse classifies *Corrosion* as a psycho-noir. It's a term that's starting to turn up more frequently lately, and even its fans seem to disagree on exactly what it means. All noir fiction is dark, harsh, and psychological by its very nature. The entirety of Jim Thompson's *The Killer Inside Me* (1952) or the shocking ending to Lawrence Block's *Grifter's Game* (1962) are as disturbing today as they were when they were twenty-five cent paperbacks. So, what exactly puts the *psycho* in psycho-noir? The short answer: the fact that things may not be as they seem. If you'd like a longer explanation of psycho-noir, it's between the covers of Jon Bassoff's debut novel.

Corrosion begins as Joseph Downs, a war veteran with a hideous, burn-scarred face, finds himself stuck temporarily in a decrepit mountain town. After he gets into a bar fight defending a woman from abuse, she turns up at his rooming-house door. Lilith is about as unappealing as they come—filthy, repulsive, and trampy—but mere moments after they talk in his room, our protagonist makes an alarmingly quick emotional leap.

She moved closer on the bed. Her face was in soft focus. Pimpled skin. Bloodshot eyes. Lovely, no. But I was in love. It happens too easily for me.

This is no love-at-first-sight Nicholas Sparks moment, but the first sign that something here is broken. There's more screwed up about Joseph Downs than just his face. His instant attraction to Lilith is only the beginning of what becomes a nightmare of violence, secrets, crime, and passion. As the mysteries of Downs' past are revealed, the story doesn't fall into place so much as it becomes more and more unsettling. Evil has very deep roots, and the further down they go—the further into the past—the more horrific the revelations. Perhaps most disturbing of all is the realization that such an abnormal past can't help but imprint on the present. Just as with traditional noir, where losers lose, lose again, then lose some more, in *Corrosion*, it's obvious that *nothing good can come of this.*

Bassoff has been called a cross between Jim Thompson and David Lynch. It's too bad that Lynch's name has become hip shorthand for "weird" (a few decades ago, anything weird was compared to Fellini), when there are so few works that are actually similar. In this case, though, there may be some truth to the comparison, as there is something Lynchian at work here. It's the small-town vibe, populated by minor characters stranger than you'll find in any big city. It's the timelessness that makes you question whether this is the '50s or today. And it's the dark secrets that lurk beneath the mundane, imbuing ordinary things with an eeriness. Though the town lies somewhere in Oklahoma, there's also an element of the Southern Gothic that's hard to ignore, reminiscent of Flannery O'Connor's *The Violent Bear It Away.*

Despite the violence and the depravity, if you look at it just the right way, *Corrosion* could almost be a love story—several of them in fact. Bassoff shows us multiple times: this is what love looks like to the damaged.

Reviewed by Kelly Robinson

SuperNOIRtural Tales
By Ian Rogers
Burning Effigy Press
ISBN-13: 978-1926611167

SuperNOIRtural Tales is a collection of five previously published short works that fuse noir with horror to create something refreshingly unique. Each story is told from the perspective of Felix Renn, a private investigator with a tendency to attract the supernatural. This would likely be bad enough in itself, but things are a little more complicated.

Felix's world is our own, with one major difference: The Black Lands, a strange and dark dimension residing alongside this one. The Black Lands are populated by a host of bizarre, terrifying creatures that make their way over here through Portals, causing mischief, mayhem and more than a little bloodshed.

Felix Renn isn't the stereotypical hard-as-nails gumshoe. On the contrary, his humanity is what makes him so endearing. He comes across as an average guy who repeatedly finds himself in, and stumbles his way through, some very strange, dark and life-threatening situations.

There's a strong sense of humor throughout the book, a big part of which comes from the well-drawn cast of secondary characters. Felix's ex-wife/current assistant Sandra, for instance, is a great foil for Felix. The banter between the two is hilarious at times. These moments of levity are much appreciated, at times feeling almost necessary, because when things get scary, Rogers doesn't hold back.

The horror escalates from the first story to the penultimate (the last story is a short and chilling little piece in its own right, but somewhat anticlimactic, placed as it is after the brilliant novella *The Brick*).

All of the stories here are well-crafted and work on multiple levels, and the mythos Rogers has created is both very frightening and very fun. Readers of horror, crime fiction and urban fantasy will find much to enjoy, and if you're as enamored with the whole thing as I am, you'll be pleased to know that a Felix Renn novel is currently in the works.

Reviewed by Josh Black

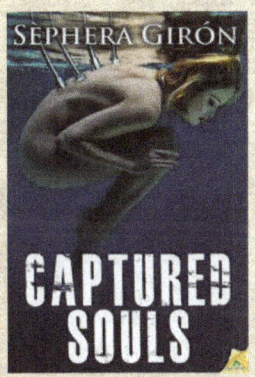

Captured Souls
by Sephera Giron
Samhain Publishing
February, 2014
ISBN13: 9781619221475

We begin in the sordid, hidden sex clubs of a big city. There, Doctor Miriam searches for connections through sex…through hookups… through passion and desire. But if you think she is only looking for a quick fix, to quench her desire for sexual fulfillment, then you're in for a trick. Soon she has gathered a pair of exquisite male specimens. Quickly, it is clear she has become a patron of pain…and an exchanger of services.

There are some very squeamish moments, and there is an honest exploration of what sexuality means. How does it connect us to one another? How does it connect us to other planes? Does it? Are we our bodies?

These are the sort of questions our doctor explores as well. She uses new methods…implants and monitoring equipment. Sex is used as nourishment and enslavement, as pleasure and unimaginable pain. The tables are turned on traditional horror. We have so many stories where men enslave women, and use them as pure vessels for their sexuality. *Captured Souls* goes beyond just flipping stereotypes. There are real philosophical questions raised. It certainly made me re-think several of my own long-standing beliefs.

The door is kicked in on traditional sexuality and spirituality. You'll want to turn away, but you won't be able to–there's a fascination to learn more about these unearthed and unspoken explorations. The exploration of submission and sexuality as a tool toward bringing someone to zero, was quite horrifying. There are many built-in beliefs that are shattered.

One last thing? Don't even think about trying to have sex with one of Dr. Mariam's lovers behind her back. She has ways to make you pay that are worse than your imagination.

Reviewed by John Palisano

Ugly as Sin
By James Newman
Shock Totem Publications
ISBN: 9780988272354

Nick Bullman is a professional wrestler adapting the villainous moniker The Widowmaker. Engaged in every conceivable bout and tawdry storyline, Bullman has enjoyed a storied career. One ill-fated day a group of overzealous fans changed everything. Now dreadfully disfigured, his reality is more horrifying than his character could have imagined in his wildest dreams. Estranged from his family and suddenly unemployed, Bullman receives a distressing phone call one day from his daughter. His teenaged granddaughter has been kidnapped without a trace. Will the ex-pro wrestler be able to overcome the odds and all adversity when it counts most, or will he simply submit to his tormentors in Ugly as Sin? As Bullman morphs into the unlikely role of bounty hunter and detective on steroids, the reader adapts the transition with little to no resistance. We want to see his character prevail as he unveils one clue after another in finding the little girl he'd never met face to face.

Author James Newman's novel, depicted as a white trash noir, emulates the realm of the squared circle in seedy, fantastical 'kayfabe' grandiosity. One does not have to be a fan of professional wrestling to truly appreciate the story telling merit of this novel, but it's evident the author is a fan of spandex and cauliflower eared ballet as he paints an often grisly and disturbing picture of social deviance. The celebrities that are idolized and the horrific fact that some fans simply cannot distinguish between fantasy and reality are the elements that breathe refreshing life into this plot. A psychological thriller at its finest, the genuine fear factors are exemplified through Bullman's confrontation.

Reviewed by Rick Amortis

Mountain Home
Bracken MacLeod
Books of the Dead Press
ISBN 978-1927112144
June, 2013;
$12.99 PB, $0.90 Ebook

A group of people are holed up in a remote diner, trying to survive a sniper attack from across the street.

That's essentially the plot of Bracken MacLeod's debut novel, *Mountain Home*. This simple scenario frames a painfully honest portrayal of some of the uglier aspects of humanity. The characters are thrust against their will into a highly stressful situation, hidden qualities and truths about them coming to light.

Point of view shifts between characters, giving each one time to develop in their own voice. Each is fleshed out well, with their own hopes and dreams, their hangups and emotional scars. Surprisingly, the sniper herself is perhaps the most sympathetic character. While the people in the restaurant are trapped within the confines of the property, the sniper is increasingly trapped within the confines of her broken mind, haunted by very human demons. Flashbacks to her harrowing war experiences are heartbreaking and give an understandable reason as to why she's snapped.

The reasons for this or anything else that happens are by no means simplistic or clear-cut. In one scene in particular, several characters argue about which of them is to blame for the sniper's actions, and none of them are wrong. MacLeod doesn't deal in absolutes, and pulls no punches regarding inhumanity. Narcissism, bigotry and ignorance figure prominently throughout the novel, leading to tragic ends. It essentially becomes a study in people's capacity to give and take physical and psychological abuse, and how quickly and drastically these things can change us. A sorrowful tone underlies the novel, at some points leaning toward being unbearably bleak. This is lightened not by humor, but by occasional scenes when humanity shines through the selfish but instinctive will to survive at all costs.

Mountain Home is a great thriller. It's tightly constructed, tense and very well-written. There's also a lot more going on under the hood than you might expect. MacLeod's voice is clear, confident, and insightful, at no time betraying the fact that this is a debut novel. It's one that all thriller fans should take note of, and comes with a strong recommendation.

Reviewed by Josh Black

Wolf's Cut
W.D. Gagliani
Samhain,
March 2014
Trade paperback,
281 pp., $16.00

Wolf's Cut is the fifth volume in a series involving werewolf and homicide cop Nick Lupo. As such it shares the strengths and the weaknesses of serial narratives. Its strengths are a solid sense of characters—major and minor—as they enter this story with detailed backgrounds, motivations, and responses to their various situations…for several, how they handle being werewolves. There is an equivalent sense of solid landscapes, mapped in earlier novels and continued in this one.

Its weaknesses, unfortunately, are intimately connected with its strengths. Many of the characters and situations continue from earlier stories, and *Wolf's Cut* devotes much of its first fifty or so pages to giving detailed flashbacks into characters, organizations, actions, and other carryovers. In addition, there are half a dozen hubs of action, until a seventh is suddenly added three-quarters of the way through. Managing shifts among the various times and locations without disrupting the threads associated with each character proves increasingly difficult as the story progresses. Add to that the dozen or so major characters and *Wolf's Cut* becomes a potentially solid story that threatens to get lost in its own minutiae.

Gagliani's take on the werewolf motif is interesting, but as with other points it sometimes clogs the storytelling. A key factor in combatting the creatures is their horrific reaction to being stabbed by one of two silver-bladed knives from the Vatican; and each time the story refers to the Vatican silvers, it stops to recount bits of their history, to describe their power against werewolves (as if *showing* it were not sufficient), and to repeat and repeat that these are the *Vatican* knives, not just any old silver blades.

Another element in the makeup of his creatures is their increased libido, based upon fundamental changes in DNA subsequent to being bitten. Again, that is an intriguing detail that should strengthen Gagliani's representation. Unfortunately, it begins to overshadow all of the werewolves, their actions, and reactions. At least one character slips into near caricature—a devastatingly beautiful sex-driven female compelled to have…and destroy…any man who crosses her path.

Wolf's Cut is also bulky, wordy at times, with a fair number of malformed sentences that, for me at least, interfere with the story it so wants to tell. And there *is* a story, almost buried under all of the difficulties. The tribe's struggle against the mob; a reservation doctor's struggle with problems internal and external; Nick Lupo's struggle with his basic identity—all of these could blend into a strong, taut, well-told horror-thriller. Just not this one.

Reviewed by Michael Collings

A Frozen World
Nick Andors, writer and illustrator
Eyekon Publishing
ISBN 978-0-9895312-1-4
2013; $15.95 PB

A Frozen World is a graphic novel that combines four stories about the various inhabitants of Irongates: a stretch of dystopian urban buildings where characters from the grotesque tradition reside.

The alternate world of Irongates is dark: the images are black and white with an inky resonance. Some pages are quite busy with many panels and small script. The language is poetic and there is a nice consistency to the drawings, making it feel as if the characters belong to a particular space and time. Andors is an accomplished artist: grief and sadness become beautiful on the otherwise unattractive visages. The city setting is gritty and desolate, yet pulsing with an unsettling energy. Irongates becomes a character in much the same way that the Overlook becomes a character in Stephen King's *The Shining*.

A Frozen World, with its violence and nudity, is for adult audiences. The ambiance is claustrophobic and bleak, countered with imaginative and visually interesting images. The sedated characters provide a curious counterpart for the energetic art. Despite being haunted by the stories, I am glad that I took the time to pound the pavement of *A Frozen World.*

Reviewed by Elaine Pascale

Evil Never Dies
Mick Ridgewell
Samhain, April 2014
Trade paperback, 264 pp., $15.00; eBook

Newsman Roland Millhouse has been given what he considers a fluff-piece assignment: to interview Patricia Owens on the occasion of her 120th birthday. Expecting a fragile if not decrepit old woman, he is startled when the woman greeting him at the door of her aging farmhouse looks to be a sprightly seventy… or perhaps younger. At first his questions are typical, including the standard "how do you explain your longevity?"

He received his second surprise of the day when she responds: "The short answer is, the reason I have lived so long is that evil never dies."

From there she begins her story—a detailed account of the summer of 1912, when the small Canadian community of Kings Shore underwent a terror that left it forever marked. Referring to a thick journal covering that summer, Patricia embarks on a tale of death, demons, and vampires.

Evil Never Dies presents an intriguing re-imagining of the vampire, specifically the Nosferatu-style creature, inhumanly swift and deadly, as first the "old one," then his newly minted followers ravage the small town, destroying everyone Patricia loves. The novel creates a deliberate pacing by interrupting the back story with present-time details—walks to the cemetery where the victims are buried; to the abandoned farmstead and the rock-capped well that contains a horrible secret; or simply to the front porch to refresh themselves with lemonade. As a result of the shift from past to present, Patricia's story reveals itself almost agonizingly slowly, paralleling her increasing debilitation and apparently rapid regressing to her true age.

As useful as it is as a narrative device, the shifts also create problems. The main story—the incursions of vampires into a small, enclosed community—often seems little more than an adjunct to drinking lemonade or taking walks, since those mundane actions are given as much attention as the horror itself. After a while, the breaks seem more artificial than essential, distractions from the evolving revelations concerning the vampires. In addition, there is a certain amount of unnecessary repetition throughout—as when Roland reminds us again and again how agile and youthful Patricia was on that first day and how much older she looks.

If one can overlook those two difficulties, *Evil Never Dies* becomes a well thought out re-creation of the late nineteenth- early twentieth-century vampiric milieu, such as was established in Stoker's *Dracula* (1897) or, perhaps more to the point, Murneau's *Nosferatu* (1922). The creatures are terrifying, the image of evil trapped at the bottom of an ancient well, the specter of graveyard headstones standing as silent witness to horror—all work to make *Evil Never Dies* a worthwhile read.

Reviewed by Michael R. Collings

Herbert Manning's Psychic Circus and Other Dark Tales
By David Williamson
Hazardous Press
ISBN: 978-0-615906836
December, 2013; £4.27/$6.29 pb;
£1.88/$3.09 ebook
97 pages

Although David Williamson's wickedly nasty tales may have a little of the supernatural in most of them, they are full of-all-too-human evil, with some of the most truly horrible sets of characters you could ever hope to find.

Like a very British Robert Bloch, Williamson is a master of the twist in the tale. "A Night to Remember" features one of Williamson's regular types of characters: vengeful, even sadistic offspring. It is easy in this story to understand why the narrator hates his parents so much – or is it? Just how reliable a narrator is he? In any event, what happens to his parents is Grand Guignol at its bloodiest. The title character of "The Chameleon Man" is able to mimic every hideous disease known to man. Yet has he gone one step too far when he is goaded into trying to mimic death itself? In "The Switch" we have a story that reminds me so much of EC Comics I could visualize it in graphic form. It has also one of Williamson's best twists. Matrimonial hatred, murder, revenge – favorite themes of the later Pan Horrors – are the major elements of "Rest in Pieces" in which a husband thinks he has found the perfect way to dispose of his hated wife, while "Boys Will Be Boys" has yet another bloody offspring whose actions are definitely not for anyone with a weak stomach! "Blind Date", reprinted from *Alt-Zombie*, is one of the few supernatural stories in this collection, a zombie tale with a neat twist. The final story, the titular "Herbert Manning's Psychic Circus", has a circus owner facing ruin in today's PC-ridden, health and safety obsessed world who is made an offer he can't possibly afford to refuse by a mysterious stranger, though he fails to realize the full implications till far too late.

These are strong short stories, graphically told, with minimal subtlety. If you like your horror full in your face, these are definitely for you.

Reviewed by David A. Riley

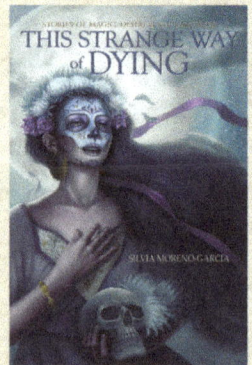

This Strange Way of Dying
Silvia Moreno-Garcia
Exile Editions
ISBN: 978-1550963540
September, 2013; $16.95 PB

In her collection of stories, *This Strange Way of Dying*, Canadian-based author Silvia Moreno-Garcia plumbs the rich depths of her Mexican homeland, the setting for all but one of the stories. These stories are subtitled "Stories of Magic, Desire, and the Fantastic," and this is certainly apt, as they are reminiscent of works by Gabriel Garcia Marquez, Laura Esquivel, and other Latin American Magical Realists. Although these stories contain the standards of horror fiction—zombies, vampires, aliens, shape-shifters, doppelgängers, and witches—Moreno-Garcia elevates them above the cliché. For example, in "Stories with Happy Endings," her vampire is a jaded resident of Mexico City, whose late night meeting with a reporter, a meeting which brings to mind *An Interview with the Vampire*, raises the question of who is the most vampiric—this rather sad character who works in a factory or the reporter herself, living off the stories of others. Moreno-Garcia's twist on the doppelgänger is also unusual, centering on a normal child with bohemian parents who—after thinking it would be great if her parents were a bit more stable—starts seeing a more conservatively dressed and respectable version of her parents. Although like many of the stories in this collection the ending of "The Doppelgängers" is left open, there is the possibility that what is wished for is not always better than what was there before.

Moreno-Garcia makes use of the whole of Mexican history, setting stories in eras starting at the Pre-Columbian and ending with a future vision of Tijuana as a base for aliens. Her brilliant descriptions convey the mysticism of the native mythology, the sorrow and desperation of the conquered, and the excitement of the Revolution (with zombies!). Even though the stories differ in plot, characters, and settings, they are all connected by a sense of strangeness that runs throughout. Moreno-Garcia has captured the essence of Mexico—its multi-layered culture, its curses and *brujeria*, its mixture of Christian and pre-Christian religious beliefs, and even its colorful plants and animals.

Those who like horror shallow and visceral will probably not like this collection. Although there is gore and violence in some of the stories, Moreno-Garcia, even at her most violent, has a more subtle touch. "Flash Frame," a story that reminded me a bit of Ramsey Campbell's *Ancient Images*, is truly frightening and will cause readers to see the color yellow in a different and terrifying way. However, many of the stories are more beautifully haunting than viscerally scary. Some are sad. Some are even funny. All of them will stay with the reader long after the collection is finished. These expertly-written stories transcend genre and would be appealing to readers who do not like in-your-face horror but do like weird tales as well as to readers who like depth to their horror. I highly recommend this collection and hope that Moreno-Garcia publishes another book very soon.

Reviewed by Leah Larson

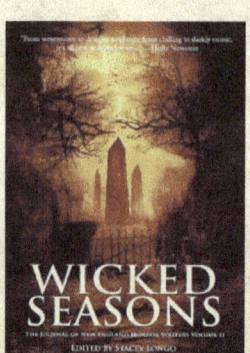

Wicked Seasons
Stacey Longo, Editor
NEHW Press
ISBN: 978-0615918839
November 6, 2013; $10.76 PB

I am writing this review during a typical New England blizzard. Having lived two decades in Boston and Cape Cod, I can recognize when something is distinctly New England, such as a nor'easter or a clam bake, and *Wicked Seasons* falls into that category.

The first New England common denominator: the booze. New Englanders have a particular way of drinking and particular response to drink. Playing armchair psychiatrist, I would chalk this up to the endless depressing winters and the insurmountable taxes. *Wicked Seasons* contains several stories featuring drunks, alcoholics, and newly sober but highly tempted characters. James A. Moore's "Spirits" handles the need for drink with a heart-tugging realness. Other stories have alcohol play a bit part, but it compels the action into often violent and delightfully surprising places.

The second common denominator: the tip of the hat to old school horror. New England's horror roots dig deep and that can be seen in this anthology. My favorite story of the bunch was Rob Smales' "A Night at the Show". This story is a smidgen Robert Bloch, mixed with a bit of Richard Matheson, seasoned with a little "Alfred Hitchcock Presents." It evoked the types of stories that drew me to the horror genre when I was very young. Christopher Golden's "The Secret Backs of Things" was another tale with a "classic tone" that stayed with this reviewer long after reading. I have always been a sucker for a clever conclusion.

Wicked Seasons is an eclectic collection, with something for everyone. There is the poetic "The Widow Mills," and the fairy-tale gone wrong "The Girl Who Wouldn't Break." There are monsters: "The Basement Legs," and "Lycanthrobastards." There are killers and dismembered bodies, and, for some reason, a plethora of maintenance men. There are equal parts violence and gore, and psychological horror. The New England writers featured here are accomplished and the stories are very entertaining.

Highly recommended.

Reviewed by Elaine Pascale

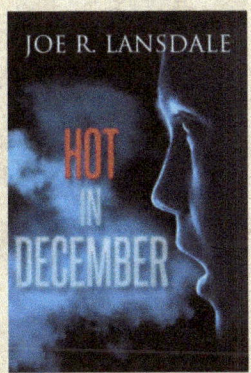

Hot in December
by Joe R. Lansdale
Dark Regions Press, 2013, 107pp

Hot in December by Joe R. Lansdale is one of those fantastic surprises that spring from out of nowhere and catch you completely off guard. Once I managed to get a copy, I couldn't wait to read the story and just spent the last two hours with my eyes glued to the monitor and another hour writing this review. The novella is reminiscent of Lansdale's earlier novels such as *Cold in July*, *Act of Love*, and *Waltz of Shadows*. There's also mention of Hap Collins and Leonard Pine in the story, and Sunset Jones from the novel *Sunset and Sawdust*, and Cason Statler and Booger from *Hap/Leonard's Devil Red*. So, it's kind of like a big family reunion. I was secretly hoping Hap and Leonard were in this novel, but instead we have Cason and Booger playing a nice substitute.

The story takes place right before Christmas when East Texas is experiencing a heat wave during the month of December. Tom Chan is busy grilling some hamburgers out back of his home when a speeding car runs over a woman out front. Tom takes a fast glimpse around the corner of the house and sees the driver dead on. Unfortunately, the neighbor is killed and the driver takes off, leaving the scene of a crime.

When Tom tells the police what he saw and takes a good look at the mug books, he's warned that the driver of the car is the son of a crime kingpin, who may be part of the Dixie Mafia. Testifying is the right thing to do, it isn't long before Tom and his family are threatened by mobsters. Tom quickly realizes that the police won't be able to protect them, and they may even be part of the problem. The only way for Tom Chan to solve the problem is to get the help of some of his old Army buddies and to take the fight to the criminals, killing every last one of them. The question is can he and his two buddies go on the offensive and live to tell about it?

You're just going to have to read the novella to find out.

Review by Wayne C. Rogers

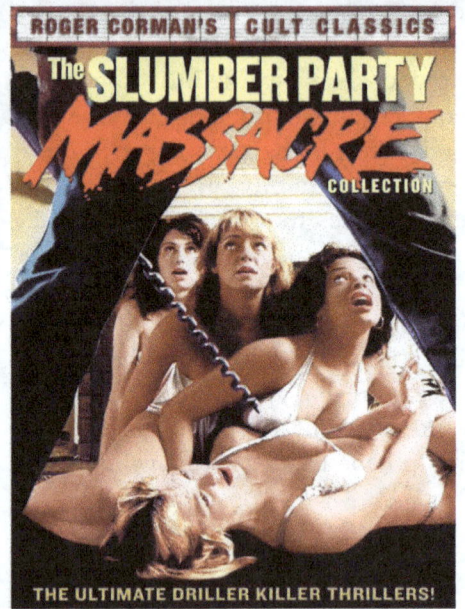

The Slumber Party Massacre
Director: Amy Holden Jones
Cast: Michelle Michaels, Robin Stille, Michael Villella

A few years back, Shout! Factory was doing their Roger Corman's Cult Classics line of DVDs and BDs. Those ran the gambit from cheesy monster movies, sci-fi farces, and masterpieces of the weird. Eventually they did THE SLUMBER PARTY MASSACRE COLLECTION, a two-disc DVD set containing all three of the MASSACRE movies. This was before their amazing horror division, called Scream Factory, came about. Now they have released the first, and by far the best, SLUMBER PARTY MASSACRE movie solo onto Blu-ray for the first time. Is this movie worth a get? Is it worth an upgrade if you already have the three movie DVD set? Well get your drill, don't answer the door even if it's the pizza guy, and let's find out.

1982's SLUMBER PARTY MASSACRE is a bona fide horror film classic. It's bloody, silly, sexy, and fun. It's everything a good 80s slasher should be. Even if you've never seen it, you know about it. It's the one with the infamous "Driller Killer" in it. He's the greasy psycho who chases around a bunch of scantily clad, or outright nude, high school girls having a sleepover. His weapon of choice is huge electric drill, and this long, deadly tool is usually held at crotch level, just in case the symbolism of girls getting drilled was too subtle for you.

Where many horror movies made during this golden age of slasher flicks were cheap cash-ins with little to no talent in them at all, this admittedly silly slice of cinema has quite some skill behind it. The acting is nothing stellar, but it is more than competent, as is the direction, no matter what the high-minded film critics at the time said in their reviews. It has more than a few moments of effective shocks and suspense as well as some nice bloody moments, but by far the biggest star of the show is its wicked sense of humor. While not really a parody or spoof, this SLUMBER PARTY is well aware of the common tropes, even back in 1982, and it plays with those. It also has some out and out funny moments. Oh and for fans of cute naked ladies, yeah, it has a lot of that too. So really, it's a win, win, win all the way around.

This new Blu-ray from Scream Factory has some nice extras on it, but most of them are direct ports from the previous DVD three-pack. There is an audio commentary with director Amy Holden Jones and actors Michael Villella and Debra De Liso. There is a 23 minute featurette called "Sleepless Nights: The Making of The Slumber Party Massacre." There are trailers for all three SLUMBER PARTY movies, and a still gallery. There is one new special feature on here, and that's a 13 minute interview with actor Rigg Kennedy. However, easily the best new feature of this release is the HD transfer. While there is still some grain on the screen, this movie does look sharp and bright.

THE SLUMBER PARTY MASSACRE is pure silly slasher gold with lots of T & A, gory kills, and a fun sense of humor. No, it's not a great film, but it sure is an enjoyable flick. If you already have this on DVD, then I can only recommend it if you're an avid videophile. Other than looking really good here, there's not enough new on this disc for me to recommend a double dip. However, if you've never seen it, and classic 80s horror moves are your thing, then you really need to check it out. So consider it highly recommended if you don't already have it in your collection, and moderately recommended to Blu-ray snobs (you know who you are) if you do own the DVD. If you fall into either one of these camps, you can get this Blu-ray on March 18th.

Reviewed by Brian M. Sammons

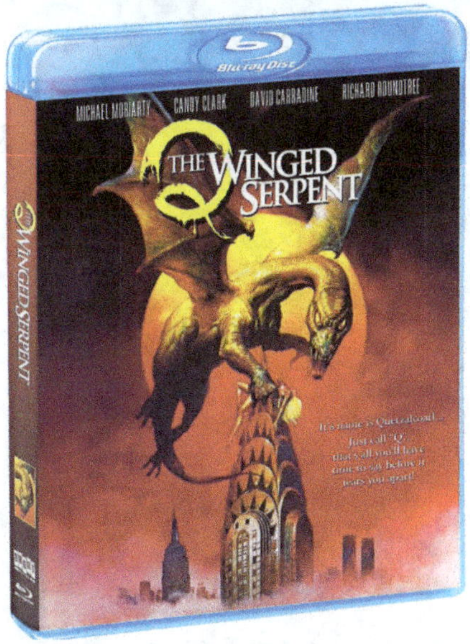

Q The Winged Serpent

Scream Factory

August, 2013; $19.97

Q The Winged Serpent is a 1982, gritty low-budget creature flick brought to you by director/writer Larry Cohen. This cult classic was released by Scream Factory on Blu-ray last August to the delight of Grindhouse genre fans everywhere. However, if you are a big fan of this film and already own the Blue Underground DVD released in 2003, then you may be a touch disappointed.

True, the Scream Factory Blu-ray is cleaned and looks fantastic with more color consistency all while keeping the nostalgic look and feel of the natural film grain. The commentary track from Larry Cohen is also new (Blue Underground's version was commentated by Larry and William Lustig) and gives some additional insights to the film and Larry's firing from the film *I, The Jury*. Unfortunately, that is where the highlights of Scream Factory's release ends.

What saddened me the most of this release was the audio. Mixed in DTS HD 2.0 – wait, 2.0? That's stereo! Sure, back in '82 stereo was the norm – and I even expect these new releases to feature a stereo track, but I also expect a full 5-7.0 surround in this day and age. Listening to this new DTS HD 2.0 track, I was disappointed in the quality. There are slight distortions at points, and the audio levels are mismatched forcing one to turn up the dialogue. Once again, compared to the Blue Underground DVD, this release falls short. Blue Underground's featured a mono, stereo, Dolby Digital 5.1 and finally a full 6.1 DTS-ES. Why Scream Factory fell short here is beyond me.

Also notably missing are any subtitles – not a biggie, but could have been added. Another standard feature missing is the scene selections. This release just has chapter breaks. The rest of the special features are minimal – the original trailer as well as the teaser. Sure, this isn't the Collector's Edition, but even the Blue Underground version contained a poster and stills gallery as well as a DVD-ROM feature called "Q Memorabilia."

As far as the film itself goes, it is exemplary of its cult following status. Michael Moriarty's performance in this film is genuinely excellent and worthy of any New York style of character such as from *Dog Day Afternoon* or *Taxi Driver*. Plus – he can play a mean piano. If you haven't seen this film already and love a good monster feature with a surprisingly good story, this picture deserves a viewing. If you are a huge fan of this film already, you won't get anything new from this version other than the commentary.

Review by Anthony Dluzak

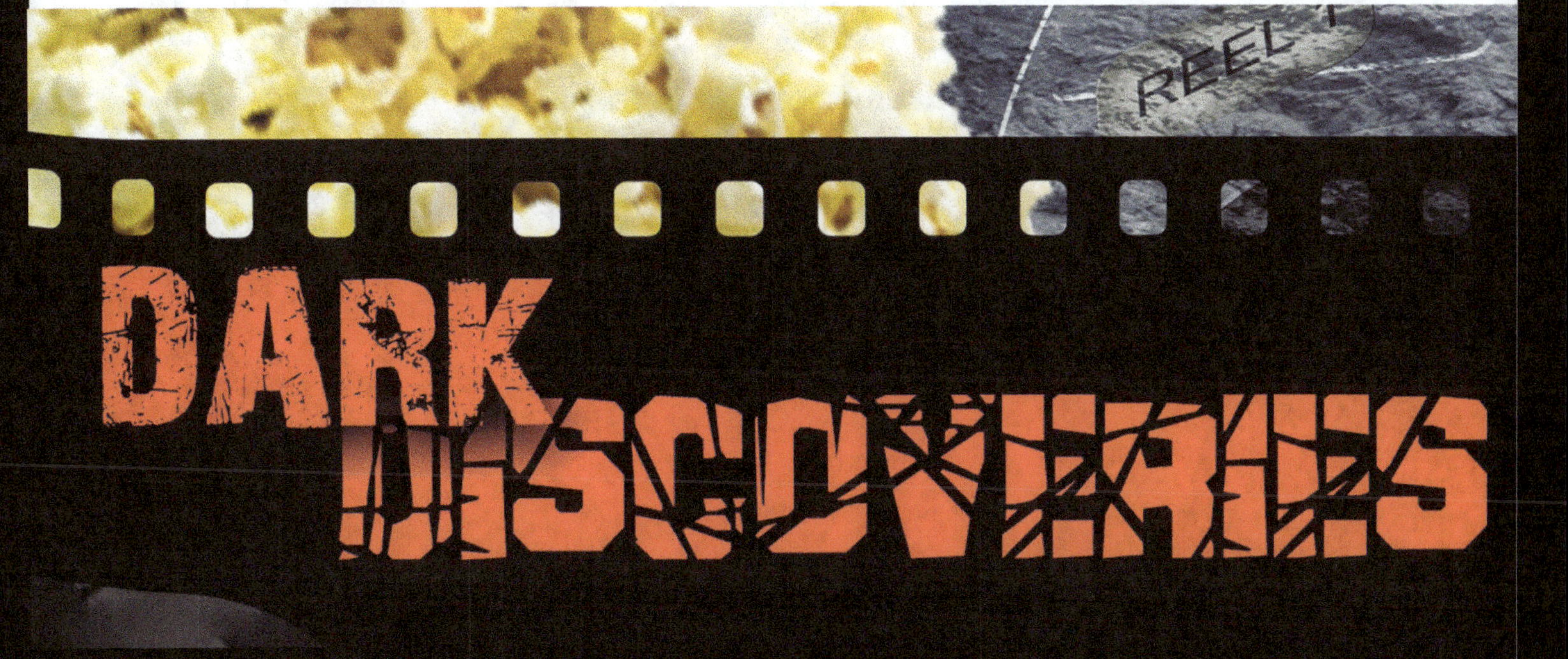

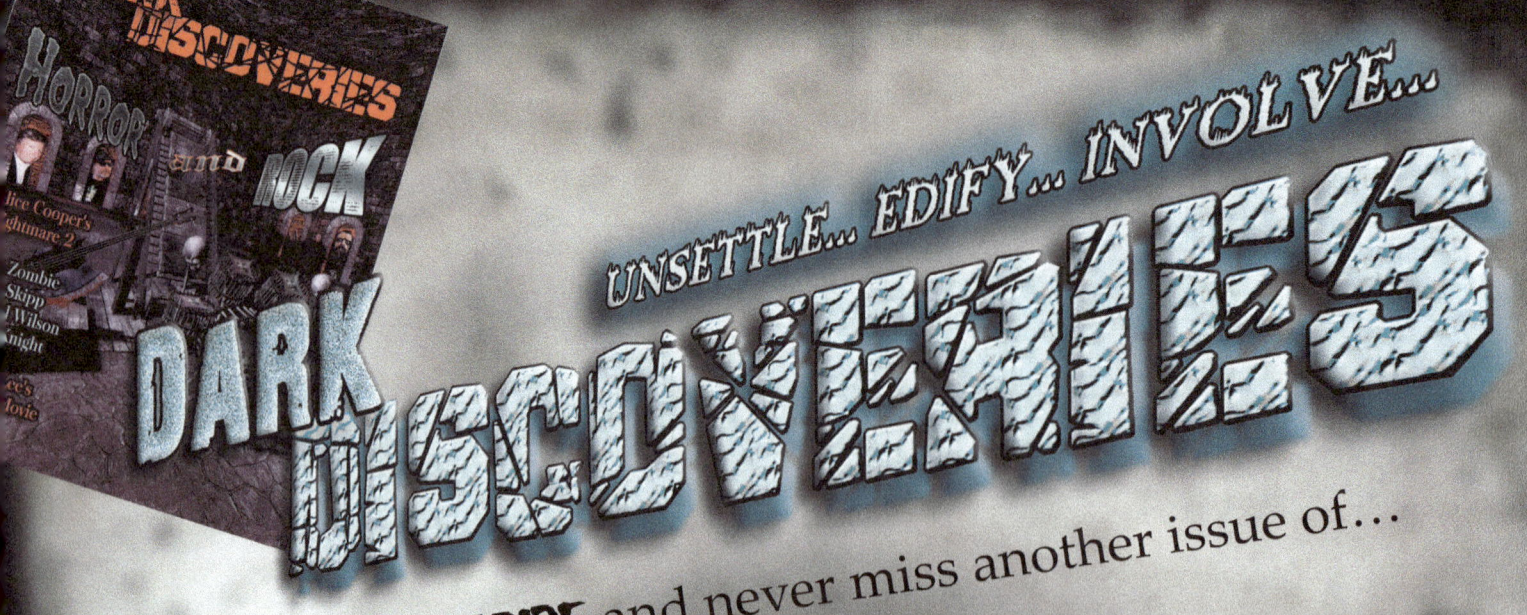

UNSETTLE... EDIFY... INVOLVE...

DARK DISCOVERIES

SUBSCRIBE and never miss another issue of...

www.darkdiscoveries.com

FEATURES:

Weird Fiction & Film, Extreme Horror, Comics & Pulps, New Blood, Dark SciFi, Twilight Zone, H.P. Lovecraft, Horror in Rock, Forgotten Horror & SF TV…

INTERVIEWS:

Ray Bradbury, Bruce Campbell, Christopher Lee, Joe R. Lansdale, William F. Nolan, EC Comics Al Feldstein, Brian Keene, Jack Ketchum, David Cronenberg…

FICTION:

Richard Matheson, Ray Bradbury, Thomas Ligotti, Richard Laymon, John Shirley, William F. Nolan, Ramsey Campbell, Joe R. Lansdale, Lisa Morton, Edward Lee…

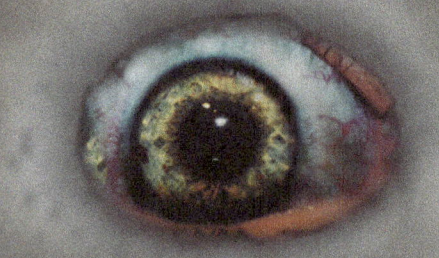

"Dark Discoveries is a very handsome publication..."

--Dean Koontz

"A bright new force in Dark Fantasy."

--William F. Nolan

"Dark Discoveries is a high quality mag... and it keeps getting better..."

--Horror Fiction Review

PRINT SUBSCRIPTIONS

4 issues (1 year): US ($37.95) Canada ($46.95) Overseas ($69.95)

8 issues (2 years): US ($74.95) Canada ($92.95) Overseas ($139.95)

(*Shipping is included on print subs)

ADVERTISERS!

Inquire via E-mail for rates!

Please Note: Future content subject to change without notice. All rights reserved.

DIGITAL SUBSCRIPTIONS

4 issues (1 year): $19.95
8 issues (2 years): $39.95
Payment accepted via PayPal: christophercpayne@journalstone.com
Also by Check/M.O. (Payable to)

JournalStone Publications, 1261 Peachwood Court, San Bruno, CA 94066, USA

JOURNALSTONE
YOUR LINK TO ARTISTIC TALENT